BORROWED TROUBLE

J.B. KOHL AND ERIC BEETNER

This book is a work of fiction. Names, characters, locations and events are either a product of the author's imagination, fictitious or used fictitiously. Any resemblance to any event, locale or person, living or dead, is purely coincidental.

Copyright © 2010 by J.B. Kohl and Eric Beetner

All rights reserved, including the right of reproduction in whole or part in any format.

Originally published January 2011 by
Second Wind Publishing.

Cover painting by Marc Sasso.
Layout and design by Eric Beetner

Special thanks to
Deborah J. Ledford and R. Thomas Brown

Manufactured in the United States of America

Praise for *Borrowed Trouble*:

"Meticulous historical detail slams you into the hard boiled world of Ray Ward and Dean Fokoli as they use hard fists and cold steel to knock the shiny off Hollywood's glitter. *Borrowed Trouble* is like a talented fighter – powerful, quick, and hard to put down."

    Rebecca Cantrell, award-winning author of *A Night of Long Knives*

"For a knockout punch of hardboiled, look no further than *Borrowed Trouble*, sequel to the period noir *One Too Many Blows To The Head*. You'll want to go the distance with Ray Ward, a tough-luck protagonist who knows how to hit where it counts!"

    Kelli Stanley, author of City of Dragons and City of Secrets

"Everyone has a short list of books that stayed with them long after they turned the last page—add *Borrowed Trouble* to mine. Eric Beetner and J.B. Kohl have vividly re-created 1941 Los Angeles, ripping apart the city's glamorous façade to reveal the cold noir heart beneath. With sharp writing, head-spinning twists, and pair of protagonists haunted by memory and loss, this is pulp fiction at its finest."

    Hilary Davidson, author of The Damage Done and Blood Always Tells

"It's 1941 and noir's hot new duo, Kohl and Beetner, return with another sure-fire winner. *Borrowed Trouble* is a relentlessly tough and lean novel, packed full with memorable characters. United by their troubled pasts, the unlikely pairing of PI Dean Fokoli and troubled boxing promoter, Ray Ward, head from Kansas City to Hollywood to untangle a dark tale of greed and exploitation, but ultimately one which offers them both a shot at personal redemption. They don't write them like this anymore. Jump onboard now."

    Nick Quantrill, author of Broken Dreams and The Late Greats

Praise for One Too Many Blows To The Head:

"*One Too Many Blows to the Head* feels like a long-lost pulp you find in a favorite bookstore. A delicious mix of classic hardboiled grit and the heart-heavy world of film noir, it's a one-sitting read that sends you back to a lost time of fight halls, Chicago boys and last chances."
    Megan Abbott, author of Dare Me and Queenpin

  "Boxing and noir once went hand in glove, but you don't see many boxing novels anymore, and that's a shame. Here's one that dredges up all the blood and spit and sweat and money of the fight game, and wraps it around a tough noir storyline full of revenge and dark secrets. Kohl and Beetner get it exactly right."
    Steve Brewer, author of the Bubba Maybry series

"A powerful tale of vengeance, rife with pounding action and colorful, complex characters. *One Too Many Blows To The Head* is a first round knock-out!"
    Stephen Jay Schwartz, LA Times bestselling author of Boulevard and Beat

"The prose is hardboiled and lean, and there's plenty of violence. There's a surprise or two along the way, and you'll want to know what happens to Fokoli and Ray. They're deeply flawed, but Beetner and Kohl keep them human, which is quite an accomplishment
when you consider the circumstances."
    Bill Crider, author of the Sheriff Dan Rhodes series

1

RAY WARD
KANSAS CITY. SPRING, 1941

I hadn't used my fists much since then. Since the night my brother died, and the days after. I guess I should say I hadn't used my fists in anger. My fists get a good workout down in the basement of my house in Rex's old training setup. I attack the heavy bag, pound out a rhythm on the speed-bag to make Count Basie jealous. I jump rope, lift weights. I shadow box.

Futile, really, shadow boxing. Still it's what I feel like my life's become. You stand in front of a cinder block wall dodging and ducking, swinging in the air at an opponent who matches your every move, who knows your strengths and weaknesses.

Pointless, fighting yourself.

But, that's what I do down there in the damp concrete gym. I beat myself up. I spar and joust with the past and the man I thought I was, trying to understand how I could have gone so off the rails.

I've been over it a thousand times and I have no regrets. I keep going as much for Rex as for me, living a life he might have wanted but never got the chance to live. I forgave myself a long time ago, but that shadow is still there.

Since that week, those troubles, I've been a model citizen. That's what made that day walking home from the grocery store such a shock. I caught a glimpse of the stranger I saw in the mirror two years ago.

I don't get out much. I don't talk to many people. I stay in the house and work out, I read, I go to the movies now and then which is good because you can sit alone and not interact with anyone and nobody thinks you're odd. On my block I've become the weirdo my nine-year-old self would have loved to ding-dong-ditch and throw rocks at his window.

Coming home from the market that day I was just minding my own, a single bag of groceries in my arms. The usual staples. I'd been living on a small rotation of about five meals I know how to cook.

I recognized the couple walking parallel to me on the sidewalk across the street. Around my neighborhood I try not to be seen, but I can see; and this marriage was not the happiest on the block. He was big. Victor was his name. Greek, I think. The kind of guy who intimidates a woman because he can. It came easy to him. Probably learned it from his father.

I didn't know her name which seemed in line with her station in life. Be quiet, sit down, make me dinner, have more babies.

The raised tone of Victor's voice was as familiar to the refrain of the neighborhood as the McTaggart's dog, so hearing him shouting didn't even make my head turn. It was the punch.

All my life I've heard the sound of men hitting men so much that I can tell you the pitch of a sock to the jaw versus a blow to the gut with a blindfold on. I can tell you if the guy doing the hitting is a righty or a lefty. I can tell you if any bones broke or if it was a knockout just by the music of a fist on flesh.

Head down, grocery bag firmly held, I can tell you it was a shot to her cheekbone thrown with a sweeping right fist. It was no slap to gain her attention, no stomach punch to prove a point. This was a strike with all four knuckles meant to do her harm.

I stopped in my tracks. I turned and heard the distant sound of the McTaggart's dog reel off fifteen barks in a row like a Tommy gun.

She knelt in front of him holding her cheek. Victor loomed over her with his fist cocked back again as if she might actually stand up or try to fight back. His breath came out raspy, ragged from the yelling. They stood like that, frozen, as if they were waiting for a referee to finish counting to ten.

I'm not one to mess in other people's business. I'm even less of one to help a stranger. I guess I do have some sense of justice and even a loner like me has his limits. This was a time when to ignore it, to not do something . . . well, it might as well have been my fist that cracked her cheek.

I kept hold of the grocery bag as I crossed the street, I don't know why. I barely felt its weight. My workouts had been intense and long and my body was never in better shape, even during my brief career in the ring. Sparring with Rex used to keep me fit but now that I had taken over his training regimen, and then some, I became taut and solid as an archer's bow. I would have fought middleweight and if my heavy bag could speak it would tell you that I can bring the hurt.

Victor didn't notice me crossing. He had that tunnel vision inexperienced fighters get. I was right up next to him by the time he turned. I broke him out of some sort of trance and when he saw me he relaxed his fist and shook it out. I could see his knuckles were thick and calloused, damaged the way a nose looks after being broken for the fifth time. I don't know what he did for a living but I want to believe it was the job that gave him those hardened mushrooms and not overuse on her face.

She still didn't make a sound, scared silent and knowing the consequences if she cried.

He waited for me to speak. I didn't. I set down the grocery bag and quickly told myself, *Don't*, but my muscles kept on moving. I reached out a hand to her and lifted her up by the arm. She didn't want to stand so I forced her.

Victor was staring daggers at me by then but I didn't care about him or his meat paws. With the same hand I lifted his wife I coiled a fist and brought it around into his gut. It was a lot of gut and he sucked wind for a moment but didn't crumple the way his wife did.

Knocking him off guard gave me enough time to square up, set my feet, bring my hands up and reach back with my right, getting just enough space between me and him to push my body forward. I followed through from my shoulder down the arm to the fist and sent a shot straight and solid with the full force of my body pivoting toward him. It landed on his jaw.

Punching a man on the cheek is a fool's game. You're much more likely to break your hand than his face. Come to think of it, that could be a good reason for his knuckles to look the way they did. Bad technique in too many bar fights. You hit him in the jaw and there's room there to give so as your punch follows through, if you threw a good one that is, it can do some real damage.

Hitting another human felt different from the sand-filled bags in my basement. A primitive spot deep in my brain thought it felt very good.

I recoiled the arm and stood ready to throw another, or to dodge whatever was coming my way. I didn't need to. He doubled over and spit two teeth to the sidewalk before following them down. He landed hard on his forehead and that started to bleed, quickly joining the flow from his mouth in a tiny creek watering the weeds in the cement cracks.

Her hand fell away from her cheek. A slight smile crept over her. I'd probably just sentenced her to another beating behind closed doors but she seemed to think it was worth it.

She spoke quietly to me. "Thank you, mister. Why did you . . .? Never mind. Just thank—"

I was already crossing the street. I didn't do it for her. I shouldn't have done it at all. It was upsetting to remember a part of me that was capable of such violence existed inside. I hated to see it roar back to life; a bear roused from hibernation.

Like I said, I guess I have some notion of justice.

It's crazy to think, but that was the same day I got the

package.

I got home and iced my hand even though it didn't hurt much. I replayed the sound in my head; the connection, the cracking of teeth, the unhinging of jawbone, the air expelling from lungs. All textbook. Enough to make you want to step back into the ring.

I'd been making my living off three fighters I owned a piece of. With the money from Rex's life insurance and his share of our purse money from his fight days, all of which went to me in his will, I laid low and didn't come out of my hole for six months after the funeral. When I did I figured the money would run out sooner or later, even if I lived like a hermit. I lurked in the fight halls and found some boys I liked the look of. I could make more money off them if I put myself back in the corner and became a full-fledged manager but I like being a silent partner. The boys do okay and none of them have ever met me.

So aside from some sore knuckles and an angry Greek neighbor I had everything well under control in my small life, shadows and all.

Then the package came.

It was in a box wrapped with twine and the return address had no name, just a street I didn't know and a city: Hollywood, California. Inside I found a reel of 8mm film and an envelope with my name scrawled on it. I opened it and read a letter than was rambling, scared and asking for help. It was signed, YOUR SISTER, AUDREY.

Thing is, I don't have a sister.

2

DEAN FOKOLI

There's a street in Kansas City, just back of 13th; the cops call it Screamer's Row. It's the sort of place a guy can go to scalp a ticket, make a bet, get a date, score some dope, or finish a deal. It's the kind of place that fills up quick at sundown and, when the sirens cry, clears out twice as fast. It's a place where the money's dirty, the drinks are stiff, and the dames are loose.

When I was a cop it was never my beat. I dealt with nobodies who were somebodies—guys who liked to grease my palm with freshly laundered money. Not that there weren't crooked cops on Screamer's Row trying to cram their fists into the till. It's just that the losers on the Row liked dealing with bad guys who didn't pretend to be something else in the light of day. There would never be much of a partnership between the riffraff and the swayback cops here. That's just the way of things.

But as a private dick? Yeah, a guy on Screamer's Row could eke out something like a living that was almost honest, if a guy was so inclined. I knew how to find people. I knew how to keep my mouth shut and my eyes open. And I knew how to make a guy talk—even when he didn't want to.

At first I went to the Row because I wanted to disappear. If I wasn't me anymore then maybe Laura had never existed . . . had never been betrayed . . . hadn't died alone. I got a room, the kind with a beat-up desk and a fold out bed, and I hung out a shingle. DEAN FOKOLI, PRIVATE INVESTIGA-TIONS. The cops left me and my corner alone most of the time. Screamer's Row boasted a murder a night so they had their hands full. Besides, I worked hard to keep my nose clean.

Guys from the street came to my office with money in hand and asked me to do things. Spy on a dame, take some pictures, follow a money trail. It was easy stuff. And legal.

But sometimes a man can be driven to do things he swore he'd never do again.

Let me put it this way: In a city where people are nothing but blank faces you'd think it would be easy to disappear. Turns out it's not.

It was a Wednesday when I opened my door to a headache, and I can't say it's entirely gone even now, two days later.

Bob White was my ex-partner, or I was his. I'm not sure how one was supposed to word it. I'd showed him the ropes and now he wanted to hang me. "Dean Fokoli. Well, well, well." He said it like we were in a movie . . . like I was some fugitive in hiding he'd managed to track down through ingenuity. Asshole. He sauntered past me and sat on the edge of my desk, one leg propped up, hands folded on his thigh, hat perched on his head like he thought he was somebody big now.

"That's what it says on the shingle," I said. "Right out in the open."

He had the grace to blush. Bob White may have been more seasoned now, may have lost some weight and stiffened his spine, but I couldn't see him as anything other than the rookie he was when we worked together. "Sure does," he said. "How's things going?"

"What do you want, Bob?" I shoved him off the edge of the desk and lit a cigarette before sinking into my chair. I didn't have chairs for clients. Chairs facilitate comfort, encourage conversation, invite civility. Nobody but me sat down in my office. Nobody.

Bob strolled around and touched things on the one and only

shelf I had in the room: nail clippers, razor, watch, a picture of me and Laura. "I got promoted," he said, looking over his shoulder at me. He put the picture down an inch too far to the left. I pretended it didn't bother me. "I'm reviewing unsolved crimes."

"Congratulations." I put my feet up on the desk.

He strolled my direction again and stood looking down at me. Bob had gotten smug in the last year. "The Ward Case."

A thousand memories fell like rain. Ray Ward, free man, murderer. He wasn't the reason I walked away from my job, but he was one of the many, many reasons I could end up in jail. Letting Ray go was one of the rightest things I'd done in my sorry life, but it made me guilty of a few things. Aiding and abetting, obstruction of justice—things that could get me sentenced to a few years or better.

I took a deep drag on the cigarette and studied the fleshy face of my ex-partner. A year ago I had figured Bob for a softy, the sort of guy who'd let me go for old time's sake. Who says teaching a guy to keep his balls in his sack where they belong is a smart thing?

"What about Ward?" I asked, blowing a plume of smoke into the air.

Bob rocked back on his heels. "I think we can prove it all real soon. We know he killed all those guys."

"You don't know anything."

"Maybe I do and maybe I don't, Dean." His face changed then. It had a tendency to do that when he was thinking about whether or not to say something. I'd learned to read him easily enough when I was showing him how to be a good cop—something I never was—and when Bob's face got like this he had something to get off his chest.

I didn't say anything because it wasn't my job to teach him how to handle himself anymore. He was on his own. I waited him out, watched him fidget, and felt a little amused by the whole thing.

"Look, Dean," he said, making like he wanted to sit on the

edge of my desk again. My cocked eyebrow warned him off. "I'm here as a courtesy. I'm going to be checking things out because of this new job. They're cleaning things up in the department and—" He shook his head. "I gotta tell you, your name keeps coming up, especially with regard to the Ward case."

I took another drag of my cigarette and met his gaze. He didn't shrink under it like he used to. "I've got nothing to hide." The phrase tasted bitter and the fact that Bob obviously knew it was a lie didn't make it any better.

After he left I smoked another cigarette and thought about Ray Ward.

I'd kept tabs on the kid since last year, wanting to make sure he kept his nose clean. Mostly he hid out in his house and didn't come out for much at all. I wondered if I could get him to leave town, to make himself scarce. I laughed out loud. Here was the great and honest Dean Fokoli ready to help a criminal escape justice . . . again. I was shitting all over that new leaf I'd turned over, but there was no help for it.

A few hours later I found myself in the back of a Pawn Shop at the edge of the Row. Bars lined the windows and the front door and the owner wore hip holsters stuffed with revolvers. I laid down my money, picked up the phony badge he laid on the table and hoped I was doing the right thing. Funny thing about that—hoping you're doing the right thing usually means you're not. But a badge in these parts equaled muscle and muscle might be necessary to get Ray Ward to leave town.

3

RAY

I read the note three times. Most of it didn't make sense to me. Beyond the desperate run-on nature of it, all the stuff about Pop and this girl, this Audrey, being my sister. It just didn't sink.

And that film reel. What was that all about? I had nothing to watch it on. It just sat there in that bright yellow can. It was like getting a warning in a language you can't understand.

The house was church quiet, like always, but I noticed it more than ever before. I was tempted to click on the radio just to have proof the world hadn't stopped spinning.

My curtains closed out any light, as usual, but a gap where the two living room panels didn't quite meet let in a shaft of bright midday sun. It caught dust motes that hung sad in the air. A moth cut a path through making swirling ripples in its wake.

I lifted the film can, turned it over, took out the reel of 8mm. I unspooled the first few feet and brought it over to the break in the curtains, held the thin strip up to the light. Tiny boxes showed the same picture over and over. Nothing seemed to change. A room with a bed in it. No people. There was an emptiness that gave me an uneasy feeling. I knew that room was no place I wanted to be.

I spun the reel and wound the film back up then set the can back down. I picked up the letter again, the paper crinkling in my hand. It looked as if it had been wadded up at one point and then smoothed out again. What she worried about was this: Girls had gone missing. Friends of hers. She was an actress, so she said. Some friends did a few films but not the type you'd see in a double feature.

Hell, I'd never even seen one. Girls stripping off their clothes for the camera. Sometimes a guy is involved. Intimate moments rendered on celluloid for the entertain-ment of lecherous men.

Starring my sister, apparently.

She made it clear that the movie she sent me didn't star her. It didn't exactly make me feel any better about who and what was on it.

She outlined, on page two of her three page handwritten rant, the details of Pop traveling out west on a tour back in 1921. He used to barnstorm around a lot in those days picking up fights all over the western states. Well, I guess he got lonely one of those nights and took up with Audrey's Mom and nine months later . . .

She said she never met Pop but her Mom told her everything and used to keep clippings of the fights he won. Her Mom had passed away and apparently Audrey kept up the hobby.

When Rex died she knew about it. When Pop died she knew about it. Now I was her only living relative and her only hope. She seemed to be really afraid that something bad would happen to her. I could feel her fear coming off the page, in her words and in the way she wrote, like she was rushing to get it all out before someone busted in and found her scrawling. The way she barely stopped for punctuation as if it would take too long and she'd get found out. The letter was written in two different pens—one blue, one black—that gave the impression she had to ditch her first attempt in a hurry and pick it up again later. I had no reason to, but I believed her.

Pop was a son-of-a-bitch and that was reason enough to believe he had messed around on Mom. Audrey was frantic enough to believe she was in some kind of trouble, real or imagined, and if she went to the effort to track me down that was proof she had no one else to turn to.

Trouble was, neither did I. Last time I set out to help someone things didn't go too well. Bodies started piling up. I managed to stay one foot ahead of the law but this is a town I know. Hollywood I don't know from Singapore.

I try not to let myself think back to that time. It's too damn easy to dwell. I can sit in the house and replay it in real-time and not even realize I'm doing it. It's why I don't need a film projector. I got a six-reeler playing in my head at all times. It's all I can do to keep the theater dark.

I thought about her request; to come out to Hollywood and help her and her friends. The more I considered her request, the more I knew I couldn't do it alone.

I didn't have a lot of options, but I had one.

4

FOKOLI

I stood on the sidewalk across the street from Ray Ward's house with the spring breeze sending my coat flapping around my legs. The neighborhood was full of sounds from crying babies and laughing children to barking dogs and scolding mothers. Doors opened and closed, cars passed, people interacted.

Ray's house was shut up tight as a tomb. Not surprising since he'd been involved in at least five murders. A guy with that kind of history might be inclined to hide out. But I'd been through Ray's actions over and over in my head—he was square as far as I was concerned. He'd killed guys, sure, but the guys he finished needed it. Ray Ward had taken care of business. I'd put away my share of bad guys when I carried a badge, but I'd done it with the help of dirty hands in my pockets. So who was the bad guy and who was the good guy?

Now I was here to try to reason with Ray Ward. By using a phony badge.

The folly of it all struck me then. He knew I had quit the force. The papers had covered my story from birth to professional death and they'd done it in Technicolor. Even now, two years later, Laura's grave had more flowers on it than the Miss America float in Macy's Thanksgiving Parade. The poor, misunderstood wife, neglected by her husband, driven to drink herself to death. Notes to Laura piled up with the flowers. Every single one touching, every single one condemning me—every single one correct.

Funny how a guy can try to go straight and can't find a goddamn straight road to walk along. There were offshoots in every direction. Forks in the road. Goddamn Robert Frost and his road less traveled. Stupid poet probably had soft hands and never worked a day in his life.

I shoved the badge in my pocket and thought maybe I'd just let Ray Ward be. When a man starts cursing poetry he's in danger of losing his marbles.

There was plenty to do back on the Row. I went to my car and headed that direction, feeling like I could clean up a few cases, maybe bruise a few of my knuckles and clear my head. Then I'd shoot some pool and think over the Ray Ward situation. Maybe I'd do some investigating and see if Ray had family out of town or something, a place he could go to ride everything out. I didn't know how deep Bob planned on digging, mainly because it felt like I didn't know Bob all that well anymore. I'd taken my finger off the pulse of the precinct and it was going to be next to impossible to put it back without getting it shot off.

As I pulled onto my street and parked the car, Ray was slipping from my thoughts. I'd get to him, I told myself. Later.

I stopped in my office long enough to grab my camera and headed east on foot. Riley's Gun Repair was a block from my office. Riley'd had some trouble with a bookie by the name of Len Kopetski who leased Riley's back room for business. Since I wasn't a cop anymore, and I had to make my living on the Row, I figured live and let live. I'd made a few bets in the back room once or twice. I even played a game of cards there now and then. But it seemed rent was slow in coming these days despite evidence of Mr. Kopetski's ever-increasing financial security—diamond ring on his pinkie finger, new furs for his women, and a gold tooth to fill the gap in front of his mouth that had been his trademark for the last decade.

BORROWED TROUBLE

I'm not a brawny enough man to take on all of the thugs Kopetski kept by his side, so eviction by force wasn't an option. Everyone knew Kopetski was scared of one thing—his father-in-law, Stan Gray.

Mr. Gray used to run book down at Riley's but had moved on to bigger things uptown. He gave Kopetski the lease to the back room as a wedding present five years earlier.

Every good goon has a wife and two or three ladies on the side. It's all acceptable. It's all understood. But discre-tion is expected.

For example: you don't buy all three of your girlfriends fur coats and forget to buy one for your wife, especially if your wife's daddy has enough pull to get you fitted with cement shoes and dumped in the Mississippi.

Mrs. Kopetski found out about the coats from Riley and then she came to see me. She requested pictures of girls in coats coming and going from the back room. She didn't care about the affairs. She planned to use the pictures as leverage to get her own coat. Let's just say it wasn't my usual request. But when a dame wants a fur coat . . .

She explained it to me like this: Mrs. Kopetski needed a coat, Riley needed his rent. They'd made a bargain to hire and pay me to catch Mr. Kopetski with his ladies in fur. The scheme would enrage Mr. Gray. Riley would use that anger to his advantage, saying that Mr. Kopetski owed him four months of rent. In the end, Mrs. Kopetski would get her fur coat, Riley would get his rent, and I would get enough in my pocket to keep me in groceries for another month. It was a walk in the park.

As I walked into the shop, Riley gave me a wave with one finger, the signal that Kopetski was in the back with one of his women. The routine was always the same—Kopetski would take bets for a couple of hours and play cards until the ponies ran. After, he'd leave through the back with a lady on his arm. I'd snap a few pictures of the woman in her coat. Piece of cake.

I headed back out the front door, moved into the alley, and

ducked into a doorway. I lit a cigarette, hoping the smell of burning tobacco would be strong enough to cover the stench of rotting cabbage and dried urine. I had the camera loaded and ready so all I had to do was wait. There were no shadows in the alley, just the glare of sun on oil stains. Early afternoon. Almost race time.

Time passed. I measure hours in cigarettes, so by my calculation it was half past six. Kopetski was still inside.

When I saw the shadow I blew out a breath. I wasn't too worried about being found. There were enough cigarette butts in the alley to make the twelve I'd smoked insignificant. I dropped the one I was working on now at my feet, crushing it with my heel and covering it with my shoe. Then I cracked my knuckles. I didn't have time for some halfwit to try to mug me, not when I was waiting to finish a job. I set the camera on the ground. It was bulky and I didn't want to drop it.

The shadow started whistling "Here We Go Round the Mulberry Bush." That's when I figured out that the shadow wasn't just a drunk looking for a place to sleep it off. I'd been here a long time. Odds were that somebody squealed. Either Mrs. Kopetski or Riley had developed a bad case of cold feet.

If I thought about it, I wasn't really worried about Mrs. Kopetski. She had her father on her side. But Riley needed business and if he messed with Len Kopetski, chances were he'd regret it a good long time. I cursed Riley for a coward and stepped out of the doorway. The goon was tall and muscular. I didn't recognize him. He stopped whistling when he saw me and finished his song by singing "Pop goes the weasel."

I sighed and put up my fists. Pointless, really. He had eighty pounds on me. I got a good shot off and clipped him in the chin before he'd even pulled an arm back, but he just gave a sort of backward nod and smiled at me.

He pulled back and landed a punch in the middle of my face. "Mr. Kopetski would like you to go home now," he said. But I didn't really hear him. I tried to dodge to the side to avoid his fist, but he was fast for a man his size and I took the force of the blow on my cheek, feeling the skin tear. After a second lightning fast shot, I was down on the ground, smelling the piss from a hundred drunks up close and personal. I groaned.

"Mr. Kopetski wants you to leave and not come back."

I was face down, feeling blood flow from my nose onto the crusted cement of the alley. I stared at the goon's shoes. He walked to the side of the alley and returned. "Mr. Kopetski says he'll make you a pair of shoes like this in your size if you bother him again."

I looked up over my shoulder at the cinder block he held in his meaty paws. "Maybe you want to see it up close." He dropped the block on my left hand.

I was quick but not quick enough. I pulled my hand far enough out of the way to avoid major damage, but the block caught the tips of my index and middle fingers. I think I swore then, but I'm not sure. I pushed the block from my hand and got to my knees.

"I'm going to take your film now," the goon said, picking up my camera and pulling out the roll. No pictures, thank God. He put it in his pocket and smiled at me before dropping the camera on the ground and crushing it under his massive shoe.

People steered clear of me as I made my way back to the office. From the feel of the blood dripping down my cheek and from my nose, I guess I couldn't blame them. I got inside and poured myself a drink before attempting to clean up. I thought about pulling out the bed and taking a good long nap—but first I'd get good and drunk.

5

RAY

I hadn't been back to the precinct since they interrogated me. I'd almost blown it then and brought the whole house of cards down around my ears. Now I was walking in of my own free will. I've had better ideas. I've had worse.

Detective Dean Fokoli was no longer with the department. I knew that. Headlines screamed it at me for a week after the mess. His indiscretions on the force eclipsed my trail of bodies by the time of the morning edition. Everyone loves a crooked cop story. It confirms their suspicions.

I'd learned enough about detective-ing from my brief experience to easily know that when trying to find someone the best place to start is the last place you know they were.

My explanation to the desk sergeant was muddy at best. He furrowed a brow at me and, annoyed, motioned for me to follow him. On his desk were two open files with mugshots in them doing a lousy job of hiding a crossword puzzle.

He led me to the homicide division. My old stomping ground.

I recognized the detective but couldn't come up with his name. Lucky for me his brass nameplate was at a high sheen like he'd worn out a half dozen ties spit-shining it all day. Must have made him proud. Guess his daddy never said he loved him either.

When he looked up and saw me I thought he was going to shit a brick. He tried to cover his surprise but it was too late. I'd seen his opening move and I knew how to proceed in the next round.

Bob White, as the nameplate said, forced himself to relax into the world's smoothest detective. His demeanor said he was a tough-as-nails, lady-killer, always-gets-his-man type. Too bad his gut and bald head were giving a different speech.

"Well, well. Mister Ward. Here to turn yourself in?" Bob went to put a foot up on his desk but nearly lost his balance in his chair and had to lurch forward to stay upright. He kept his feet planted after that.

I kept mine moving. Defense.

"Turn myself in for what?"

"As if you don't know." He smirked and reached for a cigarette.

"I'm looking for Dean Fokoli. I figured you might know where he is."

Bob struck the match on his desktop and touched it to his cigarette tip. "Still hanging out with your old pal, are you?"

"If I was I wouldn't need you to help me find him, would I?"

Bob hesitated with the lit match in the air. Flame crept lazily toward his finger as he contemplated throwing me in the basement holding cells for insulting an officer. Just before the flame reached his finger he shook it out.

"What do you want Fokoli for?"

"I loaned him a book. Wanted to get it back."

I wasn't making headway with my smug attitude but when a guy comes at you, the least you have to do is put up your dukes.

Bob chugged at his smoke as he swung out from behind his chair. The two other cops in the room ignored us. Bob stepped close to me and I held my ground. No way this doughboy was going to push me into the ropes.

"I just wonder what it is you two old pals are going to

discuss," White said.

"I told you."

"What book did he borrow, exactly?" Bob exhaled pungent smoke in my face. I guess cheap tobacco is all you can afford on a cop's salary.

"My Bible." Even though My eyes burned I wouldn't give him the satisfaction of blinking.

"You know Ward, I'd ask for your fingerprints but I just remembered, we've got you on file. Y'know, just in case I need them to match up to any evidence sitting around in storage. Wasn't that long ago when you were down here just making friends with our pal Fokoli."

"Look detective, do you know where he is or not? I told you everything I knew back then and I forgot everything since so quit wasting my time and I'll quit wasting yours."

He stepped closer to me. If there was a ref there he would have broken up the clinch. "I haven't forgotten." Another puff of smoke and Bob White turned his back on me, his way of signaling he was done with our conversation. He marched back to his desk and refused to look up at me anymore.

"Fokoli's gone private dick. Lift any rock down on Screamer's Row and you should see him scurry."

"That's it?"

"That's all you'll get from me. Am I supposed to make it easy on you? Don't worry Ward. You'll see me again soon. I've been reading up on you." He tapped a file on his desk. "Yeah, you'll see me again. And this time I'll do what should have been done two years ago."

"Thanks, detective." I turned to leave.

"Be seeing you," he called out like I was a good friend just leaving an afternoon of iced tea and conversation. His words stung with the sharpness of an ice pick.

6

FOKOLI

The knock on my door set me on edge. And then I realized that Kopetski and his friends wouldn't knock. They'd just come on in. I opened the door.

Ray Ward.

"I need your help," he said, and held out a package—like he was a house guest bringing me a bottle of wine.

Funny, but I was almost relieved to see him. He stepped back a little when he saw my face but he got over it soon enough. I gestured for him to come inside.

I looked over the package and read the letter. A sister. Hollywood. Naughty movies.

It was clear enough. He wanted me to find her.

"Why?" I asked.

He met my eye which was something not too many people did nowadays. "Because you're better at it than I am. It's your job. Last time I . . ." his words trailed off.

I turned and moved deeper into the office. He had no choice but to follow. I sat down. He stood. I put the yellow film tin and the letter on the desk. He made no move to take them.

"I've been meaning to talk to you," I said.

Ray didn't say anything at first. He just met my gaze, looking tense. It had taken a lot for him to come to me. After a minute he said, "Why?"

I told him about Bob, about the cold case files, about how they still wanted to pin it all on him, take him down and push me down right along with him. He nodded as I spoke, like it was something he already knew. "So you need to get out of town."

He chewed on that for a minute. "And you?"

I shrugged. "I get to go on doing what I'm doing." It tasted bad when I said it. What the hell was I doing? The sounds of the street rose then and it was like I was hearing it for the first time—the sirens, the yells, the traffic, the coarse music, the screaming babies from nearby flats. All of it deafening. I hated it. I hated everything about it. My busted up face hated it more.

"She's my sister," he said. "At least take a look at the film."

"Have you watched it?"

He gave a short shake of his head, abrupt and serious and somewhat disgusted.

It occurred to me that he was here to trap me. Bob White and the D.A. approached Ray with a plea deal if he could prove that I had let him go. But Bob White wasn't that smart and I didn't figure Ray Ward for the sort of guy who would snitch. I kept my guard up but I'd be lying if I said I wasn't interested in the case. Dealing with Nancy film makers was probably better than getting stomped on by Neanderthals in blind alleys.

I took the film from the can, unrolled about six inches and held it up to the light. Nothing but a bed. Not enough to say for sure the type of movie it was, but enough to suspect. I tried not to groan.

"I don't have a projector," I said, "but my guess is we don't need it to tell us what's on this film. Your sister, right?"

"No," he said. "I think something bad, though."

I massaged my aching head. "Shit."

7

RAY

It took me about an hour to find a projector. I hadn't thought of it until Fokoli really pressed, then I remembered Tommy Diggs, a boxing manager who was one of the only guys in town friendly to me back when Rex was in the ring. He liked to go over films of bouts with his boys and give them tips, none of which they ever used. He still had a small stable of kids out there slugging but none of them had gotten any smarter, just younger.

I called Fokoli to meet me over at Diggs' office and politely asked Tommy to give us a half hour alone. I knew whatever was on that film reel wasn't something I wanted being shown for an audience.

Fokoli showed up and I couldn't help seeing him hesitate at the door like he knew if he crossed the threshold and sat down with me we would become some sort of partners. I knew it unsettled him but not any more than it did me.

"Well, Ward, let's see what we're dealing with," he said.

He'd done a homemade patch job on his face and I resisted my desire to strip off the crooked gauze and tape and do it myself. Years of patching fat lips and swollen eyes for Rex made me an expert at small-time first aid. No other man worth his salt wants a grown man pulling a Florence Nightingale on him though. If he wanted help he'd ask.

The office was small, smelled of chewing tobacco from the half-filled spittoon in the corner. I sat in Diggs's green leather chair under a cluster of framed pictures of young men in silk shorts striking poses with gloves on, hands and knees bent like they maybe had a shot to knock someone out. They didn't. A glass jaw doesn't show up in a photo.

Fokoli sat on a two-seater couch with dark stains from where a hundred sweat-soaked boxers sat before to watch film of their own humiliation in the ring.

I had Tommy give me a rundown of the machine before Dean got there so I had it threaded up and ready. A roll down screen was set up against the far wall. The room was dark enough for a movie show twenty-four hours a day so all I had to do was switch off a desk lamp and flip the switch on the projector.

The lamp shone a white square on the screen which flickered and filled with dirty frames of numbers counting down before going black and then fading up on the room I'd seen before. Fokoli and I both cleared our throats. The film had no sound; just the whir of sprockets and gears filled the room.

There was that bed, only now it was almost life-sized. It stayed empty too long. I shifted in my seat and the leather moaned. A girl showed up on screen, pushed into the frame and teetering on high heels, but the camera didn't move.

She was young, probably eighteen, and attractive. Dark hair, pale skin and a lot of it. She wore only a bra, underpants and the kind of stockings with a thin black seam running up the back and fastened to a garter belt. When she regained her balance you could tell she was crying.

A man entered, the one who did the shoving. He was a heavyweight, easy. Six foot four or five and broad across the shoulders with a chest wide enough to show the movie on. He strained the seams on his T-shirt. His face was tan with wide, flat features like his face had been sculpted out of putty. He looked Hawaiian or Samoan, something like that. He finished the job of pushing the girl on the bed. As she fell he hooked the four fingers of his shoving hand into her drawers and pulled them away, leaving her naked backside exposed as she hit the bed.

He tossed the ripped garment away and undid his belt.

Fokoli and I squirmed.

His belt unhooked, he stripped off his shirt and then removed his pants revealing a part of his anatomy in scale with his upper body. The girl turned and looked over her shoulder, face to the camera showing mascara streaking her cheeks. She scrambled to get up into a crawl but he grabbed her waist with his massive hands and held her in place.

On her hands and knees, her tear-stained face to the wall, he took her violently.

The reel of film lasted less than five minutes, every second excruciating. He pounded into her with all his might. He lifted and moved her body at will as if she wasn't even a person. When he was done he stood and left the way he entered leaving the girl to curl up, knees to her chest, finally giving in to her sobs. The tiny bed shook almost as violently with her bawling as it did when he . . .

The film ran out, the screen went white and we sat letting the film spool around and around slapping the loose tail of 8mm against the projector and ringing it like a bell. In my world, a bell is supposed to save you.

After a minute I switched off the projector.

I knew what Audrey was afraid of now.

"I need a shower," Fokoli said. I nodded agreement. "Well," he continued. "Looks like we're going to Hollywood."

I thought about shaking his hand, welcoming aboard my new partner but handshakes and congratulations seemed inappropriate.

"I can't pay you much. I doubt your regular rate, let alone extra charges for an out of town job."

"No such thing as a regular rate in this business."

"But you'll help me?"

"I'll help her, your sister. It's you that owes me if I

remember right."

He had me over a barrel with that one. "I know I—"

"Keep your shirt tucked, I'm just ribbing you. It's not a bad idea for me to leave town for a little while. You too, Ward. I mean it about the hard-on Bob White has for us both. And after what I just saw you couldn't stop me going if you wanted to. We'll work out the money."

"Thanks, Fokoli."

"Call me Dean."

"Yeah, maybe so."

He smiled at me and I returned that grin, the way two fellas do as they step away from each other, afraid to turn their backs.

* * *

I sprang for the train tickets aboard the Los Angeles Express on the Santa Fe line. We met at 10:00 a.m. the next day. I dressed for the outside world, donning my one tie and jacket, holding my one suitcase, Fokoli his. It seemed both of us had the kind of lives that were easy to shutter for awhile. I wonder if Fokoli was like me and had that suitcase packed all along, just in case.

The fact that we were avoiding our history together didn't really sink in until we were sitting in our sleeper car in facing seats. It was easy to get caught up in the letter and the yellow film can and ignore our connection. Beyond that one interview down at the precinct and the night out at Pop's house, we were strangers. I'd read about him in the papers in the weeks after. Fired from the force, allegations of corruption that he didn't deny. A widower. Beyond that I might as well be sitting with the Emperor of China for all I knew about him.

I tugged at my necktie. Not my normal attire, but sweat-stained T-shirts and khaki pants aren't fit for interstate travel. Best to try to look respectable, even if a blind man selling pencils could tell I was faking it.

"So . . ." I started off but let it die.

"Yep," he added.

Neither of us was eager to start talking. We had that in common. We would get along fine sharing a mutual distaste for conversations about the past. This could work.

The train lurched forward with a blast of steam and started to gain speed. The noise drowned out any hope of a conversation and we both sighed relief.

I turned my thoughts to Audrey. All we had was the address on the package and a name. I didn't know what she looked like, didn't know what to do to help her once we got there. I was still in shock to learn she existed but I was growing more grateful I had some family left in the world, even a half sister.

Fokoli lit a cigarette. I must have grimaced because he looked at me after it was lit and asked, "Do you mind?"

"Actually . . . I don't smoke and what with training and all I'm just not that used to it up close."

He stubbed out his fresh smoke in the tiny flip-out ashtray under the window, trying not to look too annoyed. "Guess I can go out in between cars when I need a smoke. Or to the bar. Let me guess, you don't condone alcohol either."

"You do what you want. I just don't imbibe myself. You know, with training . . ."

"Yeah, yeah with training. I get it. What say we get up and explore our new home for the next two days?"

He stood and I followed. We wound our way through a maze of tight corridors and between rushing cars. Each time we passed from one car to the next, the blast of noise, the wind, and the uneven footing made it feel like the whole train was ready to burst apart.

Watching the flat Kansas plain speed by outside made me miss the days of traveling to fights with Rex. We rode economy and never saw many sights along the way but to travel anywhere for a fight made you feel like you'd made the big time. I guess Pop felt the same way; sleeping with women along the route. Made me wonder how many other sisters I had out there I didn't know about.

We reached the bar car. It was crowded, even at 10:30 in the morning. Fokoli stopped for his smoke and I went out to the space in-between the bar car and the next lounge car. I could see through the window it was more of a cigar and pipe crowd than the pack of Lucky's Fokoli smoked.

I hung on tight to the chain, all that was keeping me from falling to the tracks below. I let the wind mess my hair. I watched the land move west.

I'd never been to California. The furthest west we'd ever gotten was Wichita. Most of our fights were up and down the Mississippi. I must admit I was looking forward to seeing Los Angeles. After I got Audrey squared away and out of trouble I was planning on sticking around a day or two to get a taste of Hollywood for myself.

I can't say I'd been working hard the past two years but I still needed a break. If that was even in my nature. I figured I'd find out.

The Kansas landscape wears out its welcome pretty quick so my attention turned back to the coach car behind me. A fat man, smoking a stogie while reading a newspaper, sat taking up two seats. He pitched and rolled right along with the movement of the train and it was obvious a trip out to the coast was nothing new to a big shot like him.

A young boy with red hair and pants held up by suspenders wandered through the car. He looked like he was headed out to Hollywood for an audition to join *Our Gang*. Judging by the holes over his knees and the hungry look in his eye, he didn't belong to any of the adults inside. They all ignored him but he was seeing everything they did.

A black porter in a white jacket and gloves brought a drink to the fat man. He set it down and the fat man dropped a dime on his silver tray without ever looking up from his newspaper.

The redhead moved in. I watched as the boy, all of eight or maybe nine years old, swept in on the porter's wake and shot out a hand, quick as a bantamweight's left jab, up under the newspaper and came back out with a shiny gold pocket watch. If I hadn't been studying the boy's every action I wouldn't have seen the momentary glint of gold.

His oversized pants hid the new addition to his pocket and his suspenders sagged a little lower. A nine-year-old thief. The momentary feeling of being impressed was washed away by the certainty that this boy was on a path. In ten years time, less probably, he'd be back and holding up the whole train, Jesse James-style.

I turned back to the bar car and found Fokoli.

8

FOKOLI

Kansas is a flat and endless land harassed by constant wind. And on a train rambling along, cutting through that flat sea of grassland, I'd be lying if I said I didn't feel small and insignificant—a babe in the woods at the mercy of nature.

Wind gains no purchase in the city. Although its power is occasionally channeled between buildings, enticingly lifting ladies' dresses or causing men's hats to sail into the street to be crushed under the tires of passing cars; the wind, in general, is tamped by the skyline of downtown Kansas City.

A train in the middle of a prairie is the tallest thing for miles and the wind knows this. As the Los Angeles Express bucked and swayed with each gust I struggled to keep my bearings and concentrated on the painful mess of my face and my hand. It was better than thinking about the film Ray showed me.

But the images kept swimming around in my mind—the girl on the bed with her legs pulled up to her chest, the girl sobbing, the girl crying out in silent terror. What happened afterward, after things faded to black? Did she just get up and walk away? Was she still alive somewhere, being forced to do the same terrible things over and over? Was Ray's sister, even now, as we moved as fast as we could toward the west, being degraded and filmed?

BORROWED TROUBLE

I tried to smoke in the sleeper car but Ray couldn't handle the smoke the same way I couldn't handle being without it so I sought refuge in the lounge car. It turned out the tough boxer I was traveling with couldn't handle booze either. Or maybe he just didn't like it. Probably a little of both if I thought about it. When it came to the image of the girl on the film I needed something to blur the edges.

Women and children stared at the bruised cut on my cheek as I passed through the coach cars, avoiding a direct stare at my blackened eyes or taped up nose but sliding their eyes in that direction anyway. There aren't many places on a train a guy can go to be alone. The lounge car didn't have a nice corner booth where I could sit in shadow and nurse a bottle of bourbon while I mulled things over. So I sat across from a drummer from Indiana selling neckties. He opened his case with a flourish when I sat down, so I gave him a look and a bit of a growl and he backed off. Suddenly the prairie outside the window fascinated him.

I drank a little and smoked a lot while I tried to think about the case logically. Still the girl, curled up and sobbing, penetrated my thoughts.

I'd seen a stag film or two in my day. It was hard not to in my line of work. As a younger man I fell in love with my fair share of beauties gyrating to jazz in front of a camera. This was something more, something vile. I was old enough to have a daughter the age of the girl on that film. The fact that Laura and I never had children changed nothing about the way I felt.

I ordered another bourbon and the waiter asked if I'd like something for my face. I asked for ice and aspirin and didn't get either one before Ray Ward sidled in. He took a look at the salesman but when the guy didn't acknowledge him Ray figured it was okay to talk. "I need to see you," he said.

"So take a look," I said. But Ray only cocked an eyebrow at me. He was a literal fellow I decided, not much for tongue in cheek. I sighed. He'd hired me, after all. Although what, exactly, that meant I hadn't decided yet. I tossed back my drink, crushed out my cigarette and signed my tab. The drummer heaved a sigh of relief.

Ray led me back through the first coach car again and into the second, past the cringing ladies and their noisy children, past a sleeping fat guy, past a grungy kid sitting alone, and numerous other snoring, staring, nosy passengers. Halfway through the second car, he paused and slipped into an empty seat, then gestured for me to sit beside him.

"Three rows up on the right," he said.

I didn't need to look. "Dirty kid. Traveling alone."

Ray nodded. "He's got sticky fingers." Ray shrugged then, like maybe he was afraid to tell me what was on his mind. I waited him out. After a minute he cleared his throat. "I thought we could maybe teach him a lesson."

I watched the boy. His dirty fingers smeared the seat in front of him as he fidgeted and looked uncomfortable, like there was something big in his back pocket. I gave Ray a nod and rose from the seat. I moved up the aisle, stopping just in front of the kid's seat. Ray followed and stopped just behind so the kid was wedged. Unless he wanted to crawl under the seat and end up between an old lady's knees, there was nowhere for the runt to go if he decided to try and run.

He looked up at us from underneath dusty red eyelashes and his eyes widened when he got a load of my face. He had a snotty nose. A kid with dirty hands and a snotty nose was most likely motherless. I'd seen a lot of bad mothers in my day and even the worst ones wiped their kids' noses. Wiping your kid's nose was the best way to hide a broken home. Sympathy popped up for a minute and I couldn't help thinking Laura would have liked this brat—wouldn't have wanted him to end up in juvie.

The boy swallowed hard and his eyes shifted side to side in panic. I thought that was a good thing. If the kid was still afraid of people in charge then he stood a chance of going straight.

I could tell Ray Ward was thinking the same thing. He nodded at me and I grabbed the kid by the scruff of the neck and pushed him out in front of me. Ray brought up the rear.

The kid was short and scrawny so he was easy enough to keep quiet. Maybe folks thought Ray and I were his angry uncles. Maybe they just didn't care. But no one paid us any mind.

I shoved the kid out into the area between the coach car and the dining car. Wind howled there and the tracks blurred by underneath the tiny perch where we stood. The kid made to open the door into the next car but I held him in place and pushed him against the railing so he could feel the full effect of the wind howling by. His eyes widened with fear. "Welcome to No Man's Land," I said.

Ray loosened his tie and rolled up his sleeves, letting cords of lean muscle show through. He stood with his feet planted shoulder-width apart and his arms crossed, blocking the passage. The boy looked at him and swallowed hard. "Empty your pockets," I said, pulling him back from the rail.

The boy kept his eyes on Ray.

"Hey," I said, swatting him on the back of the head. "Empty your pockets."

Reluctantly, the kid turned to look at me, his lashes blinking in bewilderment. "Why should I?" His voice squeaked a little bit.

I pulled the phony badge out of my pocket and showed it to him. "Because if you don't," I said, kneeling down in front of him and nodding in Ray's direction, "my partner is going to get very angry."

Ray cracked his knuckles.

The boy gulped and his hands disappeared into his baggy pants. When they emerged again, he held an assortment of items, no doubt lifted from passengers up and down the coach cars. He held his cache out for my inspection—a pocket knife, a gold watch, a handkerchief, a gold pen, and a flask. I held up the flask. "Someone is sure to be missing this."

The corner of Ray's mouth turned up, barely, but it was a change from his usual hard look.

"You gonna arrest me?" the kid asked.

I chewed on my cheek like I was thinking about it really hard. "I don't know, son." I stood up and made a show of looking at Ray. "What do you think, Sergeant?"

Ray cracked the knuckles on his other hand and looked down, studying the ground sliding past beneath the train. The boy's lip started to quiver. "He has to return the stuff," Ray said. "Or he goes to the clink."

I'd had about enough of Ray's cop lingo so I stood up and put my hand on my hip, pushing my jacket out of the way as I did in order to let the boy see my gun. I rubbed my chin. "I don't know. There's a lot of stuff here. Looks like he's committed a real train robbery. They used to hang men for that."

The boy's lip quivered violently and he hung his head. "Who you traveling with?" Ray asked. He kept his feet wide and his arms crossed. The boy was afraid to meet his eye.

"My mom." We knew it was a lie and the little thief knew that we knew because after a minute he said, "Nobody. I'm going to meet my granddad."

"Where?" Ray asked.

"California."

I rubbed my chin again. "Fair enough," I said. "Let's have you return all this stuff to the folks you stole it from and my partner and I here will see what we can do about keeping you out of stir."

9

RAY

Los Angeles, at first look, was a letdown. I expected what everyone expects: movie stars waving at you from top-down cars, klieg lights and movie cameras on every corner, someone walking Rin Tin Tin down streets paved with gold.

What we got was a busy Union Station buzzing with the same porters, passengers and grifters as anywhere else.

I saw the redheaded kid get off and meet up with his grandfather. The old man seemed a little miffed the kid came off a cross-country jaunt empty-handed. I'm sure Grandpa got an earful about the two cops who busted the kid and made him take a long walk of shame up and down the cars as he delivered stolen goods back to the suckers who let it get swiped in the first place. The kid learned a lesson but the lesson may have been to work on his game so next time he wouldn't be spotted.

The main hall of Union Station was grand enough for a movie set. If you could get past the hustle and noise of the crowd and look up it was a really beautiful space. High pitched ceiling in thick wood beams, intricate stone floor, comfy leather seats, chandeliers hanging.

Out front I saw palm trees. Only place I'd ever seen them before was on a postcard.

Fokoli stepped up next to me and I'm happy to report we didn't look like the biggest rubes on the curb. Two girlfriends tittered by soaking it all in. Their eyes as big as saucers and filled with dreams. Fokoli joined me in stripping off his suit coat and slinging it in the bend of his elbow. The sun felt like it shined a little bit hotter in L.A.

I showed the address to a cab driver and he said he knew the area.

"Miracle Mile," he said. Hollywood does have a flare for the dramatic.

"Take us to a hotel nearby," Fokoli said.

The cabbie pulled away from the curb. "First time in L.A.?"

"Yeah," I said but Fokoli cut me off with a firm, "No." His eyes told me to shut up. "We've been back east, putting together some financing for a picture."

"Issat so?" the cab driver asked, suspiciously. I looked at Fokoli and apologized with my eyes. He was right. I wouldn't step into the ring and announce it was the first time I'd put on gloves. He knew better than me that cab drivers were like Western Union when it came to delivering news.

Everything was bigger than in Kansas City. Streets were wider, buildings spaced farther apart. We drove up Wilshire Boulevard for a few miles and then ducked off a side street. Spanish-style homes and two-level stucco apartment buildings sat on either side of the streets beyond thick swaths of green lawn. The horseshoe shaped apartment buildings almost all had fountains in the courtyard, hacienda style. I only know what they're called from reading it in some of Mom's decade-old Collier's magazines.

Fokoli rolled his window down, drumming his fingers on the door. He wanted a smoke bad but I'd scared him off of it.

The cab pulled over to the curb in front of a four-story stone building with a rusty sign: ST. MORITZ HOTEL.

"Here you go," the cabbie announced.

Fokoli leaned against the window, looking up. "You got anything a little less . . .?"

"Expensive?" finished the driver.

"Yeah."

It struck me then that he and I hadn't said a word to each other for the entire cab ride. We were each lost in the newness of the world outside the car and both perfectly content not to speak for fear of igniting a conversation.

The cab pulled away from the corner and continued down the street, the cabbie surely starting to worry about his tip.

Fokoli turned to me. "I charge expenses so the rooms are on your dime. Lower the rent, fewer the questions anyway."

"Fine by me." I just wanted to get to the address and find Audrey.

We turned on Pico Boulevard and stopped again at the curb in front of a building more befitting the two of us. The bottom floor housed a liquor store. A trash can on the sidewalk in front was overturned. The doorway of the building next door was blocked by two men with nothing better to do but stand and watch traffic. The White Star Hotel beckoned.

Fokoli left it to me to pay the cabbie. I handed him the fare on the meter and told him to wait for us.

We ordered two rooms, next to each other. We walked up two flights of paint chipped stairs, untrustworthy banisters and past noisy closed doors. I threw my suitcase down on the bed in my room, tugged off my tie and changed into my usual uniform: sensible khaki pants, T-shirt and a short sleeved button up shirt that had never known the heat of an iron. I washed my hands in the sink, waiting a moment for the water to look less brown, then knocked on Fokoli's door.

He answered pulling his hat on as he shut the door behind him, ready to go. I could see the bulge of his gun beneath his jacket.

He looked at me. "Going to the gym?"

"That tie was choking me."

"You're the boss."

We got back in the same cab and gave the driver the address again for Audrey's place. The cabbie sighed and did a u-turn. He wasn't buying the movie producer cover for a minute.

We passed back through the neighborhood on a different side street. The apartments all had names in fancy script or odd leaning letters on the sides. The Alexis, The Romana, La Casa Bella. Like somehow having a proper noun gave it some class. "Take me to The San Rafaello," you could say and anyone in town would know it like it was the Waldorf.

He let us out in front of one of the haciendas. The Pacifico, although the first "c" was hanging down by a single screw making it more like an "n". Two levels in a U-shape around a fountain that wasn't working. Spanish tiles decorated every surface, the courtyard was planted with exotic desert plants I'd never seen before. The air smelled different. We were a thousand miles away from a cattle yard, something you couldn't get more than a mile from in Kansas.

"You do the talking," Fokoli said.

"Yeah." I swallowed hard, not quite ready to meet my sister. My brother Rex and I had a bond I know could never be replicated. It was blood. No one else in the world had what we shared in common. Certainly not a half sister I'd never met.

I shifted on my feet side to side. I jerked my neck left, then right, but it didn't crack. I wanted a bell. Wanted an announcer to call my name. Wanted to tap gloves and run a time limit. Really what I wanted was to be back in the corner, safe behind the ropes. Managing allowed me the thrill up close but none of the danger. I couldn't help feeling I was stepping into the ring with one hand tied behind my back.

I knocked.

Round one.

The door swung open. She was pretty. Nothing like me. Blond hair, red lips, full figure. She cocked her head slightly like a confused dog but there was fear behind her blue eyes.

"Yes?" She slid the door a tiny bit more closed, suddenly unsure.

"Audrey?" I asked.

"No. I'm Nancy." Her features dropped. Then, hopefully,

"Are you Ray?"

"Yes."

She swung the door open and practically leapt out to hug me. She strangled my neck as she squeezed. I saw why knights wore suits of armor; to protect against cracked ribs from the damsels in distress.

"Is Audrey here?" I managed. I felt Fokoli smiling behind my back.

Nancy released me. "She's gone. Been gone for four days now." She looked me up and down. "I didn't think you were real."

I tried to stay focused. "Where is she?"

"I don't know. Come in, come in."

She let us in to the two-bedroom apartment. It was done up in girl chic. Lace pillows, soft colors, crystal figures.

"I'm Dean Fokoli, a detective." He must have gotten tired of waiting on a formal introduction.

"Oh, a detective. Thank God." Nancy hugged him too. He was caught only slightly less off guard than I was. She let him go and finally saw his face. She recoiled slightly then softened. "Are you okay?"

"Hazard of the job."

I spotted a photo of Nancy arm in arm with another girl. "Is this Audrey?"

"Oh, that's right. You've never met her." Nancy came next to me and lifted the silver frame off the credenza. "Yeah, that's her. Last summer down at Santa Monica beach."

A knot inside me loosened. I was glad for the confirmation that Audrey hadn't been trying to spare me in her letter—the girl in the movie wasn't her.

It wasn't a pipe dream to think she could be in pictures. Legitimate pictures. She wore long brown hair, had brown eyes and pale skin that offset her dark features nicely. She had what I've heard of as that thousand watt smile. Maybe I was just overcome with brotherly pride. She might have been an awkward bucktoothed country gal but all I saw was looks made for the silver screen.

Fokoli got antsy again. "So, you knew she wrote to Ray."

"Oh, yeah. I told her to. She knew about you but wasn't ever going to find you because of your Dad and stuff. But she had nowhere else to turn. Lloyd tried to help but—"

"Who's Lloyd?" Fokoli asked. I was glad I'd brought a professional. Already asking questions, divorced from the emotion of it.

"Audrey's boyfriend."

"Do you think he might be involved?"

"No way. Lloyd's a good man. It's Silvio."

"Who's Silvio?" Fokoli got out a small notepad and a pencil, scraped the tip with a fingernail and started writing. I couldn't yet put down the picture frame.

"He runs the studio. Banner Films. Strictly poverty row. Mostly Westerns. He gave Audrey her first parts. He also put her in her first . . ." She stopped herself, unsure what we knew.

"Dirty movie?" Fokoli cut through the bullshit.

Nancy got quiet. Her eyes went to the floor. "Yeah."

I set down the photo. "So she's been in the films? Films like what she sent me?"

Nancy snapped out of it. "Oh, no! She only danced. Just little strip tease movies. And not even the whole blow off, just down to her skivvies."

I didn't find much relief in that.

"Oh! She left you something. In case you showed up." Nancy dashed out of the room and down the hall to where the bedrooms must have been.

Fokoli finished writing in his book. "What do you think?" I asked.

"We got two names already. Should be easy to find her."

"Is that what you tell all your clients?"

"Cheating husbands, insurance cheats—tell 'em what they want to hear. Missing person? No way. Gives 'em false hope."

"Why shouldn't they have hope?" Fokoli hesitated, not wanting to answer me. "I can take it," I assured him.

"Because most missing persons aren't found. Not the ones gone for more than a day or two."

"And she's been gone four."

"But we have names. That's better than most." He held up his notebook as evidence.

Nancy reentered the room holding a package similar to the one Audrey sent me.

"She wanted you to have this in case you got here and she wasn't around. I think she knew there was a good chance she wouldn't be."

Nancy's elation at the cavalry arriving was giving way to her grief over her missing best friend. She seemed to have come to the same conclusion as Fokoli. Things didn't look good.

I opened the package. Another note. Another film, this time in a red can. I read the note silently and they let me. The whole room held its breath.

Audrey knew she was going away. She seemed resigned to it. She signed it:

> *Please help me, Ray. And if it's too late for me, do it for the others.*
> *Audrey Starling*

"That's her full name, huh?"

Nancy looked down at the last line on the note. "Oh, just her stage name. She's been using it for years. Her mom's name was Dumermuth. Sheesh, can you imagine?"

I'd sure as hell never heard Pop mention anyone with that car crash of a name. I'd remember.

The note was short on names and accusations, big on innuendo and fear. She seemed afraid to even write down certain names or maybe she didn't know them. Some sinister force was at work, though. Someone wanted her for a film. I tried not to think what kind.

"Do you have a projector?" Fokoli asked.

"No," Nancy said, worried. "Do you think it's . . . like the others?"

He ignored that one. "What about Lloyd? Where's he?"

"He's out at the studio in Palm Springs. They shoot cheap out there and there's lots of desert for the Westerns. He's a prop man doing one of Silvio's six day specials right now. He keeps calling and asking if I've heard from her. I've been trying to tell him there's nothing to worry about but I think he can hear it in my voice."

"Four days isn't nothing," I said, stating the obvious, then immediately regretted saying it. Nancy's chin fell to her chest. She was sinking deeper into a dark place.

I turned over the film can in my hand. Same size, just a red can for some reason. I had a good idea that what was on the film would look familiar too.

"So what now?" I asked the room.

"We go to Palm Springs," Fokoli answered. "But first I want to do a little checking around here. Did Audrey have a job?"

"Yeah, she and a lot of the girls worked at the Alibi Room. It's a bar a few miles up Wilshire."

"What do you mean 'the girls'?"

"Other actresses. I'm an actress too."

"You ever, uh . . .?" Glad he asked because I didn't have the balls to.

"No." She blushed and looked at her feet. "I do mostly chorus girl parts. I've been in six different movies for MGM. You blink or go out for popcorn and you'll miss me but I'm there, right up on the silver screen. I don't work for Silvio. I told her not to either. She just wasn't getting the parts. A girl's gotta eat you know."

"Okay. I'll start at the bar. Ray, you stay here and go through Audrey's stuff. Don't be shy. We're looking for something to maybe save her life. If she's got a diary, read it. Okay?" I nodded. "And try to find a projector. I don't want to see what's in that can any more than you do, but if she left it for you she wants you to watch."

"Okay."

"All right. I'm gonna go earn my fee. I'll meet you back here."

Fokoli left without a handshake or any reassurance that we'd find her for sure. I was liking him more and more.

Nancy rested a hand my arm. I noticed tears in her eyes. "She's gonna be okay. Right, Ray? You'll find her, right?"

I wasn't as good as him. I turned my body, pulling my arm away from her touch. "Yeah. Of course."

Either I was a decent actor or she was because she nodded and smiled through her tears. She believed help had arrived. I was starting to believe I'd never see my sister beyond a silver frame.

10

FOKOLI

Nancy. Audrey. Lloyd. Silvio. I chewed on the names as the cab wound its way out of the neighborhood where Audrey and Nancy lived, toward the ritzy part of town where The Alibi Room was located. In the alleys along Audrey's block, bums lounged against grimy walls, their hats pulled low over faces, sweat stains darkening their shirts. The spring wind didn't bite with cold like it still did back home; but everything else—the despair, the hopelessness, the crime—was the same.

The cabbie took a series of tight turns and just like that we were uptown. Nice shops, nice cars, nice ladies with nice legs. The cabbie dropped me off on a corner near the lounge and I paid him with cash Ray handed me before I took off. I was careful to give a good tip because I figured that's what folks in this part of town did. The cabbie tipped his hat as he drove off.

The Alibi Room was cool and dark inside and a fuzzy haze of smoke hung low in the air. It was the kind of place I knew well. I lit a cigarette, realizing I hadn't smoked since I got off the train with Ward.

I scanned the room, taking in this L.A. crowd, not so different from Kansas City after all. The bartender was a pockmarked man with a widow's peak and a flat nose and he didn't talk to anyone not sitting on a barstool. I counted three waitresses, five guys on barstools, and six couples at tables scattered throughout the bar. A guy in a tux sat on a small stage plinking out tunes on a grand piano. I slid into a corner booth where the light was dim and I could carry on a conversation if the right sort of girl came along.

After awhile a waitress sashayed over with a tray. She leaned over far enough for me to catch a glimpse of perfect white cleavage as she set a paper napkin in front of me. Her name was Rebeccah—with an "h" on the end, she said in case I was a producer or somebody important. I waited for her to bring me my drink and a fresh pack of cigarettes.

"Isn't Audrey working tonight?" I asked.

Rebeccah was the kind of girl who would never make it as an actress. She tried to look like she had no idea who I was talking about. She failed. She tossed a look over her shoulder in the direction of the bartender, like maybe she was afraid he could hear what we were saying way over here on the other side of the room, with a piano tinkling out a high-class rendition of "Minnie the Moocher." "Who?" she asked with a tight smile.

"Girl named Audrey," I said, taking a drag off a fresh cigarette. The smoke I blew out mixed with the cloud in the room.

She stuck out a hip and rested a manicured hand on the round part. "Sorry. Nobody by that name works here." Her eyes wandered lazily over my face before coming to rest on my bruised cheek. "I bet you're tough. I like a man who's tough."

I sipped my drink to buy some time, letting my eyes wander around the room. The bartender chatted up the stiffs while he poured the scotch, but his eyes slid our direction every few seconds, like maybe he didn't like that Rebeccah was spending so much time at my table.

Rebeccah drummed her fingers on her hip and studied my face. It had been a long time since I'd been interested enough to sweet-talk a dame and in a joint like this I had a feeling I needed to use my best manners. "I'm as tough as they come," I said, giving her the smile that Laura always said melted her heart.

Rebeccah chewed on her cheek and I could tell she was thinking about sliding into the booth across from me. She gave a one-fingered wave to the bartender and he scowled at her before signaling one of the other waitresses to take over Rebeccah's tables.

"Can I buy you a drink?" I asked.

She sat down across from me. She still wasn't sure what I was after. "I don't drink."

"Cigarette?" I shook the end of one out of the pack. She took the smoke between her lips and waited for me to light it. I began to wonder what sort of place this was and I wondered what Ray's sister had been doing working here.

"So, what do you do?" she asked, wrapping her beautiful red lips around the tip of the cigarette and tossing her dark hair as she exhaled. "Producer? Director?" She studied my face again. "There's no way you're an actor."

I laughed at that. "Why can't I be an actor?"

The bartender gave a sharp whistle. Rebeccah excused herself, slid out of the booth, and crossed the room. She leaned on the bar, talking to the bartender. One of the suits, a guy perched on a stool near the end of the bar listened to her, cast a glance in my direction, and slipped from his barstool and down the hallway in the direction of the back door.

I finished my drink and listened to the piano playing. After awhile the bartender sauntered over under the pretense of wiping tables. He gave me a weak smile. "Can I get you anything else?"

I shook my head and gave a smile of my own. "I'm looking for a girl who used to work here by the name of Audrey." I slid a ten onto the table, keeping most of it under my palm, but letting him see the corner.

The guy thought about it for a second. The Alibi Room was a posh place and I guessed right then that he was probably used to bigger tips. So I added another ten.

A couple of guys at a nearby table got up to leave and the

bartender moved away from me to clear their table.

I stood up and walked the cash over. "Hey, bub," I said, "I got a guy who says he's the girl's brother. All he wants is to know where she is."

The barkeep stopped his wiping and set his tray of empty glasses down. "That right?" he asked, taking the bills from me and tucking them into the front pocket of his apron. He moved over to stand toe to toe with me. The piano music got louder. I reached under my jacket and touched my gun, reassured by its presence.

"You seen her?" I asked.

He stared at me hard for a minute and then he blew out a breath and shook his head. "She owes me money. Kept all her tips five nights ago and took off."

Rebeccah pointed an accusing finger at me. "No one is supposed to keep all their tips. We all share. That's the rules. Right, Bill?"

Bill ignored her and studied my face. "Lloyd do that to you?"

Audrey's boyfriend. Interesting. "Why would Lloyd want to mess up my face?"

Bill's eyes narrowed. "Exactly." He moved to stand between me and the door.

A guy in my business gets to know when he's skating on thin ice. My neck tingled and my feet started to move on their own . . . time to go.

A couple of the guys on barstools stood up. I stood a good head above Bill, so I pushed my chest forward a little forcing him to back out of my way. The two guys at the bar moved in behind me, so I moved to put a table between me and them. I opened my coat. At the sight of my gun they backed off.

"I'm going to ask you to leave now," Bill said.

"I paid twenty bucks for information on Audrey. I'm not leaving until I get it."

"You paid twenty bucks for drinks," Bill said. "And if you don't go I'll call the cops."

I thought about flashing the phony badge, but I didn't want to make too many waves this early in the game. Besides, it was obvious they didn't know where Audrey was.

"She always thought she was so smart," Rebeccah said. "Like the stuff she did was acting. Ha. I've seen goats that can do what she did."

"Don't talk about her like that," Bill said. He looked at me. "I'm counting to five. If you're not gone, I'm dialing the phone."

I moved to the door, wondering if Ray found anything of value in Audrey's room. Maybe I'd bring him back here with me, he could hold 'em off up front while I searched the back. There had to be stuff worth looking at in the back of this joint. I studied Bill. He didn't look like the sort to make dirty films, but maybe I never looked like the sort of guy who would have his partner murdered and maybe Ray Ward never looked like the sort of guy to kill a man for revenge. The world is made up of all sorts of people.

" . . . three . . . four . . ." Bill kept count.

I stopped at the door and turned to look at him. "You wouldn't happen to have a film projector, would you?"

The last thing I saw of Bill as I pushed out the door into the bright L.A. sunshine was a bottle of beer sailing through the air at me. I closed the door just as it shattered.

"Sounds like quite a row in there," a man said as the door closed behind me. He was leaning against the wall outside the bar with his hands in his pockets.

"Yeah." I recognized him as the guy who slipped out the back earlier. I waited a minute before hailing a cab to see if he had anything he wanted to say to me. He didn't look like he wanted to talk. He was a big man, arms straining at the fabric of his jacket. Not the sort of fellow who looked for conversation. I fished in my pocket for my cigarettes and lighter and still he said nothing. I stepped to the curb and whistled for a cab. End of day traffic was picking up. It was getting on toward happy hour.

BORROWED TROUBLE

The driver pulled away after I gave him Nancy's address. Behind me, a black sedan pulled up and took the cab's spot at the curb and the man from the bar climbed inside. They tailed us all the way back to Nancy's place.

11

RAY

I didn't find much in her room. Then again, I'm no detective so, for as thorough as I was, she could have been keeping pet rattlesnakes and I wouldn't have gotten bit. No diary, not that I found. A few more photographs. That smile beamed from each one bright enough to burn a hole in the paper they were printed on.

"Those aren't cheap." Nancy stayed in the doorway.

"No?"

"Nope. Those photographers make quite a living off all the girls who come here and need head shots. More than a few of them take payment out in dates, if you get my drift."

"I do." I set the photos down on her nightstand. The bed was made to hospital perfection, a pink bedspread folded neatly and layered over white sheets trimmed in pink. A small writing desk was piled with movie magazines and lists of casting calls with more than a few circled in pencil. Cigarette cards of matinee idols were stuck in the edges of her mirror: Tyrone Power, Gary Cooper, Cary Grant. No boxers. Hard to maintain that matinee idol look when your job is to get punched in the face.

I opened the drawer of the writing desk and found the file folder she kept on me; newspaper clippings from the *Kansas City Star*. It was a strange feeling to know someone had been paying attention. I folded the papers shut and put them back.

There was a knock at the door. I turned to Nancy who was frozen with a fingernail pinched in her teeth. "I bet it's Gina."

She went to the door. I stayed back out of sight. The voice at the door was female, friendly. I came out of hiding to see Nancy taking a compact movie projector from a tall woman in a tight fitting navy skirt and gray cashmere sweater. Perfectly set raven hair, red lips freshly applied. Stunning. It's like they grow beautiful girls on trees in Hollywood.

"Thanks a ton, Gina. I'll get it back to you tomorrow."

"No rush. What are you watching?"

Nancy blanched. She stammered out the beginnings of a lie.

"Just some old home movies," I said, stepping fully into the room. Gina looked me over, then back at Nancy. I think she was impressed a little. "Hi, I'm Audrey's brother, Ray." Understanding registered on Gina's face and a little disappointment, I think, that Nancy wasn't entertaining male guests in her apartment.

"Gina. Nice to meet you, Ray."

"You an actress too?"

"Not yet. Just a secretary for a man who promises me the role of a lifetime someday soon. Very soon. It's been very soon for two-and-a-half years now. All I have to show for it so far is a parking space on the Paramount lot and chipped nails from all the typing."

"Well, whatever you were in, I'd buy a ticket." God help me I was flirting.

"I'll hold you to that when my name's in lights." She smiled at me and I grinned back like a grade schooler on the playground. "Nice to meet you, Ray."

"Yeah, me too." I found myself taking steps with her to the door. "Y'know I'd love to see a real movie studio. Maybe when this is all settled I can come by for a lunch or something."

As soon as I'd said it I felt like a heel. How could I be

asking for a date at a time like that? All settled? What was that? Keep it together, Ray. Before Gina stepped into the room I was feeling more and more like this was all going to be *settled* down at the morgue.

"Any time, Ray. It's just nice to meet someone who doesn't want me to get them an audition. What is it you do?"

"I manage boxers."

"I thought you looked athletic." God her smile was beautiful. "Enjoy your movie."

The fluttery feeling in my stomach sank like a rock. Why'd she have to say that? No way I was going to enjoy the movie.

We shook hands and I completely ignored the trouble Nancy was having holding the projector until Gina was out of the room.

"Oh, I'm sorry. Let me take that." I set the machine down on the coffee table.

"We don't have a screen so we'll have to show it on the wall."

I helped Nancy take down a painting of two horses running in a field. I placed the red film can next to the projector and plugged it in.

Nancy drew the curtains. "Guess it's show time."

"Not yet. I want to wait for Dean."

Right on cue there was a knock at the door. Fokoli came in but wasn't excited to see the projector. He knew what it meant.

He told us about his trouble at the Alibi Room and the overreaction of the bartender. I grit my teeth and wanted to ask him to take me back there; three days since I worked over a heavy bag in the basement. Working over the gut of a guy who knew about Audrey would feel twice as good. Those tendencies I'd been suppressing for over a year were beginning to bubble up again, the way a volcano gives off steam before it blows.

"And I'm pretty sure I was tailed on my way back here," Fokoli said.

"Followed? By who?" I said.

"It was more than the bartender interested in my questions about Audrey. I think they were just curious. Nothing to get too worried about yet."

I tried to read his eyes, unsure if he was telling me everything was A-OK to keep me calm, treating me like a housewife or hysterical mother of a missing daughter. His poker face was solid. He gave up a grin to Nancy and I reconsidered if he was being coy for my sake or for hers. I'd have to ask him for the straight talk on the tail later.

"Well, I guess we should roll it," I said.

"Nancy, you step out." Fokoli was the chivalrous one.

"No way. She's my best friend. I want to be here to help any way I can."

"If we see anything we might need you to help us with we'll call you. Otherwise this isn't for a woman to see." He gave her his best cop stare. She gave it right back.

"You see a lot in this town. Behind the scenes. It's not all pretty. I'm not a kid from Kansas. I know what's on the films. Audrey talked about it. She was scared it was going to happen to her. Now I'm scared it has." She shifted her eyes from his to mine, looking for a more sympathetic audience. She found it.

"I've known a lot of girls who've gotten hit on, grabbed at or very nearly raped. This town is a lure for guys who think they can get girls in bed with not much more than some promises. A lot of times it works. Sorry to burst your bubble boys, but almost everyone I know has done something they regretted. But what Audrey said was going on . . . girls being forced . . . whatever's on there can't be worse than what's in my head."

She was so wrong.

Fokoli and I caved to her insistence but what we saw wasn't like the other film. Right away we knew it was the same room and the same guy. The putty-faced man had a harder look this time. He wouldn't let go of the girl either like he did with the other one. She was a scared rabbit kicking to be let go, a gag wrapped tight around her mouth. Other than that she was completely naked.

He had to release her to unzip his pants so he swatted her a backhand across the face which sent her down to the bed, bouncing on the springs—there was no sound but I could almost hear them squeak. He slipped his belt off and put a knee on the small of her back, wrapping her wrists with the belt and pinning her arms behind her.

I looked away and caught Nancy's eyes darting to and from the image, body tightening, chewing a fingernail down to the quick. I wanted to cover her eyes, to rush her out of the room. I wanted her to be sitting next to Audrey, nervous for the other girls, not my sister.

The projector motor hummed along just as it would to a Laurel and Hardy short. No one on screen was hurling cream pies to make us laugh.

The sex act was over quickly, each of us taking turns looking away. The man looked slightly more tan than before, like he'd been sunning himself in anticipation of his big role. The girl was different but really she was the same. She cried the same. Curled into a ball the same. She suffered the same.

Fokoli and I exhaled after the worst was over. We'd survived another one. But the film did not run out. The screen did not go white.

The big man, his mouth a hard line, his brow furrowed like he was doing a job he did not want to do, left the screen for a moment, came back with his pants on loosely, no shirt, and approached the girl again. He untied his belt from her wrists but did not thread it into his belt loops. He quickly and mechanically brought the strap up around her neck.

Nancy gasped so Fokoli and I didn't have to.

His biceps flexed as he pulled tight and leaned back, lifting the girl off the bed. Her feet hung in the air and she was a rabbit again, kicking at nothing. His face contorted, pulsated, grew red.

Nancy looked away at last. She whispered, "God" to herself or maybe for the girl.

Fokoli clenched a fist though I doubt he knew he was doing it. I tried to just concentrate on the actor. His physique, his flat features, his short black hair. He'd have made a good fighter. I'd like to see him in the ring with someone his own size. Someone to tear him apart. I'd like to see him hanging like she was, her kicks becoming slower and resigned.

The actor pulled, unrelenting, until she was still and then beyond. He let one end of the belt go and pushed her away from him so she fell onto the bed. I'd seen men go down in the ring, KO'd before they hit the canvas. They collapsed the same way. No arms went up to stop her fall. No protecting of the face. No point to it.

After a few heaving breaths, the actor turned and walked off screen unceremoniously. The camera rolled, unblinking. The figure on the bed was still. Her face turned toward the lens, eyes still pleading for help even though it was too late.

The image remained unmoving exactly where two horses had run across the wild plains not fifteen minutes before, the three of us as still as the image on the wall.

The projector clicked, snagged and stopped. Gears turned but the film did not. The thin strip of film turned crooked in the gate, a row of holes showing on the right side, breaking the illusion. After a few seconds of stillness the image warped. Heat from the lamp blistered the frame and the picture melted and bloated in orange tones that quickly turned black on the edges.

I stood up and unplugged the machine. The sound stopped and left us with only the acrid smell of burning celluloid, an appropriate stench to accompany what we just saw. I only wished the pictures would leave my brain as quickly as the smell would dissipate.

12

FOKOLI

Nancy's breath came in short gasps, each higher pitched than the one before. Ray moved to put his arm around her but I got to her first and pushed him back. She was standing and pointing toward the wall where the images of a raped and murdered girl had all but burned themselves into the paint. Her mouth moved in silent, tortured contortions. There was no sound in the room but the hissing of her breath. I shoved her onto the couch and pushed her head down between her knees.

"What are you—?" Ray started but I cut him off.

"She wanted to see it. You let her stay. What did you expect would happen? That we'd watch the film and drink wine after it was over, discussing cinematography or lighting or whatever it is these whackos out here talk about?"

Ray took a step back and I realized I was yelling, my voice echoing off the thin walls, bouncing back to me in a hollow sound. I was close to becoming a madman. I had one hand on Nancy's head and the other clenched into a fist. Ray and I stared at each other. The film was what we were here for. It was what we had needed to see. He knew it. I knew it. I focused on a grimy fingerprint halfway up the wall on the other side of the room and took a deep breath.

"I'm sorry," I said after a minute. I helped Nancy to sit up. She was better, but pale in the way a dame gets when she's seen too much. Ray strode to the couch and sat down beside her.

I stepped into the dining room. A battered sideboard stood next to the tiny table and I opened it, pushing aside table linens and candle sticks, feeling in the back for what I hoped would be there. My hand closed around a bottle of bathtub rye and I pulled it out. My kind of girls.

I took a deep pull from the bottle then grabbed a glass from the kitchen and poured Nancy three fingers.

"That's Lloyd's booze," she said as I pushed the glass into her hands.

"Drink it," I said. "We need to talk."

She downed it. Her eyes watered a little, but some pink came back into her cheeks.

"Did you know her?" I asked. "The girl on the film?"

Nancy shook her head. "N-no. I never—I never . . ." She put a hand to her mouth and stifled a sob.

I walked to the window and looked up and down the street. The car that had followed me was nowhere to be seen. I'd made it easy for them. All they had to do was come back when Ray and I weren't around. I looked back at Nancy and thought about the film. There was no way to lie about any of it. There was no way she was safe.

"You need to leave here," I said. Nancy didn't speak. She just stared at me wide-eyed. A muscle in Ray's jaw worked in a way that said he was as sick about all of this as I was. I wanted to say something reassuring about being certain Audrey was still safe. But there was nothing—nothing I could say about that so I poured Nancy another drink.

Nancy swallowed the booze, her hands shaking a little. After a minute she asked, "Why? Why do I need to leave?"

I reminded her about the men who followed me and about the girl on the film we'd just watched. "I don't know what those men want. The Alibi Room was a dead end. Audrey's boss said she stole from him and he fired her." I took Nancy's elbow and helped her up from the couch, propelling her to the bedroom as I continued to talk. "You watched the film, Nancy. There's no way to lie about it, not now. You need to get out and lay low for awhile."

I pulled a suitcase from the closet and opened it on the bed. Ray pulled open drawers and dumped their contents into the open case.

Nancy revived at the sight of what we were doing to her clothes. "Stop," she said. "You'll wrinkle everything."

I turned my attention to Ray. "We've got to find this Silvio guy. And Lloyd too, if we can get to him. See if he'll talk."

Ray nodded. After a minute he said, "Audrey wouldn't steal."

I scoffed a little. "Yeah okay, pal. She's a saint." Ray stared at me. "You don't even know her," I reminded him.

"No, listen," Nancy said to me. "Ray's right. If Audrey took money from her boss it was because she'd earned it and he was holding out on her, or because she was in some sort of real trouble." She stopped folding her clothes and chewed on a nail.

I ignored them both. "Where can you go?" I asked Nancy. "It needs to be someplace safe."

"I've got a friend I can call."

"Good. Do it." I looked at Ray. "Let's call a cab."

"No," Nancy said. "Take my car."

Ray's jaw clenched again and I imagined his teeth being ground into powder with all the worrying he was doing. "What about you?" he asked.

Nancy kept packing. "I'll get a ride." When neither of us said anything she looked up and shrugged. "I have friends with cars. Important friends who can keep me safe." She went back to packing. "Keys are on the table by the front door. Now go," she said.

On the way out, Ray stopped and stared at the projector. "We should destroy that film," he said. "No one should ever have to see it again."

I pulled the reel from the machine, put it back in the red can.

"Leave it with me," Nancy said. "Like I told you, I've got important friends. They might be able to help."

I had a bad feeling about that . . . about everything. "No. We should take it, Nancy. It'll be safer. You'll be safer."

She shook her head. "I'm keeping it. I owe it to Audrey to do something about this. Go. I'll be fine." She hugged the red can against her chest.

Ray's jaw clenched and looked like he wanted to say something but I moved toward the door and he seemed to change his mind.

As I walked out, I turned back to her. "Be careful, Nancy. And get out of here as quick as you can."

She nodded, her eyes wide. As we pulled away from the curb she was busy pulling shades.

I drove. Ray sat beside me with thoughts heavy enough to hear. I felt a little guilty for doubting his sister and I thought maybe I should say something to soften it a little. But I was never good at that sort of thing and it was probably better if Ray braced himself for being disappointed—with the case or his sister or both. After awhile he turned to me and spoke. "I'm going to kill that guy."

There was nothing I could say to that.

I pulled into a diner, went inside and got us some takeout. Ray didn't seem too hungry. We sat in the car for a few minutes while he got up the nerve to speak. "What next?" he asked.

"What are you prepared to do?"

He didn't have an answer for that and I wasn't sure I wanted to hear one right then. I drove east toward Palm Springs and kept my eyes open for the car that had followed me from the Alibi Room earlier.

Spotting a tail on a dark highway isn't as easy as spotting one in the city. I kept my eyes open and my mind on the case. But here's the thing about the dark . . . in the dark, all headlights look alike.

13

RAY

L.A. lights up pretty at night.

I felt like a kid sitting next to Daddy while he drove. Fokoli in his hat with his cop chin leading the way. Me, no hat, permanently looking like I just stepped out of a gymnasium. Gee, Pop can I have a nickel for a pack of gum?

Gears were still grinding in my head. My sister mixed up with men who would do a thing like that. Made me realize how much I didn't know her. But it didn't matter. She was family. Even if Pop was our only bond that still meant something. He didn't matter worth a shit but she did.

I was a lousy navigator. My mind was too blurry to pay attention to street signs. In no time flat we were lost. Fokoli pulled into a Texaco station, asked a white-shirt who was all too eager to help until we said, "No fill up. Just directions to the highway."

He flicked a thumb over his right shoulder as he sulked away, no tip in his hand.

As Fokoli confirmed the rather vague direction of his thumb I watched the rearview as a still pair of headlights stared back at me. Paranoid. Calm down. Take back control or you'll lose this fight. I unclenched my fist but without thinking it curled back up on its own.

Palm Springs held more mysteries than Hollywood and I

was eager to get out there. My stomach rumbled for lack of food, the hamburger Fokoli brought me sat uneaten on the back seat. I swore I wouldn't eat for a week after that film ended.

Nancy's car, a Ford coupe in a red normally reserved for nail polish, was purchased for looks rather than what was under the hood. Fokoli tried to gun it but it was a cap gun at best. We managed our way onto the freeway heading east into the desert.

Fokoli cinched down his hat against the warm spring wind blowing through the open window. Back in Kansas no car window is ever open until at least June. Out here we were surrounded by convertibles with bottle blondes behind the wheel. Even at night people were out to be seen. I mean, you never know when the next gal is going to be plucked from the counter at Schwab's and taken for her screen test, right? No promises on what kind of screen test though. I'd learned that during my one day in town.

"You know where we're headed?" I asked.

"I know what direction we're going, but I don't know what the end of the line is."

"Is this what detective work is? Chasing clues off a blind cliff?"

"Mostly. You just learn to look before you leap."

"Thanks again. For doing this."

He kept his eyes forward on the road. "Don't mention it. Slimes like that, guys who made those movies, they need to be taken down."

"Not exactly K.C., is it?"

"K.C.'s not immune."

He chewed his lip. I knew there was a story there itching to come out but I wasn't so sure I wanted to hear it. I'd seen all I wanted to about the dark side of man already.

"Go ahead and smoke if you want. Just keep the window down."

Like a thirsty man to water he reached for his pack. "Thanks, Ward."

The cigarette was lit in a hurry and he held the smoke in

his lungs for a long time.

City lights faded. We passed a warehouse district, the remnants of an orange grove, and drove east into a pitch black night. The highway led off into the distance, invisible except for the headlights of cars coming the opposite direction. Highway signs read like a Spanish phonebook: San Bernardino, El Monte, Rancho Cucamonga. Finally Palm Springs, 78 miles.

I checked the speedometer: 50. Doing the math to calculate our arrival time took my mind off Audrey for a moment. I even think my brow unfurrowed and my shoulders relaxed.

The desert air turned cool and Fokoli tossed the butt of his cigarette out and cranked the roller on his window, tossing his hat aside now that his hair was safe from the blowing wind. "I hear this place is good for your health."

"Yeah, dry heat. Good for asthma."

We were getting good at small talk. Ought to have our own radio show.

I checked the rearview when a bright glow flashed in my eyes. "Looks like this guy is eager to start his healthful desert retreat. He's a little impatient."

"More like right up our ass." Fokoli cranked the window down and waved an annoyed arm signaling the driver to pass. The imposing four-door Mercury stayed pinned to our bumper.

Fokoli and I both knew it at the same time.

The sedan was black. It gave the appearance of two floating headlights and not much else in the darkness surrounding us. We crested a hill and saw a sign for the next town ahead, some Spanish-named town I didn't know visible as a bed of lights nestled in the valley ahead.

Fokoli reached up under his armpit and pulled out a gun, passed it over to me. "You know how to use this?"

"Never shot one before in my life."

He shook his head at me. Even as a rookie I was a rookie.

"I say the word and you aim for the tires. There's four of them so you have a decent chance."

I held the gun loosely in my hand, trying hard not to

remember the last time I held one. Never shot one before, yes. Never killed with one before, not true.

Fokoli lit the fuse on the tiny firecracker engine and used the downgrade into the valley to pick up a little speed but the big sedan had us beat under the hood. As soon as we tried to run he gunned the engine and bumped us. The hit was gentle but we got the message.

Dean kept both hands on the wheel, staring down the road the way you do in a rain storm.

Another bump, then the Mercury came around to our left. If I was going to shoot I'd have to shoot across Fokoli and out his window so that was off the table. The sedan tapped our left bumper and our car swerved. Fokoli wrestled it straight again and I was glad to have him driving. My skills behind the wheel were rusty at best.

As the engine on the big sedan rumbled from the opposite lane, just off our back bumper, I could see the tall chrome grill of the Mercury smiling at us, the pointy nose of the hood and the headlights eyeing the Ford. Whitewalls spun and swerved to tap us again.

A frontage road split off about halfway down the hill. No exit number, no lights. The Mercury came up alongside us and drifted closer, daring Fokoli to keep to his lane.

"You see those big whitewalls?" He was shouting over the engine roar like we were pinned down in the trenches of France. "Line up the sight and blast 'em!"

I leaned over my seat and aimed the gun at the tiny back window of the coupe. I caught my reflection for a second and the image of me behind a pistol was startling. Beyond, I could see the rings of white spinning and as I tried to aim they made me dizzy. I pulled back on the trigger and the gun blasted. The back window blew into tiny pieces and my ears rang. Fokoli kept the car ramrod straight down the incline.

The Mercury swerved back into his own lane, tires undamaged, and then came back at us with fury. Our tiny coupe was rocked with a broadside from the sedan. I lost my balance and my body tensed trying to get it back. As I did I fired the gun again, quite accidentally.

I pierced the roof of our car and the tiny hole whistled in the wind. It was like riding inside a boiling tea kettle. Fokoli flinched but resisted scolding me. It would have to wait.

I aimed out the broken window and fired two shots, both off the mark. Like poking a hornet's nest my shots only made the sedan driver angry. He pressed the car into us and began pushing us toward the frontage road. I could see shapes of two men in the car, hats on, the one in the passenger seat gesturing with his arm.

I fired twice more, this time at the front seat of the sedan. The back passenger window shattered and the car swerved away for a moment, then crashed back into us, determined to push us off the road. Fokoli had no choice but to comply.

He guided us off the highway onto a soft shoulder. The car bucked and I was thrown back in my seat, dropping the gun on the floor of the backseat as I fell. There was one good shot left in the gun but the car tossed and careened like we were suddenly driving through a tornado.

"Shit," I said as I watched the gun bounce around the floor of the back seat.

I reached down over the seat as the car bucked like a Brahma bull and my ribs took a shot that a heavyweight would have been proud of. The gun slid forward, going up under Fokoli's seat, lost like a kid's gum ball.

The sedan slowed on powerful brakes and followed us off the highway, a fruit truck blasting us with his horn as he sped past, powerless to stop on the incline. Palm Springs would get their oranges in the morning. It wouldn't get us.

The dirt road turned and cut a straight path through to farmland far away from the sanctuary of lights in the valley. Fokoli managed control of the car as we approached a ditch. He cut the wheel and the headlights lit up a steep drop off down to a small irrigation creek.

Our tires stopped only a foot before the edge. The sedan

kept pace with us for the whole wild ride over the dirt and slid to a stop inches from our back bumper, threatening to push us over if we misbehaved. At least the ear-splitting whistle stopped.

"Polish up those fists, Ward. You may have to use them."

"Gimme your tie."

"What?" he asked but I was already undoing it before he could object. I tugged the cheap silk from around his neck and made two loops around my right fist by the time they got to us.

Both our doors swung open at the same time and two heavyweights reached in and each grabbed a fistful of our clothes. I swung once with my right but inside the car and at that angle, it was no use.

As I came out into the night air, dust still settling from the fast braking of the cars, I twisted my body and tore free from the powerful hands that held me. I stepped back and could see our attackers – right out of central casting at Warner Brothers. If these guys weren't in the pictures then they'd seen too many of them. A matched set, each man six foot four if he was an inch. Chests the size of grizzly bears. Noses with a history of being broken. Skulls a few inches thicker than normal.

I spun the tie the rest of the way around my hand. No point in breaking a knuckle in round one. By muscle memory I snapped into my boxing stance and let rip a right, fast as lightning. It caught the heavyweight in front of me on the jaw and sent him backwards. His polished shoes slipped in the dirt and he fell against the Ford which kept him upright.

I could see Fokoli on the opposite side of the car struggling to break free from the grasp he was in. He twisted and turned but the ape holding him was just waiting him out, a marlin on the hook.

My guy didn't need any recovery time before he charged me. I put up my defenses as he swung for my midsection. My chest rattled, lungs and heart banging against the cage of my ribs. I hunched over. He swung for my head with a windmill punch and as long as I was halfway bent I ducked under it. I jumped up and flicked two left jabs at him, bouncing off a mound of muscle, what part of his body I don't even know. He flung another wild swing at me and I ducked under it again flashing forward with another right to his ear.

He swatted at me like I was a mosquito there to ruin his picnic and then lashed a backhand at my face, complete with a heavy pinky ring that connected to my left temple. Dazed, I leaned right. I knew I had only a few seconds to get my shit back together, but I was too late. He drove a hairy paw into my solar plexus and I went down to the ground, sucking for air and bringing in a fistful of dirt with it.

By the time I could see straight I was upright, locked again in the giant's clutch.

"Which one of you assholes was shooting at us?"

Fokoli would have made a good fighter. He put on a tough face. "If it was me you'd be back on that highway with four flat tires and a bullet in your forehead."

That earned him a solid right to the gut. Man, the crowd would have screamed for that one. Fokoli doubled over, then was quickly pulled back straight by the thick goon holding him. We were both patted down, looking for guns that weren't there.

"Get in the car," we were told. As if we had a choice.

They took little care as we were both stuffed in the backseat like wadding into a musket. Rough and made to stay put. Both goons climbed into the front.

In the back, we joined a third man. He wore a dark suit, silk tie, polish on his shoes. Despite a weaselly face he held an air of authority you find in a maître d' or a butler, the kind of guy who dresses up nice for the job but underneath is a real bastard. I was pushed up against him and sandwiched by Fokoli at the door. We both sat on broken glass from the shot I took at the Mercury. The two Neanderthals climbed into the front. We'd have to tell Nancy sorry about the car.

"Gentlemen," the Dark Suit said. "You boys sure did piss off some people tonight."

"Like who? Those two?" Fokoli asked, tossing a thumb to

the chauffeurs in the front seat.

"Oh, no. If you pissed them off you'd be down in that ravine bleeding into the ditch water. No, much more important men."

"Like you, for example?" Fokoli kept at him. I stayed the silent type.

"Not me. I only do errands for the important people. I don't know from Adam. But they want you picked up, I pick you up." He smiled and showed rotten teeth. Bad breath hung like a fog trapped in the backseat.

I felt a trickle of blood from my temple where I no doubt had the imprint of that pinky ring in my scalp.

"Where to?" the driver asked. I knew he wasn't talking to me.

"Phone booth."

Fokoli stayed quiet on that one. I heard a gun cock from the front seat and a barrel stared us down at eye level. The man next to me spoke.

"Sit still boys. I got to find out what to do with a couple of curious fellas like you."

The sedan reversed and we went back out to the highway, back toward L. A.

Still far from the city, downtown only a glow on the horizon, the car pulled off. We drove over a narrow bridge over a trickle of a creek and pulled up to a street corner where the town seemed to just stop. It was an unfinished work. As if the 5:00 whistle blew and everyone went home. There was a phone booth but not much else. A traffic light but no reason for it. Street lamps but nothing to see. A street sign hung over the intersection but the name was left blank.

The Mercury stopped by the booth and the dark suited man got out leaving the door open, daring me to run for it. That gun in the front seat remained diligent, the man holding it grinning, wanting me to try.

I faintly heard the bell ring as a dime dropped into the phone. With no traffic around except for the distant rushing water sound of the highway, the night was quiet. I turned to Fokoli and saw an urgency in his eyes that I could not interpret. Maybe he was expecting me to start taking swings but where guns are concerned he was in charge and if he stayed put so did I.

The Dark Suit got someone on the line. "Gimme Baron . . . All right then just let him know we got 'em. Now what? . . . I don't know . . . Look, all I know is he said pick 'em up. We picked 'em up . . . the guy from the bar and another guy, I don't know who . . ."

I caught Fokoli's eye again but he was deep in concentration trying to listen.

". . . Then what? . . . A red one? . . . Okay, okay . . . What if he . . . All he did was ask a few questions . . . I know but . . . Okay . . . Okay . . . Right." He hung up, came to the door. "Get out."

The two men up front kept the gun trained on Fokoli and me as they matched our movements getting out of the car. We stood near the edge of the bridge, the water below just a trickle, hardly a river to someone who grew up where the Missouri and the Kansas rivers met.

Dark Suit seemed annoyed. "So, who's got the can?"

I looked at Fokoli. He kept his eyes on the man asking questions. "What can?" he said.

"The red one."

We both tensed. I played dumb. "No one has a red can. What are you talking about?"

"You guys better start gabbing now or someone is gonna get hurt. You got stolen private property and the owner wants it back."

"You got the wrong guys, pal," Fokoli said.

"Okay." Dark Suit began pacing, already frustrated with us. "Why were you asking questions at the Alibi Room?"

"Just looking for an old friend." Fokoli sure wasn't trying to make any new ones. It earned him another slug in the gut. My arms ached, wanting to lash out with coiled left jabs and powerful rights. They were angry dogs tugging at the end of a leash but that gun kept me in check.

Dark Suit calmly asked his questions. "If you're such good friends with the girl who took the film, why don't you know where it is?"

"Let's go see her and we'll ask her together." Fokoli's voice came out weaker but the attitude was still there. Dark Suit stepped closer to him.

"Look, I want to know what you know, why you're asking questions and who has my boss's missing red can. And I want to know now."

Fokoli laughed. "Oh, the film can. Yeah, I saw that movie. A little dull at first. Really picked up at the end. I didn't see you in it though. What's the matter, dick too small?"

Dark Suit stood back, unamused. He waved a hand at the one with the gun. "Shoot him."

Before the words left the air between us, like he'd been waiting for the call, the gun erupted.

Fokoli staggered back, dipping to his left. His feet were unsteady. I'd seen it before from behind the ropes. A guy who is going down and knows it but his body won't cooperate. The legs fight the brain to stay upright but the brain always wins.

The driver, the one without the gun, must have felt left out because he stepped up and snatched Fokoli by the lapels of his suit before he hit the deck. Fokoli's head flopped around, KO'd or dead I wasn't sure. I was leaning toward dead. The driver got in a last fist to the gut but Fokoli was beyond reacting. Fokoli's rag doll body was shoved, hard, against the side of the bridge. The man I'd paid to join me, the man I asked for a favor well beyond what he owed me, hit flat against the railing, pitched backward and fell down into the shallow water.

No one punched me in the gut but I was out of breath anyway.

"Let's take a ride. You can tell me all about movies in red cans," Dark Suit said.

14

FOKOLI

When a guy gets hit with a bullet it's said that his life flashes before his eyes. I'd been hit with bullets a few times before the night on the road to Palm Springs and I can tell you my life never once flashed before my eyes. Mostly I just got angry.

I didn't know how much time I'd lost by laying there with my suit soaking up all the mud and water it could hold. My pulse was fast and weak, making the stars I tried to focus on throb wildly in the night sky above me. The shot went wide and cut into my right shoulder—high enough to miss anything vital, but low enough to pierce the muscle and hurt like hell. I struggled to my feet and took a deep breath, dizzily watching the blood run down my hand and collect in fat drops that splashed into the muddy water of the stream.

The road atop the ravine was silent, but cars moved on a road in the distance, their wheels making that humming, slapping sound peculiar to freeways. In the dark I looked around for Ray Ward, wondering if they'd capped him too. But I was alone.

I took off one of my shoes and pulled off a sock to stuff in the wound. I would have preferred to use my necktie, but Ward had it and I was guessing they'd probably put a bullet in his head by now, so the tie wouldn't do him much good either.

I pressed the sock against my arm, picturing a future case of gangrene and gritting my teeth against the pain as I made my way up the steep incline and onto the road. Follow the lights, I told myself, but that was easier said than done because my eyes wanted to drift closed. So I focused on the sound of tires slapping the pavement in the distance, hoping it was a street where I could hitch a ride.

Initially each step was about survival—move forward and don't fall down. But I've got a one-track mind. Not even a bullet could keep me from replaying the night over and over in my head.

Nancy's frightened eyes swam in front of me. We'd left her. We'd taken her car and left her alone. I told her to leave. She said she would. But did she have time? And where was the film? Had she taken it with her? Had she hidden it? It wasn't just my shoulder aching now; my gut was starting to give me a little trouble.

My heart started to race and I fought the urge to run. I wouldn't stay conscious long if I ran. I pushed on, making it to the road and walking along the shoulder heading west. At least I thought I was heading west. The cars whined past me, their headlights casting erratic shadows ahead. I waved a few times, but the effort required to lift my arm was too great so I tucked my head down and moved on, hoping I'd make it to Nancy's before it was too late.

"Need a ride, Mac?" A New York accent shouted at me from a truck window.

I nodded and climbed in. "What happened to you, Mac? Tough night? You're a helluva long way from the city."

In the darkness my suit looked muddy and bedraggled, but at least it made the blood look like nothing more than dirt and grime. "Yeah," I said. "Tough night. Can you give me a ride back to town?"

He said he could. He dropped me on a main road about a mile from Nancy's. I was in no condition to make it on foot, so I grabbed a cab. The driver didn't look happy to see a guy who looked like he'd crawled out of a sewer, but I said I'd pay him double so he let me climb in. I spouted off the name of Nancy's street and leaned back while he drove.

I don't remember if I dozed. My arm was stiff and I was weak as I climbed out of the cab. I handed over double fare and watched the cabbie drive away. The street was deserted. Lights were off. I had no idea what time it was, but I guessed after midnight. Down the block, the lights were off at Nancy's place, too. I moved around to the alley and approached her house from the rear. There were no sounds on the street—not even a barking dog or an angry cat. I had a bad feeling.

I stood at the back door of Nancy's and listened for movement, voices, or any other sign of life coming from inside. I didn't hear a thing and I couldn't wait any longer. My arm needed to be patched and I needed to sit down or I wouldn't be conscious for much longer.

I jimmied the lock and stepped into a back room filled with hat boxes, dress mannequins, and a few old dolls. It was the sort of stuff girls tossed aside when they were done with it, but not quite ready to throw it out for good. Laura had a room like that in our place. After she died I found thirteen hats I'd seen her wear only once or twice.

The kitchen and dining room were dark and empty. I kept the lights off. No sense in advertising someone was around.

I had to go through Nancy's room to get to the bathroom. As I stepped into her bedroom, I noticed the hot, coppery smell of blood. I'd been smelling it from my shoulder all along, but this was stronger—this was a lot of blood and it soaked the carpet, squishing up around my shoes as I walked deeper into the room. Nancy. She hadn't made it out after all.

I knelt next to her still form and pushed hair back from her eyes. She was naked, her hands tied behind her back. Her eyes were swollen and crusted shut with blood already beginning to dry. Her lips were bloody and twice their normal size, wrapped around a cloth that had been jammed into her mouth. And at some point her attacker had taken a knife to her gut. Wounds crisscrossed her skin in a pattern that could only mean they played with her before they killed her. When they were done they'd snapped her neck.

I didn't bother to look for the film. I knew it was gone.

I got to my feet, dizzy with the effort and sick with the knowledge that we'd left her here to face this alone. I covered the body with a blanket. I saw my reflection in the dark bedroom window and noticed it was open. Maybe somebody heard something when she was being killed. I didn't know if this was the sort of neighborhood where folks called the cops when something bad happened or if they just kept their heads down and their doors locked. But one thing was certain—I needed to patch myself up and get lost before somebody showed up to check things out.

Nancy and Audrey didn't have much in the bathroom—bubble bath, razors, stockings hanging everywhere, no bandages.

Sweating with pain and sick from seeing what they did to Nancy, I tried not to pass out as I maneuvered out of my shirt. I set it on the bathroom counter and headed to the dining room. There, I grabbed the hooch from the sidebar and doused my arm, spilling the stuff everywhere and crying out when the ache got to be too much. When I felt like I had the wound cleaned out I returned to the bedroom and sat on the bed, careful to avoid looking at the shrouded body while I pulled a pillow apart. I packed the bullet hole, now only oozing, with stuffing, then tore the pillowcase into strips and tied a couple pieces around my arm to hold the packing in place.

Then I tossed the house. I looked for anything that might give me a clue to what was going on with these films. Ray took a look around earlier, but Ray was the kind of guy who would be careful to avoid offending a dame like Nancy. He probably hadn't opened any drawers.

I started in Audrey's room. I lifted her mattress and looked under the bed. I opened nightstand drawers and dresser drawers. I looked in pockets of coats hanging in the closet. I got lucky and found a short sleeved shirt, some khaki pants, a Hawaiian print tie and a leather jacket in Audrey's closet. Lloyd must have stayed over now and then. I struggled into the clothes and then I set my teeth and went back to Nancy's room.

I refused to look at the body as I went through the same routine as in Audrey's room. I didn't get lucky until I started pulling shoeboxes from the closet shelf and tossing their contents on the floor.

It didn't take long to find something. Morphine. Four full vials, and half of a fifth. Four syringes. Rubber tubing. Four hundred dollars in tens and twenties. All nestled beside a pair of tall, black high heels. Either Nancy was a doper or someone close to her was. I drew up a small amount of the drug and injected it into my hip. I could have handled a stronger dose, but it was the kind of stuff that would mess with my head and I couldn't have that right now.

I pocketed the dough and the drugs. I found enough food in the icebox for a sandwich, so I fixed a ham and cheese on wheat and drank at least a pint of milk. My mouth watered for the bathtub hooch, but I couldn't take a chance on adding that to the morphine in my system. I felt weak, but the pain was less and I was ready to move on. The clock on the stove read 12:30. If I hurried I could make it to the Alibi Room and catch Rebeccah at closing time.

I left from the back and I didn't bother to lock the door.

15

RAY

Wind rushed in through the broken window but I found it hard to catch my breath. Fokoli was dead and I might as well have thrown him off that bridge.

I guess there was a chance for Fokoli. I didn't see a death certificate but I've seen the look of a man with only seconds to live. Maybe it was just the street lamp shadows that gave him the look of death impending.

I tightened his tie around my fist until it hurt.

"Smart guy, staying quiet," Dark Suit began. "Your friend did too much talking but nothing I wanted to hear. Now it's your turn, but I can tell you don't mince words. I think you'll tell me what I want to know."

"And what's that?" Glass crunched under me as I shifted in my seat.

"I want to know about the red can of film. That girl stole it and now my employer wants it back."

"That girl, huh? Tell you what, I'll lead you to it for a little information of my own."

Dark Suit spoke to his assistants, amused at me. "He wants to start cutting deals. Like he's some Hollywood agent or something." Everyone had a good chuckle. "What do you want to know?"

"That girl is named Audrey. Where is she?"

"Fuck if I know. They all look alike to me, pal. Especially when they're bent over."

He smiled with nubby, unfinished looking teeth. My fist was clawing at the cage again, trying to break free, smelling the blood behind his nose waiting to come out if I broke it just right.

"Tell you what then, fuck your red film can. Consider it thrown in the ocean."

"Now then, pal . . . say, what's your name anyway?"

"Ray." I saw no point in lying.

"Ray, you don't want to end up like your partner back there, do you? What did he do, hire you for muscle? Couldn't handle it himself so he has to get a washed-up puncher like you to do his dirty work?" I let him rattle. "Ray, I don't know your girlfriend and I don't much care. You crossed the wrong guys. These guys, they got the most powerful thing you can have, especially in this town. Money. With money you can buy anything, even a girl. I can tell you seen the film so you know what I'm saying. Personally I don't like it. Not one bit. I never sat through one all the way. But these guys with money, they need the thrill. Nothing else gets them off, y'know?"

The closer we got to the city the traffic picked up. Dark Suit had to raise his voice over the whipping wind and delivery trucks rushing to make deadlines.

"So this Audrey, she's for sale. Everyone is. Look at it like this, she'll finally get her shot at the silver screen. That's what they all want, isn't it?"

The one with the gun thought up a zinger, started smiling before he opened his mouth. "She'll have to go to the premiere in a body bag though." He laughed. Dark Suit didn't dignify it but I saw his mouth curl into a grin.

I probably should have grabbed the gun first but I wanted a shot at that nose too badly. My right, tightly wound with the tie, struck out like a cobra and caught him in the sweet spot. I could feel it break even if I couldn't hear it over a fruit truck passing us.

My left shot up and grabbed hold of the gun. The gunman was dazed enough at what he'd just seen and his mind was still on his joke. I pushed his hand over and slid my finger in with his to pull the trigger. Dark Suit's forehead shattered like the window behind him and spewed bits of skull the same as the glass already in our seat.

With the side of my fist I punched the gunman and got his nose pretty good though it didn't break. The driver swung the Mercury into a different lane, confused about where to go during the fight.

I tightened my grip on the gunman's hand until my fingers dug into his wrist like they were clay. He tried to swing a left hand at me but it had to cross his body and I was well out of reach. I struck out with another right and caught his ear dead center, a painful blow if you land it right. He dropped the gun to the floor of the backseat and reached to cover his ears against more punches.

I grabbed the loose end of Fokoli's tie and spun it off my hand in a magician's flourish and swung it down around the throat of the unarmed gunman. I squared myself in my seat and pulled. A retching gag came from his throat. Finally the driver put on the brakes. He bumped off to the side of the highway but my grip stayed tight. The threads of the tie were going to give before I did.

On the soft shoulder the car ground into the gravel and the brakes hit a high pitched note that would shatter a wine glass. I gripped both ends of the tie in my left hand and opened my door with the right before quickly taking hold of the silk with both hands again. The driver spun in his seat and looked at me. He was lost, still wondering what happen-ed and how I overpowered the other two men. His partner was thrashing and clawing at the tie, desperate for air, his neck muscles straining.

The driver stared at me, somehow unable to do anything about what he was seeing, but I could tell wheels were spinning and I didn't have much time. I clenched the tie in my left again and threw a right over the seat and into the driver's face. It wasn't full force between my lack of leverage and not wanting to hurt my hand but it was enough to stun him a few seconds more.

I let the tie slip out of my grip and I rolled backwards out the door. I tumbled to the gravel and ran for the weeds on the side of the highway.

I didn't get far before I heard the big engine of the Mercury rev and the tires grind in the soft shoulder as the driver made his escape like he was being chased by Welles's little green men.

I stopped running and caught my breath. It may have been foolish to let them live. I'd find out and if it was a mistake it would be too late to do anything about it by the time I knew.

I didn't have much blood on me. Most of it went out the window when Dark Suit ate the bullet, and the gun was small enough there wasn't much spray. I patted the dust off my legs and evaluated all my extremities. I was unhurt and grateful for it.

I walked the highway, nervous to thumb a ride. After only a mile and a bit I followed an off ramp and found a diner. I wasn't sure I was up for people or food but I made my way over.

I hesitated at the door, stopping to watch a moth circling the lamp hanging above the entry. Its fat body had no business being held up by wings so thin and delicate. Maybe that explained his spastic flying and repeated banging against the glass of the lamp only to skitter off and loop back around like a punch-drunk fighter who doesn't know when to give up.

I opened the door and the moth stayed focused on his goal. Before the night was up he would probably be flattened on the windshield of a semi bound for Arizona and I wasn't so sure I'd be much better off.

The place was crowded for late night. Highway business; truckers, salesmen. No cops, thank goodness. I sat at the counter. Thoughts of the fight faded away and the image of

Fokoli falling over that bridge railing rushed in. The stink of cigarettes didn't help keep the pictures at bay.

A waitress in a pink uniform held out a coffee pot and a mug. "Coffee?"

I nodded, she poured. Not normally one for the stuff but I felt like indulging in a few vices. In that moment I could have reached for one of those cigarettes.

It was quiet for as many people as were in there, like everyone was trying not to wake the cook. I looked around. Three other guys at the counter and a woman down on the end. Two booths were occupied, one with a couple getting a little coffee jolt and one with a salesman looking at a map laid out across his whole table. The smell of old grease hung in the air, not much different from the engine smells outside in the lot.

The waitress came back presuming I'd had time enough to consider a meal from the thin menu still closed on the counter in front of me.

"Get ya' something?" She was older, weathered. Not like the girls in the city with stars in their eyes. I bet this one never had dreams that would get her killed.

"What I really need is a ride to Palm Springs."

"We don't do special orders," she said bluntly. I wasn't sure she was making a joke.

"Gimme a minute."

She turned and picked up her coffeepot. I could imagine the calluses on her hands from carrying it night after night.

I noticed the man two seats down turn away from me. He'd heard. "What do you say, pal? Going to Palm Springs?"

He ignored me, slurped his coffee. I ran my hands over my face and across my scalp, feeling the dried blood where that signet ring left an indent. So far I wasn't much of a knight in shining armor for Audrey. I'd gotten my partner killed and with him all the experience of locating a missing person. I'd managed to make enemies I didn't know and who were very serious about protecting secrets Audrey was trying to tell me. I wasn't any closer to finding her and I was starting to lose faith that I'd ever see her at all.

The thought that kept me going was that I'd done nothing for Rex. My brother, killed in the ring while I stood by, mute. Even if I was too late for Audrey I wanted to be doing something, anything but standing by, flat-footed and dumb.

I rubbed my eyes so hard I saw stars when I opened them again. It took me a moment to notice the woman sitting at the counter had moved from her seat to the stool next to me.

"Rough day?" she asked.

"Yeah." She'd brought her own coffee cup with her and sipped at it.

"Know how it is. Did I hear you say Palm Springs?"

"Yeah. I did."

"Guess where I'm going?" She smiled. She was attractive. Even sitting down I could tell she was tall. Natural blonde, tight fitting pencil skirt, sensible blouse buttoned high. She was no truck stop floozy from a barroom song. I got so interested in looking at her figure I forgot to answer her question. "Palm Springs, silly." She nudged me on the shoulder.

"Is that right?"

"Sure is. Know what else? I could use a little company to keep me up. I was thinking of turning in and getting a room for the night, but if you came with me I wouldn't have to. We could keep each other company. What do you say?"

I didn't want to say anything. I wanted to grab her and kiss her. If Kansas City had this many gorgeous women there never would have been a westward expansion. It was starting to feel like the whole country was tilted to one side and all the beautiful gals rolled downhill and landed in California.

"Let's go." I said.

"Great! I'm Cindy."

"Ray."

"Nice to meet you, Ray. Now get that frown off your face. Things are looking up for you."

She winked. I swear to God she winked. I tossed down a nickel for the coffee and followed her outside.

16

FOKOLI

A guy can get pretty tired of spending time in alleys trying to keep the smell of rancid lettuce and curdled milk off his clothes. The alley behind the Alibi Room was just like any other alley—dark, damp, the ground slimy with refuse. I stood a couple of minutes in my borrowed clothes before deciding that a dame, even one who worked here, wouldn't come out the back door. She'd leave by the front and make her way home by bus or by taxi.

I shoved a couple of shuffling drunks out of my way when they got too close. "Looking for a quarter, pal," one said. "That's all, just a quarter to take the bus. You can spare a quarter, can't ya?" His breath was 90 proof and as I backed away from it I felt his buddy's hand brush my hip, reaching for the cash and the vials in my pocket. I dealt him a sharp elbow to the gut and gave the guy with the flammable breath an uppercut that took his jaw up hard enough to clip a piece off his tongue. He was drunk enough not to feel it and didn't have enough brain cells to remember in the morning how it happened. I left them there slurring curses at me.

Yeah. I hate alleys.

A cigar shop faced the lounge on the opposite side of the street. Nobody loves a smoker like a tobacconist. For ten bucks he sold me three cigars, hand-rolled in Orlando. For an extra five he said I could stand inside and smoke while I watched the bar across the street. I told him I was waiting for my sister. He cocked an eyebrow at that, so I pointed to the bruise on my face and said, "See this? A guy at work has been bothering her. I had to step in. Almost got her fired."

He gave a bark of laughter. "Does he look as bad as you?"

I didn't know if he was talking about the ugly shirt I was wearing or the bruising on my face so I just smiled.

The guy slid a hand-carved box across the counter. "I bet you'll like these. They're the best they make." He pulled a cigar out and slid it under his nose. "They smell like the ass of a princess, if you know what I mean."

I pretended I did.

The cigar smoke made me sick. And my arm was stiffening up. It was late enough that even the night life was beginning to wind down. Lights dimmed up and down the block, OPEN signs flipped to CLOSED. Couples who had been flirting with seduction for hours suddenly emerged from doorways and hurried to catch taxis—on their way to finish the dance before any minds were changed. It was 1:00 a.m. closing time, witching hour.

I made like I was ready to leave the tobacco shop but the guy surprised me by pulling out a bottle and two glasses. "She's not your sister," he said as he poured me a couple of fingers.

I cocked an eyebrow and he gave another bark of laughter. "You're watching the Alibi like it was a bouncing titty, son. There's no way you'd be watching it like that unless she was more to you than a sister."

I swirled the bourbon he'd set in front of me and puffed the cigar. "She wants to be an actress." Maybe the guy would give me something; maybe he wouldn't.

He studied the burning tip of his cigar. "Every gal in L.A. wants to be an actress. If they aren't waiting tables to foot the rent in some slum, they're sitting at the drug store waiting to be discovered." He shook his head. "Is that the case with your lady?"

I nodded. "She's got a friend who wanted to be an actress."

"And let me guess . . . the friend got discovered, right?"

I leaned forward and lowered my voice for effect. "She disappeared."

His eyes widened. "You don't say."

I had him. One thing I'd learned since quitting the force—shop keeps love to gossip. I shook my head. "My girl thinks she can take care of herself. But I gotta see her home safe."

He poured out more bourbon and looked out the window to watch the cabs stopping at the curb across the street and loading up before pulling away. Another light had gone out inside the Alibi Room.

"She'd be better off working someplace else," the man said. "You tell her I said that." He took the ashtray from the counter and picked up our glasses—not yet empty. "Time to call it a night." He no longer met my eye.

"Yeah. She'll be coming out soon." I tucked the cigar between my teeth and shook the man's hand. I tried not to wince as I lifted my arm. The morphine was wearing off and I could already feel fresh blood wetting the pillow batting I'd stuffed it with. I thanked him and stepped outside. The sound of the door locking behind me was loud in the deserted street.

What did the tobacconist see while he stood in his shop and sold cigars? Was he in on it? Had he seen a film like the one we had? My arm pulsed with pain. My head ached and my mouth was dry. The morphine sat in my pocket, tempting me. But the desire for a clear head was stronger than the temptation of oblivion. Ray Ward hired me to do a job and I'd do it. That was that.

I waved a cab over and climbed in the back. I told the driver to wait for the girl. "You'll have to make a U-turn when she comes out. Is that a problem?"

"No problem, pal. As long as your money is green."

I gave him ten bucks and told him the less talk the better.

"You mind putting that cigar out?" he asked. "Smells like

my dad's false teeth."

I crushed stogie out on my shoe and laid it on the seat beside me. We waited ten minutes in silence. Rebeccah checked over her shoulder when she came out. Was she worried someone was watching her? Who? The barkeep was who came to mind. He had enough of a temper to throw a bottle at me. And Rebeccah had been nervous about talking.

She walked a block to the nearest bus stop and climbed aboard the first bus that pulled to the curb. She looked nervous, hunted almost. I hadn't seen anyone watching her, but then I wasn't exactly in a condition to catch too much. The cabbie followed her without any problems. The streets were busy but subdued. The frantic pace of getting somewhere to drink or dance or get laid had been replaced by the reluctance of returning home and facing another morning in a few short hours.

The bus stopped after a couple of miles and Rebeccah climbed out. I had the cabbie stop a block away so I could watch which way she walked. She stopped in front of a small bungalow, made her way up the steps to the front door, fishing for her keys in her bag while she moved. Careless. It was the kind of thing I used to warn Laura about all the time.

"You gonna get out?" the driver asked me.

I was stiff and weak. Without thinking I handed him another ten bucks and climbed from the car. He coasted behind me, watching, like maybe I was a guy up to no good.

Rebeccah was still looking for her keys as I approached. She turned at the sound of my footfalls and opened her mouth to scream or cry out, but I kissed her, covering her mouth with my own as I pushed her up against her door. I spun her around and held her around her waist with one arm and pushed my finger into her back with my other, hoping she'd think it was a gun. "Hello, darling," I said. "Find your keys so we can go inside."

She started to shake like maybe she was going to drop the bag. "I'm not going to hurt you, sweetheart," I whispered in her ear, turning around to wave at the driver.

"Pig," was all she said, but she stopped shaking so hard. She found her keys and unlocked the door. The driver pulled away.

She moved into the kitchen and started a pot of coffee. It was then that I noticed she was more relieved than angry to see me. Then I remembered how she had looked over her shoulder as she left the bar. She gestured to a kitchen chair and told me to have a seat.

"I need your help," I said as I sat down.

"I'll bet." She was flip but her eyes got big when I unzipped my jacket. The entire right sleeve of my shirt was soaked in red. "Jesus." Then she looked at my hands. "You don't even have a gun, do you?"

I shook my head. "I need you to patch me up. I can't do it." When she chewed on her lip I added, "Please."

She shrugged. The coffee finished boiling so she poured me a cup before disappearing down the hall.

I forced the hot liquid down my throat and was ready for a second cup by the time Rebeccah returned with a first aid kit.

"Bullet still in here?" she asked.

"Yeah. And it's going to stay there so don't get any crazy ideas."

"Testy, testy. This is going to hurt." She pulled out the wad of bloody stuffing. I jerked violently from the pain and my stomach clenched, but I managed to stay in my seat.

She cut several bandages from an old sheet and laid them over a wad of fresh padding she'd stuffed into the wound. She looked a little scared, jumping at sounds like the wind blowing.

"You nervous?" I asked her finally.

"Yeah. Some crazy man just busted his way into my house by making me think he had a gun. Guess that might make me a little nervous."

"The way you acted I thought maybe you were expecting somebody."

She chewed on her lip, like maybe she wanted to say

something but didn't know what it was. She was saved by the sound of erratic pounding.

"Lemme in, Beck. Lemme in." The voice was muffled by the door, but desperation didn't need clarity. I was halfway out of my chair before she stopped me.

"That's Joshua," she said. "He'll throw himself inside through one of the windows if I don't open the door."

I shrugged. What was I going to do? Shoot her?

The door was just off the kitchen, opening into the living room. A short, wiry man, covered in sweat and dressed in a dirty T-shirt and chinos ran in when Rebeccah opened the door. He stood in the living room and raked dirty fingers through his greasy hair. "Oh man, I need something. I need something now."

Rebeccah looked unconcerned. "You won't find it here. You know that."

"I know. I know. I just came to sleep it off." He was disappointed.

Rebeccah came back to the kitchen and he followed, stopping short when he saw me. "There's a man with no shirt on at your table."

"Sit down and have some coffee," she told him.

"Hello Joshua," I said.

He burst into tears. "Oh my God," he said, "he knows my name. Rebeccah, he knows my name." He looked around like maybe he wanted to jump out of a window.

"Tell you what," I said. "Rebeccah's going to call me a cab. You're going to give me your shirt, and then I'm going to forget your name."

Joshua thought hard about all that information for a minute, but in the end he gave me his shirt. It smelled as bad as the alley behind the Alibi, but I couldn't wander around town in the shirt I had on earlier.

Rebeccah waited outside with me for the cab. "Joshua's my brother," she said, pulling the front door closed behind her. "He came out here to take care of me."

"He's doing a great job."

She looked like she wanted to slap me, but she kept quiet.

"Audrey's roommate is dead," I told her. We were past the time for small talk. Her eyes grew round and she looked around, again like a woman hunted.

She swallowed, a lot like maybe she was trying to keep from crying. "When?"

"Tonight."

She nodded.

"I came to L.A. with a partner," I said. "For all I know he's dead, too."

She started to breathe fast. "Oh, God."

"I don't know how deep you are in this and I don't want to talk in front of Mr. Charming in there. But I'll be back in the morning because you and I really need to talk."

She tried to get her breathing under control. "I won't be here. I'm leaving as soon you drive away." She nodded in the direction of the cab pulling to the curb.

"Fine," I said, trying to think fast but finding it hard. "Just tell me one thing."

"I don't know anything. There's nothing to tell." She scanned the street like she was searching for something . . . or someone.

"Let's say I was to hop on a bus tomorrow—a bus to Palm Springs." She met my eyes, and I could see she was still trying to get her breath. In her head she was already inside packing her bags. "Do you suppose Palm Springs would be a good place to go?"

She chewed on her lip a little bit, her eyes darting side to side like she was still afraid of the wind. "I guess Palm Springs might be a place a guy could look for . . . things."

I climbed into the cab and gave him the address for the motel.

I didn't bother to check Ray's room. He wouldn't be there. I'd get inside in the morning and collect his stuff. For now, I needed to sleep.

I wanted to barricade the door, but the bed was chained to the wall. And there was no way I could move the dresser with just one arm. So the question became how bad would the goons want to find me? How likely were they to come looking for me? I had left my ankle holster in the nightstand and pulled the compact snub-nosed revolver out now, checking the load. I laid down on the bed, held the gun close. I tried not to think of Ray Ward with a bullet between his eyes as I fell asleep.

17

RAY

I'd never ridden in a convertible before. It felt like flying, or what I imagine flying would feel like. The warm night air sent my hair in all directions but somehow Cindy's stayed in place. She drove at a leisurely pace.

Her skirt settled just above her knees as she drove, something I'd never thought about as being sexy before but I kept stealing glances under the guise of looking at the scenery despite it being pitch-black everywhere except the strip of highway leading us deeper into the desert.

"So, Ray, what brings you to Palm Springs? Business or pleasure?" She said pleasure the way it was meant to be said.

"A little of both, I guess." Hard to say what aspect of this was pleasurable but better to lie than try to explain it all.

"And what's her name?"

"What?"

"The girl. What's her name?" My mouth hung open, wind rushing in. What did Cindy know? Was she part of it? "It's always a girl, Ray. No one ends up hitching a ride into the desert unless he's chasing a girl. Did she break your heart? Or are you just afraid she's going to?"

I relaxed. "Oh, it's not like that. It's my sister. I'm going to see her."

"So you don't have a girl?"

"No. Just my sister."

She grinned and I started to come around to her meaning. With my thick head you'd think I'd been punched silly in the ring for ten years instead of standing ringside. I know everything there is to know about the square circle but nothing at all about women.

I was tired. Dead tired. The white noise of the air in my ears, the rhythm of the tires on the highway. It was like a lullaby and I drifted off. Cindy let me.

I woke to her shaking me. The wind had stopped. It was quiet. Her face was close to mine and I could smell her perfume. Somehow the top-down ride hadn't blown away the scent of vanilla, unless she had spritzed herself before waking me. Her lips were shiny red as if she'd recently applied a fresh coat of paint.

"Ray?" She spoke gently. "I hate to wake you but we're here."

I sat straight, looking around, trying to remember where "here" was.

We were parked at a motor lodge. Tiny cabins in two neat rows ran back into the barren landscape. Short misshapen trees sprouted up among the rocks and fine grain sand.

"You didn't give me an address so I just stopped here. I hope you don't mind. Palm Springs isn't that big. It will take me no time to drop you wherever you want in the morning."

"How long was I out?"

"Only about an hour. You must have been bushed."

"Sorry."

"It's okay. I like the look of a man when he's asleep. Makes me forget I don't have one next to me every night."

My sleep had been short but intense. I wasn't sure if I was up for what she'd been implying all night. I wasn't sure my assumption was real but here we were at the threshold of a room for two. All I could think of was *It Happened One Night* and I was Clark Gable. Would I be blowing down the walls of

Jericho once we got inside?

It felt like a betrayal of Audrey to think such things but sometimes biology wins out. It was hard to keep thinking about a girl who was never there as I faced one who was. And was she ever.

Cindy slid out of the car and straightened her skirt. She dangled a key from her palm. "I already paid."

I got out and tried to smooth my clothes. My slacks still had the smell of my training room in the basement, just like all my clothes. I needed a new suit. A woman like Cindy, she needed a man with a collection of ties, not just one I kept around for funerals.

Neither one of us had any bags. She led the way to the door. I followed, hoping she would continue to take the lead. My mind raced trying to remember what to do with a woman.

She opened the door on the dark cabin and stepped aside for me to enter. I did and felt on the wall for a light switch. Cindy closed the door behind me and I heard the bolt click shut. My pulse quickened.

The light came on but not by my hand.

"Hello, Cindy. You're out late." A man's voice. I spun to see where it came from. At first I missed him sitting in the chair beside the bed. My eyes ran back to him as he stood. A tall sandy blond with a thin mustache and a light tan suit, a great tie surely one of a hundred in his closet.

"Relax, Robert. I brought a friend."

Suddenly the room seemed exactly the size of a boxing ring. I kept my back to the ropes, my hands went up on their own, defending against an unknown threat.

"What's going on?" I asked.

"This is my brother, Robert. Robert this is Ray. He's looking for his sister."

"And where did you two meet?" He seemed uninterested in knowing me.

"A diner just east of L.A. He needed a ride."

"So no car, no bags. A guy with no suit on looking like a

bum out of the gutter?"

I opened my mouth to protest but she beat me to it. "Hey, knock it off. It was slim pickings."

"Oh well. Let's see what he's got." Robert brought his hand out of the pocket of his linen suit and flicked open a switchblade. I didn't know what to think other than it was a joke. I turned to Cindy who looked away.

"Cough it up, pal," Robert said.

"What?"

"Your wallet, bub. Let's have it."

I stood still, stunned. This was a shakedown. Cindy was acting. She should get a contract with Louis B. Mayer; this girl's got the stuff. Fooled me like Houdini on a good day.

She stepped up behind me and reached into my pocket to remove my wallet. I let her, not wanting to provoke the switchblade before I knew more about the man holding it. She tossed my billfold to Robert then stepped quickly away from me. She still wouldn't meet my eye. She turned to the dresser where a whiskey bottle stood, open and half gone. She splashed some into a short glass, no ice, and took it in one shot.

Robert had my cash in his hand. "Two hundred and some. Nice take."

Guess he was lousy at math, it was over three hundred. My whole bankroll for the trip. "Give that back," I said.

"What for? So you can blow it all on a dame you meet in a diner? Did he even buy your coffee, Cin?"

"No."

"What's with the bum's clothes, pal? You steal this wad? A guy with this much dough usually has on something made in New York. Nice work, Cin. Grifting a grifter." He tossed my wallet on the bed and stuffed the cash into his front pocket.

"Can we wrap this up?" Cindy was obviously afraid of him. As solid as her acting was with me she let her guard down around Robert and her fear showed through. She turned to the bottle again and refilled the glass.

"At least he knows the game. Okay, pal, you and me are

gonna take a ride. I'll let you off a few miles down the road. Don't give me any guff and no one gets hurt. I bet you'll have your pockets filled again in no time, smart kid like you. Say goodnight to your dream girl."

Gesturing with the point of the knife he pointed to the door, expecting me to obey. He must have been used to suckers who were husbands, traveling salesmen, middle aged doughboys who didn't know how to fight back.

I'm not that sucker.

I didn't have the luxury of Fokoli's tie around my knuckles anymore so when I struck out with my right I didn't make a fist. Instead, I led with the heel of my hand across his mouth. I put a slight curve into it so it wasn't a jab that would have ruined my shoulder with the impact, but a follow-through blow that took his lower jaw with it and filled the room with a bone snapping sound.

Cindy screamed and I heard the glass crash to the floor. Robert was dazed, too out of it to feel the pain just yet. He would though. His hand unfurled and the knife fell to the floor harmless as a feather. I pounded a left into his gut and he doubled over expelling a whiff of air that blew out a long strand of bloody saliva.

He reached out for balance with his right arm and I grabbed it, spun him around and pushed him down on the bed, then reached into his pocket to retrieve my money. I bent down to pick up the knife, turning it from harmless to deadly again, then hoisted him upright. He moaned as the pain finally reached his brain. Blood drooled from his mouth but he was unable to close his broken jaw.

There was no referee there to stop it. No bell to save him. I pushed him forward into the bathroom, followed him in and kicked the door shut behind us.

"Wait, Ray, wait!" Cindy called after me but didn't follow.

The thought of Dean Fokoli's body pitching over the railing and falling out of sight entered my head again. It was quickly eclipsed by the image of Audrey being pushed onto the bed in that room from the movies, my brain creating a vision of the future if I didn't make it to her in time. I was helpless to do anything for them right then. But Robert was in my hands. Him I could do something about.

I pushed him in front of the mirror in the tiny washroom. With my left hand pinning his wrists behind his back I lifted the knife to his face. I held it up just under his eye and waited for him to focus on his reflection.

Powerless to speak, his fear showed only in his widening eyes. His breathing quickened. He sucked deep and choked on the blood that ran down his throat. He coughed out in a spasm he couldn't control and a fine spray of red hit the mirror.

I could hear Cindy's sobbing from the other room.

I tried to think of what to say. Some way to warn him to leave innocent drivers alone and to stop doing whatever it was he did to make Cindy so afraid. Just like with my neighbors back home, I was mute. I couldn't find the words for my disgust, content to let my fists do the talking again. Seeing my reflection next to his, masked behind tiny dots of blood, I knew I was in no position to be lecturing anyone.

Before it got out of hand, before my anger got away from me again, I lowered the knife, pushed his head forward and broke the mirror with his forehead. I pulled him down by the collar and flung his body backward bouncing him off the toilet. He landed in a heap and remained still. I knew he was playing possum but better for him that he did. It wasn't him I wanted to draw blood from.

I stood looking down at him until the last of the mirror fell to shatter in the sink. It took a minute for all the shards to break loose and smash on the porcelain below. It reminded me of sitting on my porch back in Kansas City watching icicles fall from the eaves during a thaw. Peaceful in its way. The thought calmed me.

When the room fell silent I tore open the door and walked back through the cabin, knife in my hand. Cindy was standing by the door, weeping. She didn't run to him or nurse his wounds. She just stood hiding behind her hands.

I paused in front of her and she braced for a beating. She didn't retreat, just stood ready to take it. I shook my head, sad that I let thoughts of Cindy's lips and her sweet talk push Audrey from my mind, if only for a moment.

I picked the bottle up off the dresser and handed it to her. She tilted it and swallowed.

"Get out," I said. "And take him with you."

She moved slowly, afraid to turn her back on me. I wondered if they were really brother and sister. Doubted it.

My rage, unfocused, frightened me. Men were deserving of such a beating, and worse. I needed to find the right men. I needed to find my sister. On any other day Cindy may have been worth saving. She would have to wait.

A moment later she came out of the bathroom with his arm up over her shoulder, helping him along like some wounded soldier. With a change of costume it would have been a hell of a screen test. The tears were genuine.

I followed them out to the car. She set him in the passenger seat and he slumped down with a groan. The tears had stopped but she still sucked deep sobs now and then.

"Thanks for the ride," I said and then stabbed down with the knife, ripping a six inch hole in the upholstery. The blade was buried to the hilt in the leather of the back seat. I twisted and the metal snapped. I dropped the knife handle to the floor of the car.

The night air had gotten cooler but the top was still down. I stood and watched her pull out of the lot, tires crunching on gravel. Then I went back inside and slept the way I used to after a winning fight.

18

FOKOLI

My tongue was thick and dry and my head pounded but I rolled out of bed anyway because Joshua's dirty shirt had made the entire motel room stink like last week's sweat socks. I wadded it up and prepared to toss it in the trash but the pockets crinkled, full of paper. With my good arm I patted it down. Two rolls of cash. I counted. A little over two thousand bucks.

Great. More to be nervous about. Joshua wasn't brainy enough or conscious enough to remember me from last night, but Rebeccah with an "h" was. I'd just made off with somebody's bankroll. It was most likely drug money . . . money Joshua was supposed to deliver to someone. I swore a little, but then I realized I'd be able to buy a clean shirt. The cash would come in handy. Joshua's problems were his own.

I sponged off in the bathtub a little and did a trial shave—not easy with one arm. My face dotted with toilet paper, I strolled next door and broke into Ray's room. It smelled stale and unused and with the lights off, felt foreign and strange—like a place expecting someone any minute and that much sadder for it.

I cleared my throat and ignored the stinging in my eyes. Ray Ward. He was headstrong. He knew what he was getting into when we started this mess. He told me so. I would finish what he hired me to do and then I'd go home—wherever that was. Who knew if Kansas City was safe anymore with Bob White poking around in my old files?

I packed Ray's things—socks, underwear, a suit, two pairs of pants, three shirts, his shaving kit, and a picture of him with his brother. I didn't know what I'd do with the possessions. For now I'd hang onto them, put them in my room. I'd go to Palm Springs and find the studio where the films were being produced and I'd burn the damned place down—after I exposed everyone of course. With my bum arm I could have used Ray Ward's fists as backup, but that wasn't in the cards so I'd just have to make due.

I was sweating from the effort by the time I finished packing and had my hand on the doorknob before I stopped to think.

We'd checked into the rooms under our own names. Did anyone know we were here? Did anyone but Rebeccah know I survived the shooting? Was Ray actually dead? Was there a chance he'd gotten away?

I set the flimsy suitcase down and leaned my head against the door. I kept remembering Rebeccah leaving the Alibi Room last night, leaving and looking over her shoulder. She looked over her shoulder even when she was home. Why? Who watched the lounge? Who set the dogs loose on me and Ray?

I couldn't go to Palm Springs. Not yet.

I unpacked Ray's bags, careful to put everything back where I found it, with the exception of a pair of boxers and a T-shirt. Those I crumpled up and dropped on the bathroom floor. I unmade his bed and rolled around a bit, pushing the pillow down in the middle so it looked as if someone had slept there. I ran the shower for a few minutes and dumped some soap in the drain to make it smell used. I got the towels a little damp and dripped water on the floor. Finally, I put the toilet seat up. If anyone questioned the maid later, she'd have nothing significant to say. I took a pair of Ray's pants and a shirt with me, not entirely sure of my plan yet, but knowing it needed to look like Ray had returned and changed clothes.

BORROWED TROUBLE

In my own room I shoved Ray's clothes under my mattress to let them get wrinkled. I opened the window and tossed Joshua's shirt onto the pile of refuse spilling from the overturned trashcan on the sidewalk below. I dressed in casual clothes and called a cab.

He drove me to a store where I could buy a coat and a hat. I wasn't much for disguises but I'd shown my mug up and down the street outside the Alibi Room and I needed to blend in. When I had what I needed I had the cabbie drop me a couple of blocks from the lounge.

I picked up a newspaper, leaned against the wall across from the lounge, and pretended to read as I watched customers come and go. After about a half hour I picked up the pattern. Men would walk in. Five minutes later they'd walk out and wander off down the sidewalk. The Alibi Room was a bookie joint. Big deal. That didn't do me any good. I settled in and waited a little longer.

After awhile I noticed some of the men didn't just wander off into the distance. They moved a half block up the road and disappeared into a doorway under a flashing marquee. THE STUFF DREAMS ARE MADE OF announced itself in bold letters, circled by chasing lights. A girl joint. Might be nothing. Might be something.

I moved my way up the road, expecting a hand on my shoulder or a bullet in my back any minute. I was pretty sure I blended in, but I'd been shot once already and I wasn't looking forward to taking another bullet.

A gorilla of a man in a black tuxedo and top hat stood under the flashing lights of the theater. It was before noon and he looked absurd. Men stopped to buy tickets from a booth outside the main doors. The ape opened the door for customers, whipping his hat off with a flourish and offering a stiff bow.

I moved across the street and watched for a few moments.

These weren't lowlifes and criminals wandering into the theater to watch half-clad girls gyrate on a dim stage. These were business men in fine suits with ten dollar haircuts and shined shoes. I could only imagine what sort of "dreams" came true beyond those doors. I thought about Audrey and hoped she hadn't ended up in a place like that. I needed to get inside.

I moved off down the street, feeling the pain in my arm with every step. I was getting too old to take punishment like I used to. I was 46 years old and I felt 100. I decided that if Ray Ward was alive I'd find him and then I'd kick his ass for getting me into this.

I walked a half mile, as far away from the street as I could get within reason. I used more of Joshua's cash to buy a nice suit and a briefcase. I felt naked without a gun. I'd left the ankle holster and gun back at the hotel, figuring there was no telling what I'd run into and having a gun was always a reason for questions.

I bought another newspaper and walked with it tucked under my arm. With hat, briefcase, shoes that pinched, and the paper, I cut a fine figure.

The lights on the marquee still chased each other around. The man with the tuxedo wasn't there. I checked my watch. 12:30. Probably at lunch.

I put myself in line and tried to hear what the man in front of me said as money was stuffed through a small slit in the glass and a ticket was slid out. Was there a code? Would the guy behind the glass refuse to let me in if I requested the wrong thing? It was my turn next and I looked over my shoulder. There was no one behind me as I bent in close to the small circular hole in the glass to speak to the crooked-nosed man who could let me in or turn me away.

He raised his eyebrows. "Nice face."

I touched the bruise on my cheek with my fingers. The swelling was almost gone, but I knew the skin under the eye was a sickly yellow color. Funny how I'd forgotten about it what with getting shot and all. "You should see the other guy," I said.

He snorted. "I'll bet. What'll it be?"

My throat clenched a little. What if I said the wrong thing?

What if they fingered me for a snoop and shut the whole place down? People like this had a way of fading into vapor when the heat was on. If I screwed this up, I might lose the chance to find Audrey.

"Well?" the guy said.

"What's the special today?" I asked.

He stared hard at me for a minute and the hairs on my neck stood up.

I'd blown it.

Another customer had showed up and he shuffled his feet impatiently behind me. Lunch hour was half over.

The man gave a half smile and said, "It's fourteen fifty for the lunch special."

I slid twenty dollars to him and waited for my change. "You're in the main theater," he said. "Enjoy yourself."

I nodded and pocketed my change.

Then I went inside.

19

RAY

When I turned in the key at the motor lodge I asked about Silvio's studio, Banner Films. The pile of wrinkles and white whiskers behind the counter didn't tip to the fact that he'd never seen me before. All the customers must blend into one generic face after awhile, and this fella looked to have been on the job for a long time.

"Banner Films? You in the picture business?" he asked.

"Not yet."

"I hear they got an open call for Injuns over there today. A little makeup and you could pass." Just two old industry insiders talking shop, that was us. "I played a town drunk in three of those Westerns they shoot up there. Pays shit but I get to see myself in the movies." He laughed like a rusty hinge.

"Is it close?"

"Can't miss it. Big place." This being a motor lodge he assumed I had a car.

"What direction?"

"That-a-way. Like I says, can't miss it." He pointed down the road and went back to his newspaper. I wanted to ask him if any reports of a dead body in a shallow creek were in there. An ex-cop from Kansas City perhaps?

The morning was already heating up as I walked. An oasis for relaxation is how Palm Springs was advertised. Hot springs were the big draw. Why people couldn't just turn on a steaming shower and get the same effect I didn't know but far be it for me to tell them how to spend their excess money.

I saw the sign for Banner Films studio after about a mile and a half of short tan and darker brown buildings and dry scrub brush that looked like a witch's fingers. There was a two-story office building next to a larger warehouse-style building. A single driveway led the way in but no arching studio gates greeted me. It was no Warner Brothers or Fox Studio like I'd seen in pictures. When all this was over I really wanted to go see what I'd been missing. So far this trip to Hollywood turned up little I couldn't find under any rock in Kansas.

Security was nothing. No cars came or went. Once the driveway petered out the streets were unpaved. Behind the warehouse building I spotted a street like out of the old west. Wood buildings, a saloon with swinging doors, a buggy parked with no horse attached to it, hitching posts. It was like looking into a time warp.

A low building on the far side of the warehouse showed activity. Wide doors that ran all the way to the ceiling stood open. A power saw was cutting wood. Inside I could see half of a house, only the front, painted blue. It looked like one I'd want to live in if it had the other seventy percent attached.

A tiny pickup truck came bumping down the dirt street kicking up dust. In the back were stands and squares of black fabric on frames. I flagged down the driver. He slowed.

"I'm looking for Silvio."

"They're shooting on the north forty."

"Where's that?"

He seemed annoyed I didn't know my way around. He pointed to the time warp street. "End of Western Way and turn right." He drove off before I could ask any follow-up questions.

I surveyed the two-story building before I went hunting. Signs hung at each doorway: MAKEUP, EDITING, PROPS, MAIN OFFICE, above the double doors.

I thought of Lloyd and went to the props door.

I eased the door open without knocking. Inside the room was a jumble, like an antique store had exploded. Shelves of vases, radios, plates and cups, holsters, hats and gun belts were stacked along the walls. Out of context items like a potbellied stove and a roulette wheel stood side by side with a steamer trunk and a silver tea set.

"Help you?" came a voice.

I turned to see a young man with a gun in his hand. A revolver, open at the middle and he was pushing a wire brush through the chambers.

"I'm looking for Lloyd."

His face fell as if his long lost dad just returned from the sea.

"You're him. You're Ray." I nodded, a little leery. "I didn't think you were real." He set the gun down and came closer to me, nervous, as he forced a question from his throat. "Audrey. Did you find her?"

I shook my head. He looked down at the floor.

"I need your help."

Lloyd lifted his eyes again, shaking off his grief. "Anything." He stuck out a hand and I shook it. He was thin with a William Powell mustache that looked out of place on such a young man. His hair was slicked back and shiny with oil, another attempt at looking the playboy, but coming off as a kid who'd raided his dad's toiletries.

Lloyd locked the door and we sat at a workbench in back. Scattered props sat half painted on the table and rows of duplicate bar glasses and whiskey bottles lined the shelves around us. He saw me eyeing them.

"Breakaways." He took down a bottle and smashed it on the edge of the table with barely a flick of his wrist. It broke into a thousand harmless pieces. "If there isn't a twenty-man saloon fight in every picture the distributor won't carry it. I go through a lot of these."

"Did Audrey show you the film she mailed to me?"

"No. But I know what's on it."

"I saw another. At Nancy's. It was worse."

"What do you mean?"

"I mean worse." I didn't want to scare him about Audrey's fate any more than I had to. I had enough scare in me for two. "I'm here to talk to Silvio."

"He's behind it, huh?" Lloyd made a fist and pounded the table. "I knew it."

"I don't know for sure yet. I'm trying to find out. What can you tell me about him?"

"He owns the studio but he's always one flop away from losing it. He's been banished to the desert because no one in Hollywood wanted him. Thinks he's an actor but the only way he can get a part in a picture is if he makes it himself. So here we are breathing in dirt for Westerns that play at the bottom of a bill and everyone gets to pretend they're in the real movie biz."

Lloyd swept a pile of the fake broken glass to the floor. I was getting tired of all the tricks and lies these movie people surrounded themselves with. At least with Lloyd I knew he was telling me the truth.

"He's producer, director and star and he hasn't made a decent picture yet. Forty-one and counting. At least he knows better than to make himself the leading man. He's got three series running now. One with Johnny Starr, one with Brett Cassidy and one with Lone Star Kelly. He tried to get a singing girl on horseback out here last year but first day of the shoot the horse bucked and threw her, broke her back. She was in traction three months. Almost lost the farm on that one."

"And you think he's behind the dirty movies?"

"He's not the top man. Not in anything he does. But he holds a lot of casting sessions for pretty girls around here and funny enough, none of them end up in the movies."

"You ever see any yellow film cans?"

"Yellow cans? I don't think so."

"How about red ones?"

"Nope. Are those the ones that . . . that . . . y'know?"

"Yeah." Lloyd looked at his shoes. "Can we go see him now?"

"They're shooting, but sure."

I followed Lloyd down the Western street feeling like Wyatt Earp. Beyond the street in the low scrub was a film crew. Two horses swayed dizzy in the heat, tied to trees with no shade. A camera the size of suitcase stood on a tripod pointing at two men in cowboy hats and vests. One was handsome and tall and the other, the one in the black hat, was overweight and moved awkwardly–Silvio. I glanced at Lloyd and he gave a subtle, confirming nod.

A half dozen crew members stood around, bored.

As we got closer I could hear the two actors speaking in slow southern drawls.

The Handsome Man: "I told you if I ever found you on my property again I'd fill you full of lead."

Silvio: "And I told you this is my property now. The judge made it so."

Handsome Man: "You stole this land from my pappy on his death bed. And I got an itch in my gut tells me you put him in that bed too."

The Handsome Man went for his gun and drew fast as you can. I braced for a shot but none came.

"Son of a bitch! The damn ting's fookin' jammed again," the Handsome Man said slipping into a thick Irish brogue.

Lloyd whispered in my ear, "Lone Star Kelly. Irish as a Leprechaun. That doesn't sell tickets to an Old West show."

Kelly threw the gun into the dirt and stomped off to take refuge from the sun under an umbrella.

"Goddammit! Lloyd!" Silvio's voice was booming, in command. "Can you get me a goddamn six-shooter that actually shoots? We're running out of time here. They need this picture in New York by next Thursday."

Now that I was closer I could see dark sweat stains in the underarms of Silvio's black shirt. He took off his hat and wiped his sleeve over his forehead to sweep away a wild river of perspiration.

"I'm on it, Silvio." Lloyd ran and picked up the gun from the sand. He blew air at it to clean out the chambers, shaking his head at the actor who just made the problem worse. I caught his eye and gave him a nod. He eyed me back nervously but strode over to where Silvio leaned over a copy of the script, penciling out lines and writing something new.

"Silvio, I have someone wants to meet you."

"Who?" Silvio looked up, squinted in the sun at me.

"Ray." I didn't extend my hand.

"Casting's in the main building. Drop off a picture and we'll call you."

"It's not that."

He put down his pencil, gave me an exasperated look. "What then?"

I could smell his body odor from where I stood. I imagined Audrey knew that smell too. I would enjoy watching him squirm.

"I'm here to talk about red film cans."

The air around us suddenly felt winter cold. He held up a hand to shield his eyes and get a better look at me. He licked sweat off his upper lip. I stared him down like a gunfighter but all I had to draw were my fists.

"Come to my office." He closed the script and shouted to the crew. "We're taking a goddamn break while props here gets us a working gun so we can have a fucking shootout to end this damn picture. Otherwise we're changing the title from *Vengeance in Death Valley* to *Conversation in Death Valley* and the whole fucking studio will shut down."

The crew groaned at the prospect of standing in the heat any longer than needed. Silvio marched off and I followed. I turned to Lloyd over my shoulder. He marched along with us.

"I'll get this back to the shop, Silvio, and have it ready in no time."

"Good, 'cause that's what we've got—no time!"

Silvio's receptionist was another page out of the beauty-for-sale catalog. Neatly pressed and fully stuffed into her thin sweater she held an air of dignity in the quiet, air conditioned office that the outside world lacked.

As I followed Silvio into his oversized office the girl smiled a practiced smile at me that said: "Always be nice to the strangers, you never know who will be casting next week and need just your type." Insincerity spread out from the beach all the way to Palm Springs. How I longed for a nice Kansas City girl to give me a scowl and a good old fashioned skunk eye.

Silvio kept his office meat-locker cold. As spartan as everything else was on his tiny "lot" his office reeked of self importance and over compensation. He slumped down into a red leather chair with the high back and brass tacks. His desk was wide enough to autopsy one of those horses outside when they eventually dropped dead of heat stroke. I took a smaller chair, facing him as he pulled a white linen handkerchief from his center desk drawer and wiped the sweat that still poured from his face.

"So, we have mutual friends? Mr. Butler, perhaps?"

"Yes," I lied. Another name to add to the list. I really needed to start writing things down.

"What are you in the market for?" He thought I was there to make a deal.

"Like I said, a red can." The mere mention of it made the sweat flow heavier than in the heat outside.

"Yes, well . . . those are expensive and hard to come by, as I'm sure you know."

"A special order item?" I was following his lead, letting him unfold his strategy. If this were a fight I was giving him the first round but really he was giving me the bout.

"A very special order. One I hadn't planned to fill again, to be honest."

"Why not?"

"Well . . . it's not my line. Usually."

"But you did it for Mr. Butler."

"Well, then again that gets into the idea of . . . payment."

He mopped his brow again. It was clear Silvio was only for hire, not the one behind the films. That singer with the broken back must have set him back quite a bit. Fear of losing his little empire in the sand must have driven him to say yes to the first one.

"Maybe you've seen one of our yellow productions?"

I nodded.

"And was it to your liking?"

"What about the girls?"

"Oh, I have at least a dozen to choose from. You can do the casting yourself. I can—"

"Where are they?"

He furrowed his brows slightly, a hint of doubt crawling out of his pores like the sweat. He was slowly realizing he hadn't checked into who I was in the least. It was only the password of the red can that got me this far.

"They're safe. And you're in business with Mr. Butler you say?"

"I didn't. I'm here for a girl." I knew in any scenario he could come up with I could outfight him, outmaneuver him and outrun him. Round two was all mine. "Audrey is her name. I need to find her." I tried to read his face, watching to see if I was too late, if Audrey already had her starring role.

"What for?" His tone was getting desperate, like the walls were closing in. His breathing got shallow.

"To bring her home and get her the fuck away from you."

"She has the red film. That's where you saw it," he said like he'd just solved a great mystery.

I nodded, relieved he spoke about Audrey as if she was still alive.

Silvio didn't lash out, didn't jump the desk to go for my throat, didn't pull a pistol from the desk. He cried. Sobbed like a little girl who lost her puppy.

My fists had involuntarily clenched but now they loosened

in my confusion. Silvio purged himself of his burden.

"I knew it would come to this someday. You're here to kill me."

"I just want Audrey."

"I told them. I told them we'd gone too far. It wasn't worth it. All the money in the world it still wasn't worth it. I knew when that damn film went missing . . ."

His face dropped into his hands and he fell apart. I felt suddenly uncomfortable, like I was watching a private moment as a man let loose a stress that had been killing him. So help me I felt a tiny bit sorry for him. But he was no help to me a sobbing mess.

"Who's Butler?" The tears kept coming. I knew he wasn't that good of an actor so I believed in his guilty conscience. "Silvio! Listen to me. Who is Butler?"

Silvio lifted his face, slick with sweat and tears and snot, looking like he was between the eleventh and twelfth rounds. Spent and out of gas.

"He ordered the red film. He paid for it."

"Where is he?"

"I don't know."

"Bullshit. How did he pay you?"

"It was all through messages and couriers. I've never met him. Butler's not even his real name."

I let him go slow to try to get a grip. He explained that Mr. Butler was one of a half dozen clients for the yellow can films. They all used aliases, famous movie names. Butler from *Gone With the Wind*. One was called Mr. Heathcliff from *Wuthering Heights* and one used Mr. Chicolini from *Duck Soup*. At least they had a sense of humor.

Silvio told me that the men behind the fake names were all very powerful, very rich players in Hollywood. They met for private screenings each month. It was hush-hush. No one knew. They kept a secret even better than all the silver screen heroes who would rather have been loving the Mexican pool boy over Norma Shearer.

The yellow films had been going on for over a year. The red films, the ones the girls didn't survive, just started.

"I told them no. I swear I did. But the money . . ."

As soon as I found Audrey I had a new task. Those monthly meetings were going to stop.

"What about Audrey? Where can I find her?"

"All the girls, they stay in Los Angeles. I don't have them here."

"Stay where?"

"An apartment building. They rent the rooms out . . . to men . . . for . . ."

He didn't need to finish. Prostitution was no stranger to even a small pond like Kansas City. There's a lot less of a lure in that town than in tinsel town though. Come to Hollywood, get discovered, get in the pictures. Sure. Also get beat up, raped, held in a room while an endless line of men come in to fuck you and imagine you're Ginger Rogers for an hour. Hope you can dance.

The anger I felt began a headache behind my eyes. I rubbed the bridge of my nose to try to get rid of it. The frigid air conditioning wasn't helping.

"Take me there."

"Where?"

"To the girls. Take me there."

He sniffed thick mucus back into his nose and seemed to find a small bit of resolve. "Okay. Okay, I will."

"Let's go." I stood.

"Wait. I need to finish this movie."

"Finish it tomorrow."

"You don't understand. You're about to cost me a lot of money. Possibly my studio. If any of this gets out I'm ruined, so you gotta promise me my name won't come out no matter what you do." His eyes were pleading and scared. Scared of me. I hadn't thrown a punch or threatened him in any way and yet he feared me. Perhaps he could smell my anger as I could smell his anxiety.

"I promise."

"If I don't finish this movie my backers will pull out and I'm done. Kaput. I'm in over my head here. I got debts. Big time. Just let me get my day's shooting done. Another hour. It doesn't have to be good, just has to be done. I'm doing you a pretty goddamn big favor here."

His pitch started to rise. I was afraid he might change his mind. "Okay, okay. Go finish your movie."

We passed by the smiling receptionist on our way out. I wondered what she knew. I wondered how long it was before she ended up on the casting list next to Audrey.

Downstairs we exited the office just as Lloyd came out of the prop house with a tray of four six-shooters. Probably backups in case the gun jammed again. Another Irish temper tantrum was something to be avoided. I got the feeling Lloyd had been waiting for us to exit the building and I was grateful he seemed like someone I could trust.

He searched my face for a clue as to what was said upstairs. I just nodded a slight tilt of the head trying to tell him things went well.

Silvio took up his man-in-charge persona again. The crying simp from his office was well hidden. "Let's get this fucking thing in the can and get the hell out of here. Fucking heat is a killer. Next time I want to do a snow picture."

We reached the set and the crew stood up and milled around trying to look busy. A shape caught my eye. A man standing just left of the camera. He was big, tan. In the Indian casting they would pick him for chief.

It clicked. It was the hulking, putty faced actor from the films. The red and yellow cans.

He eyeballed me as we returned to set. He didn't squint in the sun, like the brightest thing in the galaxy was nothing to him.

"All right, let's do this goddamn thing!" shouted Silvio, still agitated.

The hulking man came to confer with Silvio in hushed

voices. Silvio shooed him away.

Lloyd brought the tray of prop guns to Lone Star Kelly and set them at a table in the shade. Kelly was busy getting a neck rub from a pretty assistant girl. He waved Lloyd away with a flick of the wrist.

The hulking man made the rounds, checking the camera, going over the prop table, giving Kelly the two minute warning. I finally heard his voice, silent in the films I'd seen. It was a thick and muscular baritone to go along with his physique. Silvio flipped pages in the script, not registering a single word. He slammed it shut.

"Let's go people. We're losing light."

The hulking man spoke. "Maybe we should call it a day."

"Fuck that!" Silvio said. "We get this done and we make the deadline. Do you all want jobs next week?" Feet shuffled in the dirt. Shoes were stared at. Unemployment might be a relief to this crew.

The hulking man stepped over to Silvio and tried to speak to him quietly. Silvio erupted.

"No, Enzo!" I had a name to go with the face I knew so well. Enzo grabbed Silvio by the arm and I could tell he squeezed hard. I stood about twenty feet away and could not hear them as Silvio was hustled away from the crew.

For a second-in-command Enzo sure gave Silvio the business. Silvio defended himself rigorously. He spoke with finality. He jerked his arm away from Enzo's grip and walked to his mark in front of the camera. "Final showdown, take two!"

The crew snapped into action as Enzo fumed and walked to the shade by the prop table.

"Where's Kelly?" Silvio shouted.

Enzo tapped the star's shoulder and Kelly opened his eyes, squinting against the daylight.

Silvio bellowed, "Get your ass over here or the whole world is gonna know you talk like a goddamn Mick and can't hold your liquor like a decent goddamn Irishman."

Lone Star Kelly stood and walked deliberately slowly back to his mark, taking his hat from Lloyd as he passed.

"Y'know Silvio," he began in his thickest brogue. "I'd t'reaten to tell the world that you can't make a fookin' film to save your cunt mother's life but that'd just be tellin' them what they already know." He hit his mark, dug a boot into the sand, held out his hand, called, "Gun."

A new six shooter was placed in his hand by Enzo. I stood by wishing they would just get on with it so I could get to Audrey. If only one red film had been made I knew she was alive. If she had been featured in a yellow film she could survive and recover. She was, after all, my sister. I knew she had strong blood.

The bad dialogue sounded a little better this time because the two men saying it really hated each other. Lone Star Kelly waited for his cue and then drew with a self-satisfied grin. The gun went off and Silvio did an award-worthy job of clenching at his heart, crying out and slumping to the dirt.

No one yelled cut. Kelly stood in an awkward freeze, his gun out in front of him at hip level. A tiny trail of smoke curled up from the barrel. He looked every bit the Western hero. The camera rolled on. I thought of only one thing: The red film. The way the camera stayed on after Enzo left the room. The unblinking eye staring out.

Silvio didn't move.

"Silvio?" the man behind the camera said.

"He's been shot!" Enzo said, somehow privy to some information the rest of us weren't.

A girl screamed. Flies already gathered at Silvio's corpse. I caught Lloyd's eye across the set. He was ready to run.

"Who did this?" Enzo yelling, looking in my direction. "Who is that guy?"

Several crew members turned to me with suspicion. A man bent down to feel for Silvio's pulse. He shook his head, adding a finality to it. People started moving around with nervous energy, unsure what to do.

Enzo marched over to where I stood. "Someone call the police."

As he stepped up to me he reached out one of his massive arms. His straightforward walk told me he was a man not used to anyone fighting back. At least I had the element of surprise.

I struck out with a right jab, caught him up under the chin directly on his windpipe. He went bug-eyed, gasping for air. It was a cheap shot but I needed a cheap shot just then. The crew began to scatter, confused as sheep in a pen when a wolf gets in. One of the men grabbed a gun off the prop table and waved it in my direction.

Kelly stood still in the madness, looking down at the pistol in his hand.

"Lloyd!" I called. He ran across the set busy with crew running in all directions.

Enzo's thick claw reached up from where he sat on the sand in front of me. His hand pinched off the blood in my wrist. I reared back my left and brought it down on his nose. My knuckles instantly ached but Enzo released me and grunted in pain. I wanted to kill him. I wanted to take him with us. Now that Silvio was dead he might be the only other person who could lead me to Audrey. My moment of hesi-tation ruined any chance of doing either.

Lloyd reached me and grabbed my arm. "Let's go!"

We fell in with the mob fleeing the scene. A woman screamed, the crowd avoided me but tried to run in the same direction back to the safety of their cars and the road out of Banner Films. The man holding the prop gun fired and a hollow bang filled the air followed by two more. They were different from those shot from Kelly's gun. Blanks.

I turned with Lloyd and we took off running. I let him lead the way while my best chance of finding Audrey bled out into the hot dirt.

20

FOKOLI

The main movie theater was dim and filled with shadowy figures of men who wished to remain exactly where they were—in the dark. It was the sort of place the owner never allowed to fill to more than half capacity, giving the audience plenty of room to spread out and remain anonymous. Hollywood's dirty little secret. One of them anyway.

I had picked up a bag of popcorn, which seemed absurd now that I thought about it. But I needed lunch, didn't I? I set the briefcase on the floor beside me and settled back into my chair.

The movie started with a warbling and distorted fanfare as the film struggled its way through the projector. Grainy images appeared before long—the figures of dancing ladies moved in jerking movements due to repeated splicing of the ancient piece. I guessed 1920s by the look of bobbed hair-styles and dark eye makeup. A chorus line bobbed and kicked and spun—the ladies all the same with their short, dark hair, dark stockings, short skirts.

But after a few minutes the film lurched and the music changed to a jazz rag. A woman with a fringed skirt and no top on gyrated on the screen. She drank from a whiskey bottle, giggling silently as the music continued. One by one, other women filtered into the frame. They were dressed in fur coats and feather boas and if the thought of girls taking off their clothes for strange men hadn't been so repugnant to me I probably would have laughed a little. The music changed to something like a calliope at the fair. The bottle of whiskey was passed around. Some of the women entwined themselves around each other. As the song continued, the dancing got slower, the movements became more languid, and the clothing disappeared. I'd seen stuff like this before in K.C. The tastes of men didn't change much from state to state or decade to decade and for the promise of starring in a movie, some young girls would do just about anything. Somewhere behind me a man breathed hard.

A movement somewhere down front caught my eye. I watched as the shadowy figure of a broad-backed man made his way down the aisle to the left front side of the theater. There, he tapped at a very plain door in the wall. Not an emergency exit. Something else. He stood at the door and tapped softly enough so that I couldn't hear a sound from that direction.

The door opened, allowing a sliver of darkness only slightly brighter than the darkness of the theatre to filter through. The man's shadow disappeared inside.

I decided to change seats and positioned myself closer to the door in question. The scene on the screen changed again to another jazzy tune and naked women danced the Charleston. I kept my eye on the door. After a few moments, yet another shadow made his way down front. This time I heard the knock. A series of short raps, easy enough to memorize. The same thing happened as before. The door opened and the man disappeared inside. The faint smell of perfume drifted out. I waited for a few minutes and then picked up my briefcase and approached the door. I rapped out the knock and waited for it to open.

A small shadow appeared. I could barely make out the pale image of a face in the darkness. "Here for the show?" he asked.

I nodded before realizing he couldn't see my head. "Yeah," I said, keeping my voice gruff.

The figure snorted and I imagined him rolling his eyes at me. I'd said the wrong thing. He closed the door and I remained where I was, wondering what to do next. I backed against the wall, disappearing into the blackness of the fabric-covered paneling and waited.

The film onscreen had run its course and was starting again. New shadows moved stealthily through the theater to find the least soiled seats. Figures of men moved out, adjusting neckties and ducking their heads a little as they passed others in the aisles. I was assured of invisibility as anyone who had taken notice of me earlier was now gone. I pressed against the wall and waited.

It was a few moments before the next customer approached the door. I held my breath. His sleeve brushed against mine and I tensed, waiting for him to notice me but the smell of gin drifted from him and I figured I didn't have anything to worry about.

He scratched clumsily at the door and when it opened the man asked, "Here for the show?"

The man muttered something I couldn't hear and the door opened wider, allowing him passage. I stifled the curse I wanted to yell and let my foot catch the door before it shut all the way, slipping in behind the man into the dark corridor.

When the door closed behind us the chaotic sound of jazz from the theater dimmed and I could hear swing music drifting from down the hall.

The doorman led on and Gin Man followed closely behind. I followed too, but quietly, afraid of getting caught and a little unnerved at the thought of what I might see.

We turned left and I figured by the way we moved that we were in an area of the theater behind the screen. The corridor widened here and curtained doorways lined the walls. I counted seven on each side. The hall was lit by a dim bulb. "You're in stall nine," the doorman said to Gin Man and turned to leave. I quickly stepped into the nearest booth, stall six, catching the peeper off guard.

"What the hell?" he said. But he whispered it, like being busted in on was nothing compared to the shame of what he was doing.

Things being what they were, I had no choice. I couldn't afford to be exposed. I struck with my left fist and knocked him down. It wasn't hard. The guy had one hand down his pants and one against the glass. He moaned when he hit the ground, down, but not out.

Even using my left arm had caused my right shoulder to throb with pain and I struggled to hold onto the briefcase. I set it down, fumbled in my pocket, and pulled out the roll of cash I had taken from Joshua. I peeled off three bills. "Here's sixty bucks. Lay there and keep quiet."

"Fuck you," he said.

After a few kicks to the gut and one to the face, he decided to accept my offer. I gave him another twenty for good measure and then I looked in the window.

The girl there had stopped moving—like maybe she'd heard the ruckus outside and was scared someone was about to be tossed through the window. Her back was turned and a mane of thick, too-blonde hair dropped almost to her waist. She wore only a pair of old-fashioned bloomers. The light in her little cell wasn't much brighter than the light in the corridor, but it was bright enough to see the curve of her hip, the smoothness of her legs. As she turned, I realized there was plenty of light for the men out here to see all they needed to see.

After a minute she must have decided the noise outside the window was nothing to fear and she began to dance to the soft show tune being piped into the wing. I had no doubt that all the girls in these rooms were dancing to the same sultry music. It was clear that, although I could see her, she couldn't see me.

I don't know how long I stood there watching her. At first it was the shock of what I was seeing. I'd busted up a few peep operations in K.C., but this was so very organized—the theater and the girls in the back—the set-up, run like a legitimate business. My skin tingled with the knowledge there could be dozens of girls in here being displayed like zoo animals. But even after the shock passed I continued to stare at the lethargic girl.

The guy at my feet moaned in pain and clutched at my pant leg. I gave him a sharp kick in the ribs. It felt good to unload a little of my frustration on someone. I needed to get moving—figure out what to do next—but there was something familiar about the girl, something I couldn't place. Her movements were sloppy and she had a hard time holding her head up. Drugged. But by choice or by force? She kept that white-blonde hair in her face as she moved and I felt certain that if I could just see her better I could place her.

The curtain separating me from the corridor opened and a thick hand clutched my shoulder.

The big hand pulled me effortlessly into the dim hallway with one hand and picked up my briefcase and newspaper with the other. He was a head taller than me and twice as broad. His hair was slicked back from his forehead and his severe widow's peak gave him a satirically vampiric look. Even in the dim light his hair shined with grease. "We run a clean shop here, Mister," he said. He nodded at a second big man he'd brought with him who ducked into the stall and brought out the pile of rumpled suit I'd been kicking around. "Get him a drink and offer to clean his suit," Vampire said. Then he looked at me again. "Come with me."

My shoulder pulsed with pain as the man propelled me deeper into the hallway. He rapped sharply on a door in the rear and the door opened.

I found myself in the middle of an opulent office decorated in oriental statues and rugs. A pond surrounded by stones and fed by a fountain filled the middle of the room. Giant goldfish swam to the surface of the water as I passed, their transparent fish lips opening and closing in expectation of food. So this was how the other half lived.

"I like your goldfish," I said.

"Koi," was the only response I got. And I have no idea why he said it because I wasn't being coy at all.

"Sit," he said, gesturing to a red chair in front of a black desk. A fat guy sat behind the desk. Why is it always a fat guy? An oriental dame in a red kimono lounged on the arm of his chair. I cocked an eyebrow. "Seriously?" I sat looking at the girl.

My comment earned me a backhand from the vampire.

"That's enough, Charles," the fat guy said.

Charles shrugged and set my briefcase on the desk. Then he yanked me out of my chair and patted me down, pulling out my wallet, a syringe, and a vial of the morphine I'd brought with me. He set everything down in front of Fats, then faded into the background. The girl gave me a half-smirk.

I waited while my wallet was searched. Fats held up one of my business cards. "Dean Fokoli," he said. "Private Investigations." He opened the briefcase and laughed when he saw it was empty. It was a hissing, giggle of a laugh that made my skin crawl. Even the cool cucumber sitting on his chair grimaced a bit. "Am I being investigated?"

"I'm looking for a girl," I replied.

He leaned back and rested his fingers on the edge of the desk, drumming them impatiently. "Let me guess. A girl has run away from home. Mother and Father have hired you to find her and bring her back. Am I warm?"

I shook my head, hoping the guys who shot me and drove off with Ray didn't report to this clown. I decided to roll the dice. "I work for a filmmaker. He wants a couple of girls. I heard this was the place to look."

He stared at me from fleshy eyeholes, his fingers

drumming, drumming, drumming. He gestured to the morphine. "Were you going to drug and steal one of my girls?"

I smiled. "That's mine. And I'd like to take it with me when I leave." I made a point of looking around the office. "I'm sure you have means of obtaining your own."

He smiled. Tiny white teeth. Red tongue. Fleshy lips. The woman smiled too and rested an arm on his shoulders. Her nails were long and painted red.

"Who employs you?"

"I'm not at liberty to say." I was beginning to think he didn't know about me and Ray's incident with the goons. But the finger drumming kept me suspicious.

"Why don't you carry a gun?"

"Because I'm not a threat. I only want to do business." I paused. "With the right person of course."

"What sort of girl are you looking for?"

Careful, I told myself. Don't blow it. "My client has specific tastes. He likes a girl unafraid of a little rough play."

His mouth spread into a hideous grin and he reached out and clutched the girl's thigh until his knuckles turned white. She didn't move; she smiled at me as if she enjoyed it. "I employ many girls who enjoy a strong hand," he said. "Did you see anything you liked during your brief visit?"

I thought of the familiar girl with the platinum hair. "I enjoyed the girl in the booth your man found me in."

"Booth six," Charles provided.

"Ah, yes," Fats said. "A bit high-spirited but a fine piece of flesh."

I was starting to feel dirty and self-loathing. I knew my face would get red soon. Something still nagged at me. "I'd like another look at her. And then I'd like to set up a time to interview her when she isn't doped. My client is very particular about that detail."

The fat man snapped his fingers and Charles appeared at the desk to gather up my wallet and briefcase. "Let him have another look at the girl. And make sure she shows her face this time. She's almost healed." He looked at me and shook his head. "Some of them are so vain."

I clenched my teeth but managed to smile and nod. Charles began to lead me from the room. As we got to the fish pond I turned around and looked at Fats. "One more thing. My client wants to a girl who will do whatever he wants."

"Oh, she will." His eyes narrowed. "You can count on it."

21

RAY

Lloyd's car kicked up dust like a stampede as we sped away from Banner Films. He drove like a bootlegger. I held on for dear life. When it was obvious no one was following I told him to slow down.

"Where can we go?" I asked. "Your place?"

"I don't know. They saw us leave together. Won't they come looking for me?"

Brilliant Ray. Jesus, I needed Fokoli with me. As a detective I was a real daisy. I should have gone out in the first round, but somehow I'd stuck around. Hell, I knew guys who went a whole career and never won a bout, but boy could they stand in there and take a licking. Guess it's good I don't have a glass jaw. Every man's got his limits though. But getting that close to Audrey only gave me a taste for more. And knowing she wasn't the only one . . . well, just the thought of other good, kind Kansas girls being held in an apartment waiting for the next trick or the next starring role in a film that would be her debut and her finale, well, that just wouldn't stand. Not as long as I was throwing punches.

"We can go see Zachary," Lloyd said.

"Who's he?"

"Works at the studio off and on. Casting. He's a pal."

"You trust him?"

"Oh yeah. He knows Audrey too. We went on a few double dates together."

"So let's go see Zachary."

Lloyd drove us past some fancy hotels, the El Mirador and Desert Inn. He pointed out a place called the Chi Chi Club, supposed to be the hot nightspot. I doubted we'd have time to paint the town red.

Zachary's place was a low beige apartment building where the city met the sand. The front side faced civilization while the rear of the building fronted a desert probably unchanged since Indian times.

Lloyd parked as far around back as he could to keep the car out of sight.

Zachary answered the door in an undershirt and linen pants with no shoes. He was a young guy, a lot like Lloyd, and it was easy to see them being friends. A waft of moist hot air seeped out from his door, hotter inside than it was outside in the midday sun.

"Lloyd? What's going on?" It wasn't hard to see by our faces, and Lloyd's out of breath anxiousness, that all was not right.

"Zachary, I need your help."

"Sure, sure. Whatever you need. Come on in." Zachary ushered us in to his bachelor apartment. A single fan blew the hot air around but had all the effect of a fly's wings. Zachary moved a scattered newspaper off the couch and invited us to sit. He eyed me up and down but didn't ask who I was.

"What's wrong, Lloyd?" He had the genuine concern of a friend.

"This is Ray. Audrey's brother."

"Oh, nice to meet you." We shook. "I didn't know she had a brother."

"I didn't either until very recently," I said.

"Zachary, Audrey's gone missing." So they were close but not close enough that Lloyd had told him about Audrey yet.

"That's awful. For how long?"

"About a week now."

"Why didn't you tell me?"

"I didn't want to worry anyone. There are a lot of unanswered questions."

Lloyd ran it down for him; the quick version. He skipped the red and yellow cans and just said, "films". Zachary knew what he meant. He remembered Mr. Butler's name and the casual way Silvio didn't seem to know any of the girls' names.

When Lloyd finished I was grateful I didn't have to rehash it again. We sat in silence for awhile, the slow fan pushing hot air in circles lazier than a fat man in a hammock. My back was moist with sweat.

"Wow, you must need a drink," Zachary said. "You boys stay here. I'll get us something. I got cold cuts too." He stood and went to the kitchen.

Lloyd ran both hands over his face and exhaled deeply for the first time in an hour. For me the bell hadn't rung yet, I needed to keep my feet moving.

"We need to find that apartment in Los Angeles," I said.

"Yeah, but how?"

"We talk to anyone who knew Silvio. Someone else has to know about it. You said he wasn't the top man in anything he did." I'm sure there was a better, more proven method that a real detective would have known but it was the best I could do at the time.

"I guess you gotta start somewhere." Lloyd's eyes stared into space, calculating the number of people we'd have to find and question if we wanted to make any progress at all. He looked daunted.

Zachary returned with a bottle of whiskey, three glasses and three ham and cheese sandwiches on white bread.

"Eat up boys. You stay here as long as you like."

"Thanks," I said. "But we've got to get back to L.A. as soon as we can."

"You really think that's safe?" Zachary asked as he lifted a glass and poured an inch of the dark liquor into it and handed it off to Lloyd. There was no ice, the one thing the room needed most in the world.

"It's their safety you should be worried about, the men behind this." It came out too *tough guy*, not me at all. Bragging is the final refuge of a man with no means to back it up. I wondered if my little slip meant my subconscious knew something I didn't about our chances.

My whole career in the ring and managing Rex I never uttered a threat or promised a win. Leave that to the others. Let them get their hopes dashed by two talented fists. Now I was just some Saturday night undercard braggart with no fist in his glove.

I turned to Lloyd and he was already holding out an empty glass. Zachary refilled it then filled a second and handed it to me. I shook him off.

"You sure? From that close call it sounds like you could use it."

Lloyd downed his second shot and wiped his mouth with the back of a hand. It seemed to be just the medicine for him. He slumped back into the couch, eyes closed.

I took the drink.

If I was going to break one rule to myself, why not all of them?

I sipped. My throat closed and wouldn't let the whiskey down. The alcohol burned in my mouth until I forced my throat open and muscled it through, searing my insides along the way. What the hell do people see in this stuff?

I came up gasping like I'd taken a punch to the gut. Zachary laughed then poured his own drink.

"So where do you think Audrey is, now?"

"Los Angeles. I don't think she's here. It sounds like Silvio didn't really keep any girls out here."

"You know, I always wondered why he had me finding so many young girls like that. Always wanted them fresh off the bus too. I just figured it was so he could get them cheap. He's not out paying Jack Warner money you know."

I sampled the drink again. It went down smoother this time but not by much.

"We all knew Silvio was into blue movies," Lloyd said. "No one knew it involved any rough stuff." He reached over and tried a sandwich. I left mine on the plate. I wanted to eat about as bad as I wanted to watch another red can film—zero.

Zachary took a token sip of his drink then set the glass down. "Listen, fellas, I gotta come clean," Zachary said. Lloyd and I leaned forward to hear his news. "I knew Silvio made stag movies. But like you said, no rough stuff. I earned a few extra bucks running deliveries. I'd put the reel in my hubcaps and run them into L.A., pick 'em up after the party. You don't think I could have been running these other films, do you?"

"Were any of the film cans red or yellow?" I asked.

"No. I don't think so. I wasn't really looking."

"I doubt you were carrying them. I think these items are special order. Expensive. I bet they got a fancy limo ride all the way into town."

Zachary noticed my untouched sandwich. "You gonna eat? You guys aren't heading out just yet are you?"

"We should get back to L.A.," I said.

Zachary jumped up and went to his desk. He was eager to help us and seemed to be just as eager for us to stay. "I got more deliveries scheduled." He lifted a sheet of paper from his desk. "Next one tonight, and then one on the weekend."

"You already have the films?"

"Yeah."

"And no red or yellow cans?"

"No. Just gray metal. I have to tape them down inside the hubcap or they rattle like the devil's bones." He laughed nervously.

Something about him was eating at me but I got distracted when I heard crying. For a split second I thought there was a woman in the room but then I looked to my left and saw Lloyd, head in hand, weeping. It was fast for the drink to get to him but he was crying full-out like any schoolgirl I'd ever seen.

"I should have done something. She said she was worried. Said she thought there was gonna be trouble."

Zachary looked at me, his eyes asking questions. "Audrey," I said, answering one. The rest I was just as ignorant about.

"Lloyd," I said. "Did she ask you to help?"

"No, not really. She just said she had a bad feeling. I offered to. She said it wasn't my line." I could tell he was embarrassed about that. It shocked him into the present and he sat straighter and tried to clean his face and stop his sobs. "She said you would help if you could, Ray."

If I could. Exactly what I'd been saying to myself. I downed the rest of the drink. It wasn't helping. I began to wonder if that's how some guys get lost in the bottle. They drink their way to the bottom and it doesn't help a damn bit so they start over at the top of the next one and keep on looking.

One was enough for me. I could already feel my body reacting to the new substance. My liver had been shocked out of a coma and didn't know what to do with itself.

Zachary didn't ask, just poured me another. I let it sit.

"I could have helped. I could have helped." Lloyd started to spiral again. "Silvio and fucking Enzo."

I wasn't sure what kind of reliable partner Lloyd would be. It was looking smarter and smarter for me to leave him in Palm Springs. "Lloyd, why don't you stay here and I'll take your car back to L.A. No sense in both of us risking our lives."

I wasn't helping his bruised masculine ego. "No," he snapped. "I have to come with you. I have to help find Audrey."

He was starting to get that slight drunk in his voice. The celebration after a win or the birthday party for a friend. He wasn't New Year's Eve drunk. I didn't know what I was. Not drunk but my brain felt a slight confusion I wasn't used to and the alcohol made me feel even hotter in the sticky room.

There was a knock at the door. Zachary stood quickly. "Hey, I hope you don't mind. These guys can help us out." He opened the door and a chill ran through the room. Enzo filled the doorway, two dark figures standing behind him on the landing.

My eyes ran to Zachary but he looked down at the carpet, ashamed. Guess he made a phone call in the kitchen along with the sandwiches.

Lloyd sat up straight. "Zachary, what the hell?"

"I'm sorry . . . I—"

Enzo pushed into the room, his two shadows followed. They all wore suits, no ties, a nod to the year-round heat. I stayed sitting, very still. My only plan right then was to let Enzo take the lead. I couldn't beat this man one on one. I had to pull a rope-a-dope. Chances were fifty-fifty that the dope was me.

I studied his face, looking for a sign of weakness. There was none. Even my punches from before left almost no impression on his face. The slightest of bruises, that was it.

Samoan. That's what he was. The dark skin, the size, the wide featured face. Had to be. Not sure why it struck me right then but it sure beat thinking about what was to come.

"What's your name, friend?" Enzo asked me.

"Ray."

"Well, Ray, you caused quite a mess. I had cops crawling the studio for an hour."

"Did you tell them you switched guns to knock off your boss?"

His jaw tightened. I could hear tiny sobs from Lloyd next to me but I didn't turn.

"I told them it was an accident. A stupid prop man made a stupid mistake." The insult went unnoticed by Lloyd. With three more bodies the room became even more humid. Enzo removed his jacket, calm as you please, never taking his eyes off me. "A lot of people lost their jobs today. Hope you're happy."

"You don't know me very well. I haven't been happy in a long time."

"You know, in a way, you might have done me a favor knocking Silvio off. And then my good friend Zach does me another favor." Zachary stared even harder at the carpet. He was concentrating so hard I bet he could see China. "I was all set to be done with this shit desert town. I was even going to forget about you. Me and the boys were packing up to move our operation back to Hollywood where it belongs. Then my friend Zach rings me up and says you're here. So I get a second chance to do what I should have done this afternoon."

The room was dynamite and a fuse had been lit. I could almost hear it hissing. We all chose to stand by and watch it burn all the way down and wait for the explosion.

"I guess I'm supposed to come with you now," I said.

"That would be good."

He bought my excuse to stand. I did so slowly. "Then what? You kill me right away or do we make a few stops? You gonna take me to the same bridge where you killed Fokoli?"

"I don't know who that is. And when I want you to know our plans, I'll tell you."

"Zachary, you fucker!" Lloyd spat through tears.

"Hey, these guys pay me, okay? A lot." It was enough of an excuse for Zachary. He turned to Enzo. "You didn't say anything about killing."

"They killed Silvio."

"Aw, cut the crap," I said. "There's no cameras rolling here."

I could see Enzo's face turning a darker shade of clay. Blood boiling just below the surface like a hot spring outside. A trickle of sweat appeared on his temple. If I were managing this fight I'd be pleased. He stood stone still, off balance mentally. That's half the fight.

"Let's go," he ordered.

"You sure you can kill someone with your pants on?" That one got him good. The two men with him arched eyebrows, not understanding the insult. I felt confident the red cans were still a secret to everyone but Enzo, Silvio and Mr. Butler. And me.

The fuse ran out. Something was about to happen in the apartment but it came from a place I didn't expect. Lloyd leapt off the couch and charged Zachary.

He was so skinny that he practically flew. His arms were flailing before he reached Zachary, bits of his half-eaten sandwich flying off like shrapnel. Lloyd came in like an untethered windmill and landed slapping punches on Zachary who went into girlish defense mode.

Enzo, his thugs and I were shocked into stillness for a beat, then the fight was on.

During my brief time in the ring and throughout managing my brother's career I put a real emphasis on fairness and good sportsmanship. Rex had never once been accused of hitting below the belt. There, in Zachary's bachelor apartment, three against one—all bets were off.

Enzo threw the first punch and I dodged it easily. It was hard to keep my eyes off Lloyd. He had Zachary pinned against the wall and flung fist after fist at him, not a single one had the power to do much damage but the onslaught kept Zachary balled up for cover. At the rate he was going Lloyd would be out of breath and his arms would be rubber in about ten seconds.

I curved a left into Enzo's exposed flank, landing one right on the kidney. Just because I never use dirty punches doesn't mean I don't know how.

Enzo's shadow closest to me bent down and pulled a knife from his cowboy boot, still dusty from the set. I grabbed his wrist before he could stand fully and twisted. He grimaced in pain but kept the blade tight in his fist. Dumb for him. I spun his wrist a quarter turn more until the knife was angled back at him and I drove the blade down into his thigh. The four-inch blade sank to the hilt.

I released him but not quick enough. The second thug aimed a thick fist at my head. I had time enough only to duck slightly and raise a shoulder which took the brunt of the impact. The blow threw me off balance and I teetered. As I fought to regain my balance I saw Zachary try to run and Lloyd pounce on his back like a mountain lion. Lloyd took him down onto the coffee table and it smashed beneath them like a prop in one of Silvio's saloon brawls.

That fleeting thought gave me an idea. I let my body keep tilting and ended up on the floor. Enzo stared down at me and reared a foot back as if to stomp a cockroach. I rolled toward him and his foot caught me on the way down but only bounced off the back of my thigh. The kick hurt but not as much as a shot to the ribs would have.

With one hand I snatched up the whiskey bottle that had fallen when the table smashed. I rotated my body, still on the ground, and swung the bottle by the neck into the nearest knee I could see. It was the second thug. The bottle didn't smash like Lloyd's fake one. It made a loud cracking sound against his kneecap as it sprayed whiskey over me and the floor. The thug put out his hands and fell forward onto all fours, grunting loudly through clenched teeth.

Enzo grabbed the back of my shirt and hauled me up. Turning my back on him was not the smartest play. I had a fleeting wish for the razor I used to carry in my pocket. My back was still to him so he couldn't reach my face to start pummeling so he wrapped a heavy arm around my neck and squeezed. Flash frames of the red film can sparked on my eyelids, like the whole world had caught in the gate of a projector and was burning. I saw him strangle the life out of that girl and I knew what I looked like in his clutches.

I threw my head back and my skull slammed into Enzo's nose. He screamed what could have been more frustration than pain and his grip loosened but didn't let go. Through the bright burning edges of my sight I saw the first thug rip the knife from his leg and come at me like a pirate in a Douglas Fairbanks picture.

Enzo made the mistake of not lifting my feet off the ground, any good wrestler will tell you that's a key to the grip he had me in, and yes, I took in a few wrestling bouts in my day. I spun my body and leaned forward, lifting Enzo's feet off the ground momentarily as I spun. The knife dug into his side, but the thug was pulling up as the contact was made so it had only sliced through the skin, not deep enough to do any real damage. The pain was enough for him to let me go.

I fell to my knees in time to see Zachary get the upper hand on Lloyd who was clearly exhausted just like I thought he would be. Lloyd was on his back surrounded by the destruction of the coffee table. Zachary pounded a fist down on Lloyd overhand like he was chopping wood. It landed on Lloyd's face and he grabbed at it with both hands. Exposed midsection. Rookie mistake.

I was useless using only fists against Enzo and his pals. I snatched a table leg off the carpet and brought it straight up into Enzo's formidable crotch. I knew exactly how much of a target I had there and I couldn't miss. I felt a little bit bad using such playground tactics on him but you need to adapt to each fight you're in.

Enzo brought his bloody hands from the slice in his back, down to his crotch and doubled over, wheezing out all the air from his lungs.

I stood and swung out at Zachary who was rearing back for another chop of wood. The table leg creased his forehead and he went backward, arms flailing and legs trying to stand up but not quite finishing the task. Zachary was rocketing back fast and the thug in his way had no time to react since he'd been staring down at Enzo with a mixture of sympathy and shock. Zachary hit the thug and they both fell, backs first, Zachary on top.

There was an ear-splitting screech when they hit the floor, Zachary's mouth opened wide in a painful howl. I'm sure that sound carried miles across the desert. He had landed on the knife. His whole body weight had plunged the blade into his back. The scream weakened as his lung collapsed. The thug pushed up and tossed the body off to the side. The knife stuck there so deep and solid it would take King Arthur to pull it out.

I held the table leg like a club and faced off against the remaining thug. He reached into his back pocket, drew a sap. The worn leather grip surrounding a ball of lead had gotten some use and he twirled it in his hand, waiting for his shot at me.

We sized each other up. I tried to ignore the cries of grown men all around me. We both circled, lifting our feet high over the obstacles on the floor. Sweat poured off our bodies. It was hotter than any fight hall I'd ever been in. I noticed our heavy breathing was in sync, each waiting for the other to make the first move, neither of us sure we had the best move in us.

From the floor next to me a glass rocketed past. My second shot of untouched whiskey.

Lloyd must have been a pitcher in school and this was his fastball. The glass broke across the thug's nose and split the skin between his eyes sending an immediate river of blood across his face, over his lips, down his chin. He went down to the floor to join the others.

I was the only one standing as I saw an open door.

As tempting as it was to kill Enzo I couldn't bring myself to stop my escape in order to slaughter four men. The longer I stayed in the room the better chance one of the four would get the upper hand, decide to throw his own whiskey glass, or use one of the three remaining table legs. I reached for Lloyd's hand which he was already holding out for me. I pulled him along like a damsel in distress and we made for his car.

I checked Zachary's front door as we bumped out of the parking lot but no one emerged. The three men still alive inside weren't in any shape for a foot race with a car.

Lloyd again drove like there was a fire he had to get to but I didn't tell him to slow down. The faster I got out of Palm Springs the better. We needed to make it back to L.A. and start looking for that apartment building.

"Head for the highway," I said.

"Yeah." Lloyd's eyes soberly focused on the rushing road ahead.

I wondered if Fokoli would have been proud of me. I was about to embark on some real detective work. Hunting down known associates, checking addresses, getting tips. I kinda wished I'd taken a few more notes from him while he was alive.

A thought hit me like a message from beyond the grave.

"Wait! Turn around. We're not going to L.A."

"We're not?" Lloyd sounded desperate. He braked and slowed to a normal speed.

"No," I said. "Not yet."

22

FOKOLI

Charles put me in a dim room furnished with a creased leather couch and a low coffee table. "Wait here," he said.

It was only a minute later when he came back, carrying an ornate chair of dark wood with a red cushion. He placed it to the right of the couch and disappeared again. After a moment the fat man entered on legs that struggled to keep him upright. He made his way to the chair and sat down. He'd put on a red brocade robe. It must have taken twenty-five yards of fabric to make the wide sash with yellow tassels he had cinched around the general vicinity of where his waist should have been. He blew air out like a bellows as he sank into the chair and wiped the perspiration from his brow.

Charles cleared his throat. "Will there be anything else at the moment, Mr. Baron?"

The fat man shook his head. "You may go get the girl," he said, waving Charles away.

Now alone, Baron studied me. "Are you older or younger than you look, Mr. Fokoli?"

I leaned back on the sofa and squared my jaw. "I'm as old as I am."

He chuckled and rested his fleshy hands on his thighs. "You have a lean and angry look to you. Can you act?"

I resisted the urge to squirm. "When I need to."

"Can you please a woman?"

I took a slow deep breath—the kind that no one can hear but that keeps me calm. This was a game. Baron wanted to test my mettle—make sure I was used to working in the flesh-peddling business. I gave him a hard look. "I can please a woman anytime. I generally concern myself with whether or not she can please me." I held his stare. "My employer concerns himself with the same thing."

"Right." He stroked his chin with a sausage-like finger. "Your employer."

I could see that Baron's wheels were turning. I thought of Ray's empty hotel room. Would this guy believe Ray was my absentee boss? They would check on me now—maybe follow me. Years of training at weaving layers of half truths and lies had left me adept at keeping a hundred stories straight at once. I started to piece together a plan and tucked it into the back of my mind to stew while Charles returned with the girl.

"This is the one you requested," he said.

She was supported by Charles, conscious and alert but weak. The blood drained from my face and at the last second I caught myself and managed not to mutter her name. I realized now I had recognized her in the booth, the way she moved, the way she stood, the way she held her shoulders.

Glenda.

She'd been beaten, I could see that much. Besides bruises on her arms someone had haphazardly tried to cover with makeup, there were dark circles under her eyes and she was wraith thin. I reckoned Baron kept her doped. With a girl like Glenda, these clowns would have their hands full if they didn't subdue her in some way.

Glenda had connections to Ray's family. She'd been Rex's girl—as much of one as someone like Glenda can be. Two years ago, after Rex was killed in the ring, I'd bullied her in my search for Ray and she'd stayed tough. I thought she was unbreakable . . . until now.

"Would you like to inspect her?" Baron asked, shifting in

his chair to look at me.

I forced myself to look disinterested in her and made a show of standing and walking to where she stood. Charles let go of her arm and stepped back. I examined her skin, her neck, breasts, back, everything. She remained still, but the sharp defiance in her eyes told me she recognized me. I needed her to trust me but she was young—only twenty or so. I didn't know if she had enough sense to keep her mouth shut. Would she sell me out to get in good with Baron, maybe be allowed to miss a beating now and then? Her breath came in slow shallow waves and her hand trembled a little as I picked it up and pretended to inspect her nails.

I looked at Baron. "You've been drugging her."

He gave a slow nod. "She has a loud mouth." When I didn't respond Baron cleared his throat. "I hope that won't affect our ability to do business. If you don't like this one, we have others." He snapped his fingers and Charles stepped forward. "Mr. Fokoli might be interested in number two."

Glenda's eyes widened, like she was watching her one chance at escape vaporize. I turned my back on her and moved back to the couch to sit down. I lit a cigarette and crossed my legs, staring intently at Glenda and hating that it made her squirm.

After a few minutes I could see she was getting angry—and anger might make her stupid. I turned to Baron. "What if I want a closer inspection of these girls? Is that permitted?"

Baron gave a half smile. "We can arrange something."

Charles came back with the second girl. She'd been hit on the head at some point. Dried blood had caked her hair to her scalp. A finger on her right hand was misshapen from a previous break. I swallowed my disgust.

Charles pushed her to the center of the room and backed up.

"She's in bad shape," I said. My voice sounded far away.

Baron studied me. "Yes. She had a tussle with one of the doormen. She lost."

I saw how it was then. A test. I smiled. "Excellent. And if, while acting for my employer, a girl becomes unruly?"

Baron waved his hand. "I would request that you avoid unnecessary damage." He pushed himself to a standing position and hobbled across to the new girl. She closed her eyes as he drew up next to her, pushing his face close to hers. I could sense her revulsion from where I sat and I shared in it. Charles's eyes were on me. I tried to think boring thoughts . . .

In a flash, Baron's fist shot out and hit the girl in the stomach. She crumpled to the ground in a heap. Terror lit up Glenda's face. I covered my own terror with a deep drag on the cigarette.

Baron wiped his hand on a silk handkerchief, as if touching the girl had somehow soiled him. The girl had fallen in a heap, her black hair touching Baron's shoe. He kicked angrily at her. She cried out and grabbed at his leg, trying to keep him from hitting her face. My toes clenched in my shoes. Charles cocked his mouth in a half-smirk like he knew what was coming—a test he expected me to fail.

I rose on trembling legs and moved to the window. Baron looked at me. I can still see it all—the girl with blood in her hair, trying to catch the breath Baron knocked from her, her hand on his leg, trying to ward off another kick, Baron's red face and wild eyes. He grinned at me and jerked his leg from her grasp.

She cried out at the first kick, but it was a weak and pathetic sound . . . she hadn't caught her breath yet. The sound sent Baron into a frenzy. He kicked again and again and again, focusing on her face and chest.

Glenda covered her mouth to stifle a scream and ran to the couch. There, she curled up into a ball and closed her eyes. My eyes burned, my heart pounded. Baron stopped kicking and started stomping. Even after the girl was long dead he kept at it.

And me? I lit another cigarette and examined my fingernails.

It was dark when I opened my eyes again, screaming Laura's name and thrashing about like a toddler having a nightmare. The morphine syringe was still in my hand. I'd filled it with enough drug to kill a horse and had held it to my vein for an eternity, sweat standing on my forehead and running into my eyes, my clothes scattered around the hotel room. I didn't go through with it, of course. I told myself there was still a chance to bring them all down, to save Glenda, to rescue Audrey. But mostly I was a coward. I didn't want to die naked and alone like so many of the bodies I'd seen back in K.C.

The girl would have died anyway. That's what I told myself. I would never have been able to save her and Glenda and still infiltrate the group of bums running the mess. But I'd let her die. The thought disgusted me. I ran to the bathroom and threw up again, heaving and coughing and retching until all I could do was collapse on the floor.

After awhile I checked my watch. 9:00. Charles was bringing Glenda at 10:00. I pushed myself up and stumbled into the shower. When they knocked on the door I was dressed, my suit neat, shoes shined, seated at the small table and chair pushed against the window. I busied myself with smoking a fresh cigarette and drinking a glass of wine.

Glenda wore a pale green dress. I'd seen her apartment back in K.C. Glenda was a girl who wore pink. I guessed now she was probably happy just to be in clothes. She refused to meet my eye as she came in. There was no anger in her eyes now—just weariness and a newfound knowledge that the world is a pretty ugly place.

Charles kept his arm wrapped tightly around her upper arm. With his free hand he snapped his fingers and a man in a dark hat I recognized from the theater lumbered in. "Money?" Charles asked.

I nodded to the briefcase on the bed. Joshua's money, combined with my own meager funds amounted to little more than two thousand bucks. The cost for Glenda was four thousand. I'd stacked money on top of newspaper cut in the size of bills. Charles would inspect it all, and then he'd kill me.

"It's locked," Charles said.

I fished in my pocket for keys while I looked at the goon. "You want a glass of wine?" I gestured to the open bottle on the table.

"We don't drink while we're working," Charles said.

Sweat popped out on my palms. I tossed Charles the key to the case and gave Glenda a sad smile. Things were about to get ugly and I wanted to warn her. No help for it now.

I crushed out my cigarette and casually put my hand in my coat pocket, fingering the syringes I'd filled with morphine. I moved over next to the goon near the door. He spread his feet apart and crossed his arms over his chest, eyeing me suspiciously.

Charles thumbed through the cash and we all held our breath. His nimble fingers paused for a second as he discovered the phony bills on the bottom of the stacks. He looked up and grinned. I grinned back. He shook his head and I shrugged. Then I lunged forward, picking up the ashtray on the table as I moved, swinging it in an arc that landed squarely on the second thug's nose. He raised his hands to his face and blood seeped between his fingers.

Charles straightened, the sudden movement knocking the case to the floor. I flew at him, the syringe in my hand. I drove the syringe into his hip as we both fell over onto the bed. He fumbled for the gun buried beneath him in a hip holster. Already he was becoming clumsy, his hands flailing aimlessly. I rolled him over and pulled the gun out, tossing it across the room. It skidded harmlessly onto the bathroom tile a few feet away.

Glenda backed as far into the room as she could. I figured she was trying to make herself invisible.

The thug lunged for me, his hands clenched into tight fists. I pulled the second syringe from my pocket as I dodged out of his way. He laughed and circled around, keeping the bed—and Charles—between us. Glenda's breathing sounded erratic and I was afraid she might be on the edge of hysteria. The goon's smile faltered when he realized he'd trapped himself. I moved to the foot of the bed; the thug had no choice but to move back toward the door or to come straight at me.

I slowly put the syringe in my pocket and then dove into the bathroom to retrieve the gun. He raised his arms, but a smile creased his face. "I don't carry a gun," he said. "But when you turn your back I will break your neck."

"Pat him down," I told Glenda.

She sniffled and made her way over to him. She was weak and off-balance, her bones making sharp little lumps against her dress. She patted him here and there and he looked amused, moaning as if he enjoyed it.

Glenda finished checking him and then moved to sit down in the back of the room again. The thug touched his nose which was still bleeding. I gestured for him to sit. Charles snored heavily on the bed.

"I'll take that glass of wine now," the thug said.

I nodded to the bottle of wine. "Help yourself."

Glenda said nothing and I couldn't afford to look at her. I forced thoughts of her dead friend from my mind and concentrated on the thug. "This tastes funny," he said, finishing the first glass and pouring a second.

I kept the gun pointed at his chest. "It's the morphine," I said. "Gives wine a chemical taste."

The goon's eyes dimmed before he had a chance to react to what I said. When he fell over onto the floor I looked at Glenda. "Let's get out of here."

23

RAY

Banner Films looked even more like a ghost town than before. Lloyd and I sat in his car across the street watching the evening breeze blow sand and the occasional tumbleweed across the dirt driveway. I felt bad for all the employees but most of them were probably thanking me for giving them an excuse to leave the desert.

"I like the idea of going to back to Hollywood better," Lloyd said.

"Yeah, well, this is our best chance to learn something about where to find Audrey. We head back to L.A. and we might as well start knocking on random doors."

"Y'know I did props for *The Saint Strikes Back*."

I waited for the rest of the story. It never came. "Yeah?"

"That guy can solve any case in about an hour."

"Is that right?"

"Yeah." I held my breath, waiting for the other shoe. "This ain't like that, is it?"

I knew it wasn't an insult, even if it came out like one. "You watch too many movies, Lloyd."

Lloyd and I waited in his car a discreet distance away for ten minutes, then a few more, watching to make sure no one else was going to come out or go in. Every now and then Lloyd would burst out with some detail of the encounter at Zachary's place, just to get it out of his head. I knew he was running and re-running the action back in his mind like a projector on an infinite loop.

I'd been there before. The things you cannot unsee. Amazing thing though, eventually, you get used to the pictures that never leave your head. Not that I wished that on Lloyd.

Dusk moved quickly and the sky turned from golden to pink to blue which slowly drained of pigment toward black all in the fifteen minutes we'd been parked. Time to go in. I wasn't sure exactly what we'd find. More than once I looked over at Lloyd and wished he was Fokoli. A man of experience.

Lloyd parked in the shadows and we went in through a back door which took us through the prop warehouse, a sort of funhouse playroom of clashing cultures and odds and ends. With just a bare work light on, it cast shadows worthy of *Dracula*. I was glad Lloyd was with me. He knew how to navigate the maze.

We took an interior doorway that led us into the main office building, then climbed the stairs up to Silvio's office, past the empty reception desk and to the inner sanctum.

Once there Lloyd looked to me for guidance. I had none to give.

"Start looking around," I said. "If anything seems like it might relate to Audrey, holler."

Sage advice. I might as well have just said, "Toss the joint."

The place already looked halfway tossed. Enzo said he was getting packed up when Zachary had called. The desk was piled high with scripts and accounting paperwork. None of it meant anything to me. A cardboard box was perched on the edge of the desk.

Lloyd started looking at the bookshelf that lined the back wall of the office.

In the center drawer of Silvio's desk I found a silver lighter, three cigars, two fountain pens, a package of chewing gum and a pearl handled revolver. The kind you'd see in a

Western but not on the hip of the sheriff, the kind carried by a lady. I left it in place, afraid if I had a gun with me it would be an invitation to use it. I got myself in enough trouble already.

Two filing drawers were on the left side of the desk. The top one was open and contained hundreds of photos of girls. Most were modest, some were in bathing suits. None of it was organized. Each had a red number scratched in the upper right corner; a rating system. One through ten. Some of the nines were underlined.

I pushed the drawer closed revealing the bottom drawer which was empty except for a single yellow film canister. I picked up the can. Empty. Enzo must have gone for this drawer first and cleaned it out, taking the most damning evidence with him for his big relocation to Hollywood. I cursed under my breath.

"Hey, look at this," Lloyd said. I went to him and he pointed to a wall safe embedded behind a stack of books on the shelf. Not a bad bit of detecting.

"Just one thing missing," he said.

"A combination?"

Lloyd nodded. "What about the secretary?" I perked up. Maybe a little of *The Saint* rubbed off on Lloyd.

I went out to the reception desk which still smelled of Claire's perfume. A friendly way to greet visitors but also, I guess, a way to keep the stench of Silvio out of her tiny corner of the office. She must have sat all day in a cloud of spray-on jasmine and imagined she worked at RKO.

On top of her desk was a leather bound address book with all the pages ripped out down to Z, which was blank. Enzo must have gotten rid of Silvio's contacts already.

I dug around in drawers but didn't see anything like a combination or a key. Might be in Enzo's back pocket with the address book pages and the contents of that second drawer.

I returned to the office.

"Nothing," I said.

"Crap," Lloyd said. "What's in there?" He pointed to the

cardboard box.

It was closed but not taped up. I lifted the cardboard flaps and nearly gasped. A neat row of ten yellow film cans and beside them two red ones. The missing contents of that bottom drawer, I assumed. Lloyd and I exchanged a look. I lifted a yellow can out and opened it. This one was full. The thin 8mm film slid through my hand as I spooled it out and raised it to the light. I recognized the tiny boxes showing the same sparse bedroom I'd seen before. I wasn't sure if that meant it was the same film or if they only had one location. Before it got too unspooled and I couldn't put it back again I began to spin it back into place and I turned to Lloyd, "You do another one. See if it's the same."

Lloyd rolled out a few yards of film from another yellow can. He lifted the strip to the light and squinted an eye. "This one's different."

I looked and saw another room, also spare but different, almost like a cabin in the woods.

"There's got to be a projector around here," I said. I hated him thinking I wanted to watch one of the films for pleasure and I added for Lloyd's benefit, in case he got the wrong impression: "So we can try to I.D. Audrey on any of these. Y'know just watch until the girl enters the room." Lloyd nodded.

He started looking around the room then out in the lobby for a projector. "Very least," he called from the reception area, "they have a screening room downstairs for dailies. Not sure if they have eight millimeter though."

With him out of the room I opened a red can. I let several yards of film fall to the ground and gather like snakes mating around my feet. I held the gray strip up to the light. It was all too familiar. Same room, same girl. It seemed true that only one of these red films had been produced.

As I spooled back the red film reel I noticed more papers under the cans. I pushed some yellow tins out of the way and lifted out a small stack of more headshots. Fifteen girls, all beautiful. All just as bright eyed and eager as the faces in the other drawer but for some reason, and I think I know what, they were kept separate. It felt like they were marked for death, like I was reading the morning paper and the accompanying photo was describing a dead girl found floating in the river.

I flipped through the pictures, ignoring the names and focusing on the eyes, the hope and glint of a dream in them. Give me my big break mister, they all seemed to say, you won't be sorry.

Second from the bottom was Audrey. Gold embossed lettering in elegant cursive ran across the bottom: AUDREY STARLING. The signature was a long way from the cement in front of Grauman's Chinese.

She'd made the short list.

Lloyd came bursting back in to the office and closed the door quickly but quietly behind him. "They're here."

"Who?"

"Enzo and another guy."

"The closet," I said, dropping the photos on top of the film cans, I shut the box and threw a stack of scripts back on top the way I found it.

We both soft-shoed it over to the closet next to the bookcase. Lloyd pushed in ahead of me and as I moved in behind him I remembered the pearl handled revolver. I turned quickly and made it back to the desk. I was just rounding the corner when I heard Enzo out by the reception area.

I had no time to get the gun, no time to make it back to the closet. Behind me was a window with full length burgundy curtains, thick to keep out the heat of the desert sun. I slid behind one panel and with my toe I pushed a stack of scripts on the floor in front of where my shoes were at risk of betraying me.

I thought of the breathing techniques I used to work on with my brother to calm him before he entered the ring. You can breathe deep but slow and lower your heart rate when you need to. It takes practice. I had years of it.

Enzo was still angry from the fight at Zachary's.

"You get the safe. I'll finish with this shit."

I heard the second man's footsteps shuffle across the carpet. He sounded like he was limping. I heard more paper being pushed around, drawers opening and closing.

"You know Silvio still owed me a lot of money," the other man said.

"What the fuck do you want me to do about it? Silvio owed everyone money. When we get set up in L.A. we'll all be back in the pink. We never should have come to this desert wasteland. Should have stayed in Hollywood."

The limping man returned to the desk. "Yeah."

"Well, there's gonna be changes now. But we gotta lay low for awhile."

"What about the film for Mr. Heathcliff?"

"Yeah, we'll finish that, but then we take a break. We need time to set up a new studio. I'll go tell Baron that I'm the new man, now. He won't miss Silvio. No one will. Me and Baron, we can do business without middle men anymore."

I breathed steady. My heart stayed slow and even, despite the drops of sweat beading my forehead. I wasn't anxious for another round with Enzo. It was tempting to want to leap out and finish what I started back at Zachary's, but this was his turf. If he had been packing to leave town in the next hour or so surely he would be carrying a gun. Plus, I couldn't see a damn thing. Nope, stay behind the ropes on this one. Don't enter that ring blind. I only hoped I could learn something from the radio show on the other side of the curtain.

"You got everything?" Enzo asked.

"Yeah. Got it. My leg still hurts like a sonofabitch though."

"Fuck it, you'll be fine. Now let's get back to civilization."

"What about the guy?"

"Ray? Fuck him. I *want* to cross paths with that bastard again. Let him try."

"What if they go to the cops, him and Lloyd?"

"If they were gonna go to the cops they would have by

now. Besides, between Baron and Mr. Butler we've got enough L.A.P.D. on payroll to make anything go away. Come on."

Footsteps left the room and descended the stairs. Lloyd and I both waited a solid minute after they left before poking our heads out from our hiding places.

Lloyd saw me step out from behind the curtain. "I kept waiting to hear them find you and kill you. Christ I didn't know where you went. One second you're right behind me and—"

"They took everything." I pointed to the empty drawers and desktop. "We have to follow them."

"Where?"

"Back to Hollywood." I pulled back the curtain a sliver and could see the taillights of a car on the dirt lot below. I pulled open the center drawer. The gun was still there. I took it this time. Learned my lesson.

I waved with the gun for Lloyd to follow me.

"What's that for?"

"Just in case."

"In case what?" He couldn't take his eyes off the revolver.

"In case we need it. Now come on."

Lloyd led us back into the maze again. We passed through the storeroom and heard a car start outside. Lloyd got us to the exit quickly.

We opened the door a crack and peeked through in time to see tail lights pulling away from the building. As their car bumped down the dirt road away from Banner films me and Lloyd rushed to his car and pulled out from behind the building just as Enzo's car pulled onto the main road.

I should have been driving. Lloyd was scared and that made him timid. I knew he didn't want to be caught, didn't want to feel Enzo's wrath, but the car on the black streets ahead of us kept getting farther away.

I urged Lloyd to speed up, wishing again I had Fokoli back with me. There were too many turns, too many unmarked roads out in this desert oasis. Lloyd let the car disappear around a bend and when we got there it was long gone and with them, my only link to finding Audrey.

I punched the dashboard. Lloyd squeaked out an apology I didn't accept.

"Maybe we should call the cops," Lloyd said.

"And say what? I think some men are making movies of girls dying, but I can't show you one and I don't know who the men are. The only one I did know is dead now and the cops are probably looking for me as the killer. And you as my accomplice."

"Well, I don't know what else to do, Ray." He was on the verge of tears again. This kid could use a few rounds in the ring to toughen him up. Maybe he should start with the pee wee golden gloves. Even they'd probably knock him silly.

I leaned out the car window and looked up at the sky, hoping for some inspiration.

As hot as it was during the midday sun, the desert cooled quickly at night. The heat vanished into the air as the stars came out and I couldn't help thinking they looked like little drops of condensation on the night sky.

"I got one idea," I said.

"What's that?"

I pulled my head back into the car. "Turn around."

"Again? Where to?"

"The scene of the crime."

Lloyd shook his head, resigned to my crazy schemes. "And you say *I* watch too many movies."

24

FOKOLI

Glenda slept like the dead. Poor choice of words, but I wasn't in the mood to try to come up with something different. I was on the edge of panic. Since Laura's death I'd had attacks—like being shell-shocked in a way. Poor concentration on a good day, raw panic and terror on others. The feeling gnawed at my insides like a hungry rabbit most of the time—insistent, but quiet—now, with Ray gone, Glenda asleep on the passenger seat beside me, and two of Baron's men sleeping it off back at the hotel, it was all I could do to keep my eyes on the road. The crushed face of Baron's girl floated in front of me, the dashed lines in the center of the road coming through her face like spears. I blinked until it went away and I concentrated on Glenda.

She didn't speak when I collected all the cash from the floor and pulled her from my room over to Ray's. I shoved some of his clothes into her hands and pushed her into the bathroom to change. When she opened her mouth to protest, I raised my hand as if I'd strike her. She shrank from me and did as she was told. Now a trained dog. I stashed my suitcase and Ray's bag in the alley behind a dumpster, piling boxes on the top, hoping bums wouldn't come and snatch anything before I got back. I refused to let Glenda stay there. She tried to keep up with me as I dragged her seven blocks away to a quiet neighborhood—poor but respectable—the kind where folks park on the street. I chose a sedan. Chevy. White. Like a million other cars on the road. It was easy enough to start. After three blocks Glenda said, "These clothes are too big."

"They're Ray's." That shut her up.

I went back to the alley to get me and Ray's luggage. I had Charles's gun in my shoulder holster and my snub nose tucked safely at my ankle so I was ready for a fight if any bums had laid claim to my stuff. The bags were right where I'd left them. I tossed everything in the trunk and drove on.

Glenda didn't ask where we were going. Makeup had smeared under her eyes making her look like there were two huge black holes in her face. I didn't know L.A. at all, other than the few square blocks I'd covered since I started this mess. Fuck you Ray Ward. Fuck you very much. I swiped a hand over my face. I didn't mean that. I didn't. I'd find his sister and get her out. First I needed to feed Glenda. She was like a mangy dog on the seat beside me—flea bitten and scraggly and underneath Ray's baggy borrowed clothes she was dirty. God was she dirty. She smelled like she hadn't bathed in a week or more.

Laura used to keep an assortment of mysterious jars in our bathroom. Face cream, cold cream, lipstick, and God knows what else. I pulled into a drug store and picked up some things. My shoulder was bleeding—had bled through my jacket and I hadn't noticed. "Might want to get some bandages too," the guy behind the counter said. I gave him a tight smile and picked up some supplies.

Back at the counter, I said, "You should see the other guy."

He didn't laugh.

I changed jackets and took Glenda to an all night diner—the kind where guys sit at the counter hunched over their plates and don't look up—like this is the first time they've crawled out from their rock all day and they can't wait to get back under it.

I gave Glenda the bag and told her to hit the bathroom. She

didn't argue so I didn't have to raise my hand again. I ordered food—lots—and waited for her to come back.

She showed up a few minutes later, cleaner but haggard looking. Her legs were so thin I wondered how they could support her weight. When the waitress brought our food, Glenda eyed the plates, picked up a fried egg sandwich and took a deep bite. "I like ice cream sodas," she said around the mouthful of food. "Always have."

I ordered an ice cream soda for her.

She waited until the waitress brought her order and left. She played with the straw before saying anything else. "You let Baron kill that girl."

"Yes."

A tear leaked out of the corner of her eye and rolled down her cheek. I waited for Glenda to throw that damn soda in my face. She didn't. She just sat there and looked sad.

"When you don't work at the theater," I said after a minute, "where does Baron keep you?"

"Glendale."

"Where is Glendale?"

She shook her head and wiped her nose. She pushed the glass away from her and pulled a plate with a piece of apple pie close to her and took a bite. "I don't know exactly. I think it's an apartment building. They gave me shots twice a day. Morphine." She put her fork down and blushed. "He did things to me."

I cleared my throat. "Did you know anyone named Audrey?"

She shook her head. "I didn't know anybody's name."

"There were other girls there?"

"Yes." Barely a whisper.

"How many girls?"

"Fifteen. Maybe twenty."

"He kept everyone drugged?"

"I don't know. I think so. I can't imagine anyone would willingly . . ."

I cleared my throat again. "Do you know how much morphine he gave you?"

"No."

I blew out a breath. "Finish up. We've got to go."

"Where?"

"First we need to rest. Then, we've got to get those girls out."

She shoved her plate away and shook her head. "No way. Count me out. You saw what he did to that girl." Her eyes narrowed. "Remember? That thing you let him do?" Her voice was loud in the small diner. The hunched figures out the counter stirred. Someone was interrupting feeding time.

I leaned forward. "I don't give a shit what happens to you, Glenda. Ray Ward hired me to help his sister and that's what I'm going to do. Now, seeing as how Ray seemed to have a fondness for you, I figure I better keep you with me." I didn't mean it. Of course I cared what happened to her. But she was this fragile, broken thing sitting across from me with legs like a colt's. I hoped my words would toughen her up.

She looked down at her clothes. "You said these were Ray's. Where is he?" She already sounded a little tougher.

"I don't know. We got separated." And that was the truth. I didn't know where he was. The fact that I was sure he was dead was irrelevant.

"Rex and Ray have a sister?"

"That's what I'm told." I stood up and laid some bills on the table. My shirt stuck to the wet bandage on my shoulder. We needed to find a place where I could clean up—where we could sleep. When Glenda just continued to sit I said, "I'm in sort of a bad mood. I'm tired and I've got a headache. If you don't get up I'll club you and drag you out to the car."

"Yeah, you tell her mister," a guy at the counter said.

Glenda swiped at her nose, which had started to run. "Keep out of this, you."

But she stood up and we walked outside and climbed into the car. She was asleep before we got a block away. I circled through unknown streets, not knowing where I was or where to go. I just needed a place to sleep. After a half hour I found the kind of place I was looking for. A sign flashed off and on – OTEL it said. I checked us in, carried the bags up, and let Glenda get settled. Then I abandoned the car in a public lot. Glenda was asleep on top of the bedspread when I returned. I showered and re-dressed my shoulder. I put the snub nose on the night stand beside her and then curled up on the floor with Charles's gun in hand.

25

RAY

We arrived back at Zachary's apartment with the desert a black curtain behind the building. It was a dark void where light went to die. A fitting shroud to what awaited us inside.

Enzo and his pals hadn't bothered to lock the door when they left; a sight I wish I'd seen. The three of them limping out, applying pressure to stop the bleeding, a portrait of defeat.

A cool breeze blew in off the desert. When the door opened a waft of heat belched out like we'd popped a cork. The stench of blood came with it.

The lights were off and inside was as dark as the desert beyond. Lloyd and I sucked a deep breath of fresh air and stepped in, but not before I drew the pearl handled revolver.

The heat of the day was still thick and swampy in the tiny apartment. As I felt along the wall for a light I noticed a sound. It was wet, almost animal. I feared Zachary was still alive, clawing off the inevitable as he listened, drop by drop, to his life flowing out.

I found a switch, flipped it on, and saw eyes. A large dog or something. It hunched over Zachary's body and was staring at me with wide reflective eyes behind a blood soaked muzzle, baring white teeth. I pushed back against the wall and hit hard, dropping the small gun and instantly forgetting I ever had it. I measured the distance between me and the table leg on the floor I'd used that afternoon. Reaching for it would have been a lunge in the animal's direction and the beast didn't look friendly to that idea.

The creature snarled once and snapped, flinging blood as its jaws clamped shut, then turned and ran out through the kitchen. I could hear the scrambling of claws on the counter and then the banging of the body as it escaped.

I snatched up my table leg and held it like Babe Ruth.

"Coyote," Lloyd said. "Must have smelled the blood."

I peered around into the kitchen and saw the open window above the sink; a futile attempt to cool the place down during the day. I lowered the table leg and shook my head. We don't get coyotes in Kansas City.

I finally saw the rest of the room and was treated to a replay of the day's ten-rounder. I remembered each punch, each swing with the table leg. Saw the ruins of the coffee table, the remnants of my uneaten sandwich and Zachary's impaled body.

He was face down and I was thankful for that. It seemed the coyote had chewed on his neck. The back of his shirt was soaked through with blood. The edges were dried but a small ring of wetness still surrounded the knife protruding from his ribcage. I wondered if the owner of the knife even tried to get it back.

I turned to Lloyd who was staring at the wall, then went to Zachary's desk and found the paper he showed me earlier—the schedule of deliveries for the stag films. There were four dates along with addresses. No names. The top of the list was dated that day with a 12:00 A.M. penciled in next to it. That gave us almost three hours. Plenty of time.

I pocketed the list. "Let's get the hell out of here," I said.

"Wait." Lloyd crossed through the apartment and entered the kitchen. He shut the window, keeping the coyotes out. Lloyd had a good heart, Zachary was still a friend. For the man who sold us out to Enzo I'd just as soon open all the doors and windows and burn a neon ALL YOU CAN EAT sign.

BORROWED TROUBLE

We locked up when we left.

On the highway back to Los Angeles the stars blended with the approaching city lights like we were on the outskirts of a galaxy headed toward its star clustered center.

Los Angeles was growing fast. Hollywood lured count-less starlets and working stiffs in search of the bright lights and promise of discovery. From where I sat watching the city crawl up around us along the highway, it was growing faster than it could handle. The edges of the city were like a skeleton still waiting for skin to grow over it.

I made a fist and punched my knee, angry when I realized I'd left the pearl handled gun on the floor of Zachary's apartment. At least no one could connect it to me. Let them trace it back to Silvio. Pinning a murder on him would be the easiest thing a cop did all day.

Lloyd stared far ahead as he drove. I could tell he wasn't watching for cars but for where his life took a turn into a ditch. Keep looking kid. I still haven't seen where mine took a dive yet. Doubt I ever will.

"Funny, y'know," Lloyd said. "Every time I'm in the desert I can't wait to get back to the city and every time I hit the city I want to be back in the desert."

"Yeah, funny."

"Guess I won't be going back there for awhile."

I let that one hang.

"So where's the address?"

"Let's try Nancy's place first. We've got time before the delivery. She might have heard something else. At least it's a friendly face."

"I could use one of those about now."

"Me too."

I thought about going straight to Butler, but I didn't know enough to storm the castle gates just yet. I was tired of being in over my head. I needed to tread a little water.

We passed downtown. I recognized City Hall from the

movies. Lit up at night the strong central spike stood like justice itself had claimed the land. To me it seemed like justice had holed up inside and barricaded the door, refusing to come out where the rest of us live.

Lloyd knew where he was going so I had nothing to do but stare out the window. We veered off onto surface streets once we hit Hollywood. The city's concentrated center was awash in lights and people. For a place known for the sunshine, people sure did seem in their element in the moonlight. So did werewolves. Or coyotes.

Night clubs were hopping. On Sunset Boulevard we passed between Ciro's and The Trocadero where I saw a woman dressed in mink slap a guy wearing a tuxedo. He just kept on laughing which I suspected was what got him in hot water to begin with.

Lloyd turned off Sunset onto Hollywood Boulevard and I finally got to see some real Hollywood glamour. We passed by the Egyptian theater where a show was letting out. Big spotlights swept into the sky in crisscrossing patterns, a huge throng of people stood on the sidewalk behind wooden barricades. A big sign announced the premiere of a picture called *A Rage In Heaven* and my hand to God I saw Robert Montgomery step out, wave to the crowd and get inside a limousine.

"Did you see that?" I said to Lloyd.

"Yeah. Some kind of premiere." He was unimpressed. "I bet she never had to audition for Silvio."

"Who?"

"Ingrid Bergman. Didn't you see her?"

Somehow admitting I had no idea who she was seemed like a bad idea. "Oh, yeah."

We wound down away from the glamour and back to the simple side streets and Nancy's building. Lloyd parked and we both scanned the street for anything or anyone suspicious. It was dark, quiet. I wasn't sure if that was a good sign or a bad one. I could see the windows of Nancy's corner apartment and the lights were off. Not unusual that late at night, but the darkness gave me a queer feeling.

I knocked quietly so as not to rouse the neighbors. Something in my bones knew it wouldn't have mattered how hard I knocked. I tried again, a little louder.

Across the courtyard a door opened. A man was pushed out and his jacket came sailing out after him.

"But, honey, come on now." His hands were out, palms up and pleading, but the smirk on his face said he didn't really care.

"Amscray, Peter. This casting call is closed." It was Gina, the raven-haired beauty.

"Rain check?"

"How about snow?"

"But, baby, this is L.A."

"Then we understand each other." The guy got the hint and walked away, pulling his jacket on as he passed us.

"Hope you have better luck than I did tonight, pal." He aimed a finger gun at me and pulled the trigger. He left whistling.

Gina was still in her doorway. "Hey. Tell Nancy she still needs to give me back my projector."

"Have you seen her? No one's answering."

"Not since I was with you. What was your name again?"

"Ray," I said, a little hurt that she had forgotten all about our connection earlier.

"Uh-huh." She looked at me through a furrowed brow like she was memorizing my face for an eventual lineup. She went back inside and her light switched off.

"What do we do?" Lloyd asked.

"We break in."

I tried the doorknob. Locked up tight. My body was still a little sore from my tussles over the past few days, but one more bruise to my shoulder wouldn't make a difference. I leaned back to get a bit of a run at it then hit the door hard. The lock held but the frame splintered. A quick scan over my shoulder to make sure I hadn't woken anyone up and we were inside. I set the chain to keep the door in place.

The apartment reminded me of my house back in Kansas City. A certain fog of death hovered inside. In my house it was every familiar piece of furniture and picture on the wall that reminded me daily of my Mom and of Rex. Here it was a ghostly feeling, the air was thick like walking through mud. Maybe I still had Zachary on my mind. I was tense waiting for a snarling coyote to leap out.

I couldn't see much. I made it to the kitchen and snapped on the light. It cast long shadows into the living room but there was nothing to see except the movie projector still aiming at the wall. No red can nearby. No evidence of what was last shown there.

I went to Audrey's bedroom. Someone had been there. Photos were on the floor, her mattress was crooked, the drawers on her desk sat open. The stone in my stomach got heavier.

"Ray." Lloyd tried to whisper but I could hear the urgency in his voice.

"Keep quiet," I said as I followed his voice to Nancy's room. He had the closet light on. He was standing next to the bed over a wide stain of dried blood. The bed was soaked with it and the carpet had grown hard with a dark coagulated pool. In the center of it, a shrouded figure. I knew it was Nancy.

I was two for two. I felt like the grim reaper. You did not want me knocking at your door.

As freely as L.A. grew beautiful women, it disposed of them just as quickly. Nancy, whose crime was nothing more than living with Audrey and helping me try to find her. I felt partly responsible, like she was paying for my butting in.

If I was Fokoli I would have searched for clues, turned the place upside down. I'm not him. I wanted the hell out. Sharing a room with a corpse was getting very old. To make it official I lifted the blanket that covered her and waited to see her chest rise and fall or her eyes flutter. She was unmoving and naked underneath. I expected any second she would stand up and slap me, then collapse again into her bed of dried blood.

Lloyd needed my help out of the room. He was breaking down.

"Hang in there." I wasn't ready to throw in the towel yet so I had to keep him upright and swinging. I walked us both out into the living room. I noticed a clock on the side table. 12:30. Later than I thought.

"Let's go to a stag party," I said. "Zachary's list had the address. You know where it is?" I held out the paper for Lloyd to inspect. He nodded.

An idea came to me. My first real detective inkling and I was proud of it. I went to the movie projector and opened the gate. Inside was a tiny strip of burned film. I counted fifteen tiny squares, many of them were nothing but blistered orange blobs but several held the frozen image of a girl's face. I wasn't sure how I would use it but I knew it was a good thing to have in my corner.

I lifted the projector and carried it out.

The door swung open behind us, the lock unable to catch on the ruined frame. It didn't matter. I told Lloyd to go ahead and start the car.

Alone, I knocked on Gina's door. A light switched on and she opened up angrily, pulling on a frilly robe, ready to confront her suitor who wouldn't take no for an answer. She stopped, mouth open with an insult caught in it, when she saw me.

"Here's your projector. I'm bringing it back so you'll see I'm a good guy. Then maybe you'll know I had nothing to do with what's in Nancy's apartment. You should call the police though."

She took the projector from me. "What happened at Nancy's?"

"Just call the police. Don't go in there. And remember when we first met. I'm trying to find my sister. Trying to help her. I'm going to make sure the same thing doesn't happen to her."

She saw my intensity and nodded so I knew I was understood. The fear in her eyes wasn't for me, it was directed at the open door to Nancy's. With good reason.

26

FOKOLI

Me and Laura—in our happier years—liked to cook. Sometimes I would come home from work with a bottle of merlot. We'd sip wine and cook and eat. Sometimes just standing at the stove and nibbling the meat away to nothing while we talked, rather than carrying everything out to the dining room. In the later years, with cop parties and card games and weekend outings, we switched to bourbon and vodka. Laura liked vodka.

Nights standing at the stove talking and eating turned to nights of silent ambivalence that grew into noisy hatred. Empty bottles were a prop in every scene. When you see a drunk on the street it's easy to walk away—easy to ignore it. That's not the case when the drunk is your wife—and you're the guy who helped to make her that way. I'd finished beating myself up over it, but my past was with me all the time, like some big ugly gorilla on my back, with strong fingers around my neck.

Laura floated in front of me and somehow I knew she was just a dream, that I was asleep and she would leave like she always did. When Baron's face appeared behind her I opened my mouth to tell her to run, but I couldn't move. My arms and legs were stuck fast and I watched, helpless, as he knocked her to the ground and kicked her. She didn't cry out; she just laid there as he lifted his heavy feet and kicked again and again.

In the dark motel room, I sat up with a start. -OTEL lit up on the back wall and then died out only to flash on again. I swiped a hand over my face and let the thoughts of Laura vaporize.

From the bed, Glenda moaned. I stood and checked on her. She was shivering and bathed in sweat. Withdrawal from the morphine. The room had gone cold and she was in for a long night. I lay down beside her and pulled her to me, covering us both with the blanket.

She went still and then moaned a little bit. "Please. Don't hurt me."

It was nothing more than a whispered plea—acceptance of what she felt to be inevitable. Like strange men crawling into bed with her was something that happened all the time. It probably did. And I'd done nothing to help her feel safe since picking her up. I'd done nothing to make her feel like she had worth. I thought about what Ray would say to her if he were in my position.

"I'm not going to hurt you," I said.

She shivered convulsively. "I'm sick."

"It's withdrawal. I'll keep you warm. It will pass. Try to hang on."

She started to cry. –OTEL flashed on the wall again. "My head hurts. Oh, God, my head hurts." She sat up and was sick all over me and the blanket. She looked at me, shocked, embarrassed. A sheen of sweat covered her pale skin. She was in bad shape.

I stood up and tried to check my temper. "God. Damn. FUCK."

She didn't react, just laid back down on the bed and sighed. My shorts and T-shirt were soaked in half digested egg sandwich, apple pie, and ice cream soda. Her breathing grew rapid and a million images of Laura and booze and all the shit that went along with it settled over me like a plastic bag.

"Goddammit. Fucking fuck FUCK shit."

Glenda writhed in pain on the bed, crying and holding her

head. I fished in my jacket pocket for the vial of morphine and the syringe. I drew up two milligrams and injected it into her arm. I had no idea how much they had been giving her, but I was sure the amount I was pumping into her was nowhere close to the dose she was used to. "This will take the edge off," I said through clenched teeth.

I left her there while I turned on the shower. This was like Laura all over again and in a panic I wondered if this time maybe I could keep my disgust at bay and try to make myself useful. I stripped down and scrubbed off.

I held onto the anger to try and keep my hands from shaking, but I turned it away from Glenda and focused on Baron. I'd kill him first chance I got. I pulled on a clean pair of shorts and left the shower running. Glenda had relaxed a little by the time I got to her. The bedding smelled terrible and so did she. I sat her on the toilet and pulled off the dirty clothes of Ray's she was wearing. They would have to be sent to the laundry. Would we be around long enough?

Glenda cried a little more. "I'm sorry. I'm so sorry."

"Can you stand?"

She could, but she was weak. I helped her into the shower and let her wash herself. When she was clean I handed her a towel and another clean shirt of Ray's. She sat in a chair while I went to get clean linens from the night clerk.

Glenda watched me change the sheets with a cocked eyebrow much like the Glenda I remembered from Kansas City. "You could have been a nurse," she said. "You seem to know your way around a patient and her sick room." Her voice sounded raw.

"Yeah," I said, thinking about Laura. I finished the bed and looked at Glenda. "Lay down."

I tucked her in, set a trash can next to the bed, and turned out the light before beginning to make my own bed on the floor.

"Fokoli," she said and waited for my response.

"Hmm."

"Will you lay beside me? I'm scared."

I blew out a breath. Typical. I climbed in bed and pulled her close. "Go to sleep. And if you're going to get sick again, use the trash can."

27

RAY

L.A. at night is like a theater gone dark just before the show starts. You know you're surrounded by people, but you can't quite make them out, and everyone is waiting for something to happen.

Lloyd drove us to the address on the sheet I took from Zachary's. It was in a place called Culver City, one of the many towns within a town that comprised L.A.

Lloyd was quiet. So was I. For me the windshield was a screen playing an endless loop of Nancy's corpse frozen on a carpet stiffening with blood. Funny thing about blood, it's meant to flow. The faster it moves, the faster people around it move. I've seen plenty of guys with blood pouring down their faces, in the ring and out, and in that moment every-thing speeds up. Rush to get him help, rush to get away, rush to tell a friend. But when blood is solid, dark and crusted over, everything else slows down too. People move slower, talk quieter, bow their heads. Or drive in silence with the windows down, hoping fresh air will clear out the images.

But it won't.

When we drove down Washington Boulevard through a little downtown area Lloyd spoke up like a tour guide, his mind spinning anywhere but to the task at hand.

"See that hotel?" He pointed at a triangular building seven

or eight stories high. "That's where all the munchkins stayed for *Wizard of Oz*. I heard they trashed the joint."

I watched the hotel go by and imagined marauding bands of midgets swinging from the chandeliers.

"That's MGM up there," he said as we passed by a row of colonnades. "Back behind us is Hal Roach where they make the *Our Gang* films. I'd have killed to be one of those kids growing up."

He almost cracked a grin but his face couldn't seem to let him. Could have been the nostalgia of not being part of the gang or could have been the unfortunate use of the word *killed*. Death was already riding shotgun with us, no need to call it out.

He made a left and turned into the lot of the Elks lodge listed on Zachary's delivery schedule. I had no idea what we'd find inside, but if it led me one step closer to Audrey I'd brave anything.

The party was in full swing. Ten men stumbled around in shirtsleeves and loose ties, beer mugs sloshing over in their hands. A haze of smoke hung like fog and each man puffed away on cigars and cigarettes, adding to the cloud. A record player was blasting some Fats Waller. The ten men were loud the way only drunks can be and sounded like a crowd of fifty.

A tall man with a mustache and a crooked straw hat saw us enter.

"Are you the boys with our movie? You're late!" He threw an arm over my shoulder like we were old pals. I also think I helped him stay on his feet. "That's okay though. As long as she's pretty." He slapped my back. "And naked!" He roared with laughter and several other men joined him though I doubt they heard a word he had said.

I noticed the white square of a movie screen in the corner behind a pool table. My new pal announced us to the crowd. "Hey boys, these fellas are here with our movie of the lovely Lolita!"

A rowdy cheer rose up from the boys. Glasses were raised high in the air. It didn't seem like a crowd waiting to watch a girl get raped.

A voice called out from the crowd. "Hey, Mack, is she a natural blonde?"

"We'll find out soon enough!" More howls of laughter.

I waited a moment before crushing his dreams and telling him I didn't have his movie. "What kind of film are you expecting?"

"Oh I don't care, mister. Just so long as she's naked as a jay bird!" A man at the bar spit beer out of his nose.

"You're not looking for one in a yellow can?"

"A yellow can? What damn difference does that make?"

"I'd like to see her can!" someone shouted. Two men, arm in arm by the record player, laughed and slapped each other on the back so hard they bumped the phonograph and sent Fats to skipping. "Ain't misbehavin'—Ain't misbehavin'—Ain't misbehavin'"

"Who'd you buy the film from?" I asked. The man with the mustache was starting to get annoyed.

"I don't know. Look, are you gonna show the movie or not?" He looked to Lloyd for some help but found none.

"I just want to know how you found a film like that."

"Jack found it. Jack!" A sturdy man with a thick neck behind the bar perked up, a bottle in mid-pour. The mustache man pointed at me. "He wants to know where you found the film at!"

Jack came out from around the bar puffing smoke from a cigar.

"Is there a problem?" His collar and underarms were ringed in sweat.

Behind me, two men shoved a drink into each of Lloyd's hands and led him away to join the party. I let him go.

"I just wanted to know the name of the man who sold you the film."

"Hell, I don't know. One of the boys at the studio gave me

a phone number, I rung it up, said I wanted a real hot number dancing the cooch and that was that. Fella said he'd run it in from Palm Springs. What's the rumpus?"

"Was his name Silvio?"

"Sounds about right. He gave me a deal on the movie and the dancing girl. Didn't hurt when I told him we do these parties about once every other month."

"What dancing girl?"

"She ain't with you?"

"No."

He checked the clock over the bar. "Well, she's supposed to be here soon. We wanted to show the movie first, then get the live show. What do you say you thread her up and let's get going."

With the phonograph broken the men broke into an impromptu rendition of "Chattanooga Choo Choo".

"What's the girl's name?"

"What?"

I shouted over the chorus. "What's the name of the dancing girl?"

"I don't know, pal. Look, what's with the twenty questions?"

I'm a lousy liar and I'd never done any acting before in my life. But, when in Rome . . .

"I'm a private investigator. I'm looking into a missing person's case. This man Silvio is behind her disappearance."

Jack was suddenly sober. "Aw Jesus Christ! Is this a bust?"

"No. I'm not a cop. I just want to find out where they keep the girls."

"Well, do it on your own time, pal. We're tryin' to have a party."

My instinct was to let him have a right hook across his jaw, snap it in two for him. I kept my cool. The singing, the beer stink, the cigar smoke was all getting to me though. And the idea they could order up a girl like a Chinese menu made me a little sick. Partly because it wasn't that far from parties I'd been to before. Men get together, they get a little drunk—or a lot in this case—they like to pay a girl to take off her clothes. What do they say, the oldest profession?

"So are you telling me you don't have my movie?" The slur was back in Jack's voice.

"I don't have your movie." I wished I had a red can film to show him. That would sober these chumps up real quick.

Behind us, the door opened. A man stepped in with a girl on his arm. He was a heavyweight, dressed in a sharp dark suit, black shirt, black tie. He was straining at his clothes from hours in the gym. I looked closer and saw he was holding the girl's arm at her elbow, guiding her along and gripping tight.

The girl was not Audrey. That out of the way, I could look at her. She was thin, too thin, her dress was tight so that her bones showed through. She was not as excited to be there as the men were to see her. A roar went up from the small crowd that sounded like the main event on a Saturday night. That or someone rang the dinner bell and this gang hadn't eaten in awhile.

She was pretty. Red, red lips. Straight black hair. Long gloves that ran up past her elbows. Better to tease off during her routine, I guess.

The Heavyweight vice-gripping her arm spoke to the mustached man. "You Jack?"

He pointed over my shoulder to Jack who puffed his cigar back to life.

"This is Jeanie."

"Jeanie with the light brown hair?" Jack asked, his eyebrows pumping up and down. "I been dreaming of you."

The Heavyweight noticed the way I was looking at him, how I wasn't drunk like everyone else in the room. "What's the matter? You don't like what you see? Maybe you wanted a blonde."

"I don't like what I see, that's for sure."

Jack saw his party breaking up before his eyes. "It's time you moved along, friend. This is a private party." He put a hand on my shoulder, felt it tense under his grip. He could feel the years of pounding the speed bag in my dingy basement.

"This guy a party crasher?" the Heavyweight said. "Maybe trying to get a look for free?"

I turned to the girl. "Do you know Audrey?"

She flinched like I'd hit her. The Heavyweight went red, started puffing up his chest. "No talking to the girls."

I sensed I was running out of time. I tried to get Jeanie to focus on me. "I asked if you know Audrey. Do you?"

Jeanie, frail as a baby bird, seemed to wake up to her surroundings. Whatever they had her on was wearing off, or just wasn't strong enough to overpower the sensory overload of the Elks lodge. Morphine? Heroin? Opium? Whatever it was, she couldn't be on much if they expected her to dance and that tiny window was what I needed to get through to her.

All around me the crowd was growing angry. They'd been promised something and I was standing between them and that something.

The Heavyweight put a firm hand on my arm. He was very persuasive. "Private party, mister. Time to blow."

"I'll go as soon as I get my answer." It was going to take more than just a politely phrased question to Jeanie. She needed about four cups of coffee and a few miles distance between her and this place.

I made eye contact with her and saw the fear. It wasn't a fear of me or even of the Heavyweight, but of the whole Male species.

I reached into my pocket and took out the thin strip of film I'd liberated from the projector at Nancy's place. I held it out to Jeanie. I asked a question with my eyes: "Do you know this girl? Do you know if Audrey is next?"

Jeanie looked up, seemed like she couldn't focus on the tiny squares. The Heavyweight was eyeballing me and trying to get a look over Jeanie's shoulder.

Her eyes went wide. Recognition flashed on her face. It must have been like looking into a crystal ball and seeing her future. She thrust the strip of 8mm back at me. It fell to the floor as she recoiled but the Heavyweight had a firm grip on her. He stomped a foot down on the clip of film and bent down to pick it up. He held it up to the light. My muscles tensed, my fingers drew into fists.

The Heavyweight registered the images, his jaw muscles tensed. He put the film strip away in the pocket of his suit coat and came out with his fist wrapped in brass. I'm a good puncher but even at my best I'm no match for brass knuckles.

The situation was moving out of my control. I did a quick scan of the room searching for Lloyd. I spotted him by the bar shrinking between two men who patted his back and told dirty jokes in his ear. Lloyd wasn't laughing.

I knew I couldn't count on him. This night was too much for him already. It was going to be me and the Heavyweight alone in the ring.

He let go of Jeanie's arm and passed her off to Jack who escorted her through the crowd like a hunter parading his latest kill. She jerked at his touch, every noise in the room—and there were plenty—shocking her system. Those little squares of film, the girl's dead face, woke her up.

No sense waiting for the Heavyweight to throw the first brass-covered punch. I hooked out wide with a left. I made it too wide and too high, an amateur's swing. He took the bait and reared back his brass knuckles as he ducked away from my fake. As he hunched forward I stopped the trajectory on my left and shot out a quick right like a cannonball to his middle. I was right on target. You catch a guy right up under his sternum and you can momentarily paralyze his diaphragm. Makes it impossible to breathe for a few seconds. Those few seconds feel like certain death when you're on the receiving end of a punch like that.

I spun and followed the wake Jack was making through the room. Like a pied piper all the men were turned to follow Jack or, more to the point, Jeanie. No one pawed at her, no one tore at her clothes, but the looks she got would get a man slapped anywhere else. She might as well have already been naked.

I shoved drunks out of my way and grabbed her free arm, yanking her away from Jack. I knew she would be scared but I had no time to explain, and I doubt she would have believed me if I did. She had as much reason to trust a strange man as the three little pigs did to trust the big bad wolf.

Jack turned when she was suddenly not at his side. I found myself in the center of an angry mob.

I understood why real private eyes carried guns. Guns they could hang on to.

A thunderous cascade of shouts and "Booos" hit me before any fists did.

Then Jack: "Get him boys!"

I had to let her go. I threw a punch at the first face I saw. I landed a good one, but my knuckles paid the price. I couldn't take on ten guys with no gloves.

I spun and threw a right into a soft belly. He doubled up and I snatched the beer mug out of his hand. I was doing so much dirty fighting I'd have to go to boxer's confession and do a hundred Hail Joe Louis's.

I smashed the mug across the nose of guy I realized after was the mustache man. He went down with a combination of beer foam and blood soaking his soup strainer.

Arms grabbed at me from the crowd but they were wet noodles. Drunken staggering and unfocused eyes. A fist hit my back. I spun and swung the mug at him. This time the glass cracked on the jaw of my would-be opponent and he hit the deck, down for the count.

I lost Jeanie in the crowd. The men were giving me more room. Once the sight of their friends sleeping off a K.O. with blood on the side sunk in through the alcohol haze the fight went out of the boys a bit.

I heard a roar from behind. I knew the Heavyweight was up.

I turned. Over the shouting I heard Fats Waller start up again playing "Honeysuckle Rose".

The Heavyweight charged. Those brass knuckles led the way which made it easy to dodge. Can't let them do all the fighting for you, but I doubt he was in the mood for any coaching from me. I sidestepped and swung down at the passing body with the broken handle of the beer mug. I caught the jagged glass on his shoulder as he passed and pushed him to the ground. I fell on top of him and straddled his chest, dropping the broken mug handle and pinning his brass knuckled hand to the floor.

Above us the crowd became spectators, content to let the pros do the fighting.

I bent down close to the Heavyweight. "You know where Audrey is. Tell me!"

"Fuck you."

I kept his dangerous hand pinned and thrust a left jab at his nose. It trickled blood.

"Tell me where she is."

He spit a bloody wad to the wooden floor. "If you wanted her, you should have ordered her. That little twist is the fifty cent special. Anything you want just a nickel extra in the slot."

Something snapped. My ears became muffled. I got tunnel vision. I could smell the blood on the floor. I inhaled deep, taking the scent into my lungs, feeding the animal buried deep, but not too deep, inside me.

I wrestled the brass knuckles off his hand, head butting him in his already damaged nose to keep him still. Any referee would have given me the forfeit.

A familiar rage surged through me and the room went black. The noisy crowd went silent to my ears. I slipped on the knuckles and started punching. He may have known where to find Audrey, he may not have. I'd never learn.

Blood spat up from his face and each time I pulled back to load another punch tiny lines of red flung up and onto the faces of the men watching. Men who lurched backward away from the fight, the party atmosphere tarnished.

His nose went flat, then his cheeks caved in. His teeth gave way and slid down his throat. His temples crushed, his eyes swelled shut.

I stood. Blood dripped from the knuckles back onto the face where it came from. I struggled to catch my breath.

Cigars hung slack in the mouths of the men looking on. Someone lifted the needle off Fats Waller.

I scanned the room. Looked for trouble. No more was going to come. To them, *I* was trouble.

By the bar I saw Lloyd. On his arm was Jeanie. He wasn't useless after all.

The Heavyweight may have been dead, maybe not. Probably was. I didn't feel bad. I felt a kind of relief. That beating had been pent up in me for too long. It was meant for Enzo and for Silvio but they both robbed me of my chance. Now I had my blood. A fraction of the payback for whatever Audrey had been through.

And there on Lloyd's arm was the answer to where she was.

I pocketed the brass knuckles. A gun just wasn't my style. It was time to admit that the knuckles were.

I stepped through the crowd which parted for me, took gentle hold of Jeanie's other arm, and led her and Lloyd to the door.

28

FOKOLI

Glenda rolled over in bed and pulled the blankets over her head, shrinking from the sunlight.

"Get up." It was the second time I'd said it. I took a drink of the thick stuff the guy at the diner down the street called coffee and tried not to look toward the bed. It had been a long time since I'd held a woman close to me while I slept and it felt wrong to think about how much I liked holding Glenda when everything was such a mess.

I didn't seem to have the same effect on her. From under the covers she said, "I suppose we have to go look for bad guys?" Then she peeked her head out and looked at me with her big blue eyes. Her hands were trembling. Her mouth cocked up in a small, fragile smile. "You're a nice man. Thank you for last night."

It was an endearing thing to say, almost child-like, and my heart squeezed a little bit. I took another drink of coffee and disappeared into the bathroom to shave. The less said to her at the moment the better. The room was beginning to feel very small.

By the time I finished she was dressed in more of Ray's clothes and had finished off my coffee as well as her own cup. "Feeling better?" I asked.

"Yes."

"Well, go easy on the coffee. I don't need you getting sick all over me again." It sounded harsher than I meant it to, but Glenda didn't seem to mind.

She smiled a little as she pulled her hair up into a ponytail. Our eyes met in the mirror and she blushed. My neck felt hot.

Dames.

I blew out a breath. "Let's get you some lady clothes. There's a shop a couple of blocks over. I think you could find something there."

"Hmm," she said, putting the finishing touches on her hair with my comb.

"How well do you know your way around this city?"

She shrugged. "Not very well." She cleared her throat and put a hand to her head.

"Oh, hell. Are you gonna . . . ?"

She sank onto the foot of the bed. "I'll be fine. Just a little faint." She'd thrown up all the food she'd eaten last night. I handed her the Danish I'd picked up for her and she took a couple of nibbles at it. She gave me a weak smile. "Bet you never spent so much time with a dope fiend before, huh?" She looked at me with her huge eyes and for a minute I found it very difficult to swallow.

"Glenda, I . . ." I cleared my throat and moved away. No sense in complicating things. "Yeah, well, we all have our faults. And I don't think your condition is one of your own making."

She blushed and held my gaze for a few seconds and then went back to arranging her hair.

We didn't have a car anymore, so an hour later we were on the bus—Glenda in a new dress and hat and me in a clean suit.

"Is this the right bus?" I asked her when we were seated.

"I don't know. We'll have to ride around until we find the place."

It was easy to be invisible on the bus. I was just another pervert hustling a young girl. A couple of men even winked and gave me the "'atta boy," nod as Glenda and I passed. I nodded back and tried to smile. Glenda looked less haggard with makeup on, but she was still frail and she looked like she might collapse. I moved her to the back of the bus and put her next to the window.

Then we rode.

And watched.

When an hour passed the bus turned around to backtrack its route and we got out and climbed on another one.

"We'll never find it," she said.

I knew she was right. The buses stayed on the main roads. The apartment building we wanted was probably a block or two away from any bus stop—if we were lucky. What did I know about L.A? What we needed was a car.

We changed buses again and then made our way back to the hotel. I dosed Glenda with a bit more morphine to keep her comfortable and collected the rest of the cash from Joshua . . . $1700.

I bought a Ford for $300 from a lot where the sign said I was sure to get a "square deal." The car ran and that's about all I cared about. We collected our luggage and checked out of the hotel. I bought some sandwiches at a nearby deli and we ate in the car. I let Glenda stretch her legs out on the back seat while she ate.

I asked her about Baron. "What's his story?"

She shrugged. It was the kind of shrug meant to show she didn't know and she didn't really care. Problem was, I knew she cared. She was terrified of the guy. "I need to know," I said.

She looked out the window and sipped her Coke from a straw.

"Fine," I said. "How about the other girls? How many were kept with you?"

She met my eyes in the rearview mirror. "Shall I count the girl you let die?" And just like that, the "nice Glenda" was gone. So was the "nice Dean". We were back to our tough girl and angry cop roles.

I pulled to the side of the road on squealing tires, causing a car behind me to swerve and honk. The driver leaned out his window and shouted at me.

I took the Ford out of gear and turned around to stare at Glenda. She met my eyes and I had to force myself not to flinch from the look she gave me. Maybe she was trying to do the same. There were things I could have said—hateful things that would have made me feel justified in letting that girl die—but that wouldn't have made it any easier to sleep at night. And I supposed that's what I really wanted, just a good night's sleep. So I stared at Glenda and she stared at me.

A pastrami sandwich lay on the seat beside me. I hadn't touched it yet. Now, I unwrapped it and took a tentative bite. I told myself Glenda was just a kid, but I also understood her anger over what happened with Baron. I shared her disgust—with Baron and with me. I took another bite of my sandwich and chewed.

"You bulls are all alike," she said. "What's the matter? Don't you have anything to say? Cat got your tongue?"

"Sounds like you're feeling better."

She didn't say anything, so I finished my sandwich and drank my soda, and then I turned to look at her. "Look. You and I can throw stones at each other all day long. I'm sorry for what happened to that girl. Sorrier than you'll ever know. But I need your help to keep something like that from happening again."

"Gretchen."

"What?"

"Her name was Gretchen. I didn't know her that well. She was one of a bunch of girls kept in the same building as me."

I thought about that for a minute. "Glenda, there were at least nine, maybe ten or eleven girls in that peep parlor. Do you all work every day?"

She thought for a minute and then shook her head. "No. On days I didn't work there were as many as six girls with me."

I figured it up in my head. Say there were eleven girls at

the theater—ten booths and a girl in each one, plus one extra in case somebody got tired. Maybe two extra. That meant an even dozen at the theater. Six left behind. Eighteen. Minus Gretchen. Seventeen. Plus the next girl they'd pull off the bus. That made eighteen again.

"Did you know everyone by name?" I started the car and pulled away from the curb while I waited for Glenda to answer.

"Not everyone. I knew Gretchen and Candy. Patty and Rachel and Sandy. I think one girl was named Barbara." She was silent for a minute. "What's Ray's sister's name?"

"Audrey."

"Audrey . . . I don't know any Audrey. What's she look like?"

I turned onto a side street and drove slowly past rows of stucco houses with sprinklings of apartment buildings here and there. "Any of this look familiar?"

"No. What does Audrey look like?"

I thought for a minute. "Pretty. Dark hair. Dark eyes. Full lips. High cheekbones. I only saw a picture from the neck up, so I don't know her body size or height."

Glenda said at least half of the girls had dark hair and dark eyes. I figured even if Audrey wasn't with this group of girls it didn't matter. They still needed help and Ray wouldn't have turned his back on them, so neither would I. We drove in silence, up one street and down another, over and over and over again.

"I think it's farther out," Glenda said.

The sun was sinking, casting long angular shadows on the streets. The car was getting low on fuel and I was starting to get hungry again. "What do you mean farther out?"

She climbed over the seat into the front and sat beside me. "I don't know. This looks familiar. But I . . . I'm just not sure." She chewed on her lip and watched the scenery pass. And then, "No, wait, turn here."

A narrow road set between tall hedges lurked in the shadows to our right. I struggled to turn the Ford in time, hearing branches scrape against the paint.

"Ah, yes," Glenda said. "Keep going."

I kept going, pushing the Ford through low branches and over deep ruts until, after a half mile or so, everything opened up again. The road widened, the branches lifted, and Glenda pointed straight ahead.

"Old section," she said. "I think this neighborhood used to be something special."

The road curved slowly downward toward what I could see was a scattering of decaying two-story houses and several square apartment buildings set in a neighborhood that looked all but abandoned. A huge sign was posted at the its border: FUTURE SITE OF HIDDEN ACRES LUXURY HOMES.

"This is going to be torn down?" I asked.

Glenda shrugged. "I have no idea. Looks like it."

That meant at some point they'd have to move the girls. I continued downward through the fading daylight and pulled into the shadow of one of the buildings.

"I think we'd better walk from here."

Glenda paled. "What if they catch us?"

I reached out to touch her. She shrank back at first but I held my hand steady. When she relaxed I touched her face. She rested her cheek in my palm. "I can't imagine what you think of me," I said. "It's probably no worse than what I think of myself. But I promise I won't let anyone hurt you."

She held my gaze and looked like she was considering what I said. After a minute she nodded and we climbed from the car, taking care to close the doors softly. Then we walked. We passed a house, then another and another, and all the while I was aware of the lengthening shadows on the streets overgrown with weeds and strewn with litter.

After a couple of blocks, Glenda turned right. "There," she said, pointing to a building of fading pink stucco. "I think that's it."

We circled around the rear, keeping our backs pressed against the building.

Three cars were parked in the lot behind the building. Glenda's breath hitched and she reached for my hand. I clasped her fingers in mine and kept moving. She pulled me back. "There are balconies on the other side," she said. "They have drinks out there." She was shaking now. "I'm remembering things."

"Stay with me." It was all I could say right then. I couldn't have her falling apart. We backtracked the way we had come, skirting around the deserted front of the building until we reached the far side.

Glenda's breathing rasped and I turned and pressed her to the wall with my body. "Shh," I said, leaning into her. "Please. I need you to be strong now."

She bit her lip and nodded. And then, God help me, I kissed her nose.

I peeked around the corner. The apartment building was three stories tall. The second and third stories had doors opening onto iron balconies, once white, now chipping and rotting like the rest of the neighborhood. Three men in suits stood with drinks in their hands on the balcony closest to us. A breeze whipped their neckties over their shoulders. "Shit," I muttered.

I was still nose to nose against Glenda. Her hands were on my chest. At the sound of my words, her fingers clenched and I could feel her nails through my shirt. "What is it?"

"Three men," I said, meeting her stare. "Do you know if there could be more inside?"

She shook her head. "I don't know. I'm not sure."

Three men. I leaned out as far as I could to see if there was a fourth hidden farther back on the balcony. My movement caused me to pull away from Glenda. "No," she cried and then immediately covered her mouth.

As one, the men turned, probably catching a glimpse of my hat as I ducked back around the corner.

"I'm sorry," Glenda breathed.

There was a shout, "Hey!" from the balcony followed by a

gunshot. Stucco powdered and flew from the corner next to my head. Glenda screamed. I grabbed her hand and we ran.

Four blocks. We needed to make it four blocks. I pulled her along behind me. "Oh God, oh God." She said it over and over again.

"Shut up and keep moving," I barked.

The sound of footsteps pounded behind us, mingled with shouts from the men. They were splitting up. Divide and conquer. It's what I would have done. It's what would get us killed if we didn't get to the car.

We'd had a head start, but Glenda was slow and very weak and running on legs like toothpicks. She stumbled and fell, sliding forward on her hands and knees. I pulled her up. She was scraped but she'd live.

We pushed on. Two blocks to go. The hum of a car's engine swelled behind us. More shouts. Glenda was crying, no doubt already seeing in her head what they'd do to her if she got caught. We had to cross the street to get around the next block where the car was parked. I cut hard, dragging Glenda with me. Away from the cover of the buildings, the guy on foot was free to shoot. A bullet whizzed by, kicking up dust in front of me. Glenda didn't scream but she tightened her grip on my hand.

The car roared, growing in my peripheral vision as we jumped up onto the sidewalk again. It raced ahead and spun around, launching a cloud of dust behind it as it prepared to take another pass at us. I fumbled for the keys. Glenda fell again and refused to let go of my hand so I could help her up. Her eyes were wild. I pulled her up and held onto the keys. We made it to the car as another shot rang out.

I opened the driver's door and shoved her in, climbing in myself as she slid over. I brought the Ford to life and we fishtailed, racing along the street and up the hill toward the main road. I glanced in the rearview and saw the thug's car stop to pick up his passenger. They followed us out onto the highway. I merged with the steady flow of cars Glenda told me were headed toward Pasadena and tried to catch my breath. It was dark now and I hoped ours would be nothing more than an anonymous set of headlights moving along the road.

I was on a stretch of highway I didn't recognize. This wasn't the way we'd come. We were on a four-lane road. It hugged the edge of a hill for westbound traffic. Heading east meant my side of the road dropped sharply beyond the shoulder. In the rearview I watched cars weave in and out of lanes behind me, moving ahead or dropping back, depending on how big a hurry the driver was in. It was impossible to tell the make or color of anything and I wondered how I would lose them if they were behind me. Then the road curved sharply and just like that we were in city again. Traffic clogged the streets, slowing and then stopping.

We were four cars deep behind a red light and I had the crazy memory of being a small boy and biting my nails. My mother always slapped my hand and told me to stop. I wanted to bite my nails now more than anything, but I waited with my hands clenched around the steering wheel and the needle on empty.

It's funny how bullets can come out of nowhere—how you can be sitting quietly, convinced any danger you faced is now behind you, but the obstacle actually looms in the front, waiting for an ambush.

The first bullet pierced the passenger side windshield, traveling through and poking a hole in the back window before puncturing the grill of the eighteen-wheeler in back of me. The second bullet hit the windshield dead center and embedded itself in the center of the front seat just as the light turned green.

The truck driver climbed down and stood waving his cap and swearing at someone in the distance, far in front of me, and another bullet hit the hood of his car, sending steam into the night sky like a fountain.

Cars in front of me crawled past the light. I cranked the wheel hard to the left, cutting across oncoming traffic, clipping the sidewalk and knocking over a newspaper rack. The bandage on my shoulder tugged at tender skin. Glenda cried out.

Cracks spiderwebbed out from the bullet holes in the windshield, making sounds like cracking ice. Cars skidded out of my way. I turned sharply onto another side street and pulled into the nearest gas station, cutting the lights and engine.

"Did you lose them?" Glenda asked.

My shoulder pulsed angrily. "I think so."

The gas station attendant didn't look twice at the bullet holes in the car. I gave him twenty dollars to forget he ever saw us.

An hour later we were at a diner.

We ate without talking. When we were done I wrote the number to the diner's payphone on one of my business cards and drove back to the hotel where Ray and I first stayed. It seemed like a year ago. Ray's room was vacant. I paid the clerk for another three nights, hoping Ray would somehow, some way come back.

I stuck the card with the phone number on the bureau's mirror after I scrawled CALL ME on it.

"What are you doing?" Glenda asked, touching my arm. She hadn't let me out of her sight and I doubted she would.

"I think I'm praying," I said, taking her hand.

29

RAY

She woke up with a start, like someone had turned on a cold shower with her under it. She looked around the strange room, saw me and Lloyd, and cowered. She was as scared as a cat dropped into a room full of hungry dogs. I doubted she had any memory of the night before, of us bringing her to this motel, or the hour I spent trying to get information from her and the fight, also very catlike, she put up until I let her just pass out on the tiny bed.

Lloyd and I slept on the floor like gentlemen bums. If I hadn't been so tired I never would have gotten a minute's rest between the hardwood floor and the scratching of rat feet. I debated whether to go back to the room I rented with Fokoli or to Lloyd's place but both seemed a little too hot with all the new friends I was making since hitting Hollywood.

The girl pulled the sheet up around her, drawing some sense of protection from the thin cotton.

"It's okay, it's okay." I held my hands out in an I-mean-no-harm way. "Do you remember me?" The wide pupils in Jeanie's eyes told me no. "My name's Ray. We took you out of the party last night. Away from the guy who brought you. I didn't get his name . . ."

"Richie." Her voice was small, thinner than she was. The darting of her eyes slowed a bit.

"Yeah. Well, he didn't seem like a close acquaintance of yours. You feeling okay? Want some water?"

She nodded and I raised my chin to Lloyd who brought over a glass from the sink. I was suspect of the water in this joint, but desperate times and all that jazz.

"You starting to remember now?"

She grabbed her head, as if the act of remembering hurt like a loud noise in her ear. Probably best for this girl to forget as much as she could.

"Okay, Jeanie, I'll give it to you again. I'm Audrey's brother. I'm here to get her out, and anyone else who wants to come. You know Silvio?" She nodded again. "Well, he's dead." There was no shock on her face that I could see. "The movies, the ones he used you girls for? They're done. It's over if you help me find where the girls are being held."

She took another sip of water. "Audrey told me about you." I flinched like a punch was headed my way. Someone who knew Audrey. "I thought she was lying."

It was like a waft of her perfume floated into the room. She felt so close, and yet, would I even recognize her if she walked in now to change the sheets? Wasn't much risk of that happening from the looks of the place.

It struck me that I'd been chasing a ghost. I'd gone down a very crooked road for a girl I'd never met, wasn't sure I'd ever meet. I was coming to take her away, or so I said. First time I'd said that as a part of my plan. But to what? To where? Back to Kansas City?

Aw to hell with it. Why start planning now?

"Jeanie, I need you to take us there. There's an apartment building?"

"Yeah. It's where we live. It's rent free, but . . ." She didn't have to finish.

"Silvio?"

"No. Baron. Silvio was just the movie guy. So I heard. I never met him. Guess I didn't rate a screen role."

"Be thankful. Is Audrey there? At the apartments?"

"As far as I know. I haven't seen her in a few days. I've been pretty out of it though. Speaking of . . . you got anything? Y'know?" She held up her glass. "I usually start my day with something a little stronger than water."

"I can have Lloyd go down and get coffee." I knew what she meant.

"A little stronger than that, even."

"Can't help you there. You take us to your apartment and we'll stop for coffee on the way. Tell 'em to make it extra dark."

"Will that make the headache go away?"

"No. But all this will go away soon. If you'll help us."

Her eyes were unfocused but all I needed was a moment of their time. She gave it to me.

"Let's go," she said.

Lloyd drove, a silent chauffeur. I got the feeling he wanted to quit on me, to his credit he stuck it out. On the way out he made an offer to go visit a friend of his in the prop department at Warner's and get us some prop guns. I turned him down. No sense walking in with a fake. If things are going to get bad I want both my hands ready for business, not holding a paper weight.

I appreciated the help though, even if it didn't express the most confidence in my ability to keep things from getting out of hand. What did I expect? He'd seen me in action. Where I go, trouble follows right on my heels.

"Turn up Central, then right on Dryden," said Jeanie. A slick of cold sweat greased her forehead but she didn't complain. Chances were she had something in her room to help get her head straight again. I rethought that. If they really wanted to keep the girls in control only they would dispense the goods. It was a short leash and it kept all the girls in the yard.

"Here," she said.

Lloyd pulled to the curb in front of a three-story, pink

stucco apartment building standing like an oasis in a crumbling neighborhood. I counted ten windows across the top and ten windows along the bottom. Behind one of those was Audrey.

I stepped out and looked up at a palm tree swaying the breeze. Paradise. The lure of sunshine and stardom. I'd been fishing before. I know what happens when you bite down on the lure.

Jeanie said, "I don't have a key." I stopped. "Richie or whoever else took us out always had it."

"It's okay. We came this far. I need to ask you . . ." I hesitated. I looked at her swaying like the palm tree, her weak limbs about to break. "Do you ever do any . . . work . . . here?"

"Yeah. They bring the guys around. Getting out for a party is a treat." She was beyond shame about it. It was a matter of fact.

"Okay. That's our in. Lloyd?"

In case they knew me from all the trouble I'd caused, I stayed in the car. Lloyd went with Jeanie to the door and, armed with the little scenario I'd scripted for him, pressed the button.

He was a better actor than me.

I watched him speak into the intercom, asking about a girl. "Who sent you?" a voice asked through the crackling speaker. "I'm with Jeanie. I picked her up but she ain't my type," Lloyd said.

The door buzzed and they went in. I hoped like hell I didn't just send Lloyd into the lion's den.

A minute later the window opened. Second from the end on the bottom row. I saw Jeanie's hand wave me over.

I climbed through the window into Jeanie's room. It was small and all bedroom, no living space. Shared bathroom down the hall. Jeanie was already digging in her chest of drawers for something to put in a needle.

"Jeanie. Jeanie! Where's Audrey?"

She kept digging. I put a hand on her arm, she jerked it

away at my touch like my hand was a lit match. I spoke slowly again, I had to convince her all over again that I was no threat.

"Just tell me where to find Audrey's room and I'll leave you alone." Her face was stricken for a second. "I'll come back for you. I'm not leaving without you, okay? First, I need to find my sister."

"Second floor. To the left. I don't know which one. I've never been inside."

"Thanks." I reached out slowly the way you do with a frightened puppy and laid a hand on her shoulder. She accepted my touch, but not happily.

I opened her door and peered around to search the empty hall. Coast was clear. Behind me I heard her search begin again.

The stairs were at the end of the green painted hall. It didn't look much like a brothel, more like a hospital ward. Symmetrical, dull. Behind every door was a broken dream. A promise of the big break that would get a girl noticed by Darryl Zanuck. I wondered how many girls still held out hope, thinking this was just a pit stop on the way to stardom. Why surely Ginger Rogers went through this, right?

Behind me I heard Lloyd and another man. I hustled into the stairwell and stopped to listen.

"What you want, pal? Blonde? Redhead? We got 'em all. Just pick your poison."

"I . . . I'm not sure. I'll know it when I see it."

"Okay buddy. It's your dime. Wait in here. You can get all acquainted and pick one. Mean time you can pay R.J. It's fifty. Seventy-five for the back door."

The man knocked on a door. "Showtime! Into the parlor. Now."

I tiptoed the rest of the way up the steps, thinking Lloyd ought to be nominated for an Academy Award. I started with the first door on the left, my heart pounding with anticipation. I tried the knob. Locked.

I knocked lightly but there was no answer. I went to the

next door. The knob turned. I opened into another all-bedroom space with a girl sitting on the edge of the bed. I knew in an instant it wasn't Audrey. She had brassy blonde hair and a blank stare. She turned to me like her head was in quicksand, the frilly white robe trimmed with feathers barely moving.

We just stared at each other. She said nothing. I could have gone over and pushed her down and she wouldn't have fought me. I could have done a lot worse. That was the idea behind her customers, I bet.

"I'm looking for Audrey," I whispered.

She kept staring blankly. I backed out of the room.

The next door was locked, too. I knocked. No answer.

I heard footsteps. The man I heard downstairs was climbing the steps at the far end.

I reversed and slid back into the open room. The blonde in the white nighty didn't move. I listened at the door to the hallway, heard him knocking on other girls' doors.

"Come on, Patty. Customer to meet."

"All right hold your horses!" a girl called. I heard doors open and close.

"Candy, you too. Come on, chop chop."

He was getting closer.

He banged loudly on a door not next to me but probably one more down. "Let's go, Audrey. Showtime."

I almost burst out the door into the hall, decided against it. My hand strangled the doorknob but I wanted to do it right. I knew I'd only get one shot and if she was being led right to Lloyd then it was perfect. The man banged again.

"Audrey goddammit! You ain't been out in two days! You're pissing me off now. I guess you don't really want to be in pictures, do you?" Another gunshot-loud pound on the door. "Fuck it, I'm getting the pass key. It's time for your close up, bitch."

His feet stomped down the stairs so I knew exactly when it was safe to emerge.

I crossed two doors down and tried the door. Locked. This

was it. My sister was just beyond the threshold and my biggest task was to get inside without her braining me with a lamp or something before I could explain.

I knocked lightly. "Audrey. It's Ray."

Nothing. "Audrey it's me. Ray. I made it. I'm here. I made it."

I thought about the catatonic girl in white and pictured Audrey sitting on her bed, head swimming with drugs. I slid my hand into my pants pocket and took out the brass knuckles. I slipped them on and punched down at the doorknob. It bent and I punched again. The knob came off but the door stayed shut.

No time for subtlety. I kicked hard at the wood just above the knob and the door splintered inward. I stood back, primed and ready to explain through a morphine haze who I was and remind her that she had asked me to come. I was here for the big rescue. Cue the music, hit the lights, camera, action!

I saw two feet. Hanging. An exposed pipe was enough for her to throw a makeshift rope over and tie it around her neck. Her body turned in a slow circle after the gust of wind from my entrance.

My feet were as anchored in place as hers were floating free. My blood didn't boil, my fists didn't clench. Instead, I sank. My shoulders drooped, my lungs emptied, my mouth dried. I tried to make my eyes close or at least look away but I kept watching her swing, waiting for the girl in the photos to wake up, her eyes to shine at me.

Two days he said. Two days too late. Too late to save her.

Save my sister.

30

FOKOLI

Glenda was tired so I let her go to sleep in the back. I drove around for a couple of hours and eventually stopped back at the diner for pie and coffee. There was nowhere else to go and the place was starting to feel safe. Besides, maybe Ray would call.

I parked under a streetlight and cut the engine. Glenda was dizzy and weak after she woke up, but I helped her inside and just like before, giving her food was like watering a plant. Wilted leaves came back to life, her eyes focused, her cheeks got pink. She even smiled once or twice, but watched me like a hawk, jumping when I got up to use the restroom and trembling with fear by the time I got back.

She finished her meatloaf and mashed potatoes and moved over to sit beside me in the booth. "I'm scared," she said.

The waitress came back to check on us. "Pie," Glenda said, leaning closer to me.

I swiped a hand down my face. She was needy, mistaking me and the protection I could give her for something else—something more. But to be touched, to be near someone soft and lovely, and to have her look at me with trust . . . that was something I liked.

The waitress turned to leave but I touched her arm. "More coffee too," I said. She scratched it on her pad. "Anything else?"

"My name is Dean Fokoli. Has anyone called for me?"
She shook her head and moved on.

When she was out of earshot I came clean with Glenda about the card I left on the mirror at the hotel—about how I feared Ray was dead but hoped there was a chance he was alive and that maybe he'd already found Audrey. I blew out a breath when I was done. It felt good to unload.

I expected Glenda to cry . . . to say how much she loved Ray. Jealousy pinched my gut for a minute when she got a faraway look in her eyes. But all she said was, "Ray is a good man. I hope he's okay."

When we finished eating Ray still hadn't called. I wasn't surprised, but I'd be lying if I said I wasn't disappointed. Maybe I had expected him to magically appear and let me know he found Audrey and we could go home. Maybe I expected to fall asleep and wake up in Kansas City again. I tried to smile at Glenda but it felt forced. So I ordered two big cups of coffee to go and we stepped out into the soft night.

"What now?" she asked, eyeing the bullet holes in the windshield as she slid into the car.

I opened the door and climbed into the driver's seat. "I'd like to watch the apartments . . . see what happens there at night."

"Please don't." Her eyes were wide and scared. "I can't go back there again."

I wanted to go back to the apartment so bad I could taste it, but I couldn't put Glenda through any more. And the truth was I didn't know how much more she could take without cracking.

Laura had been a Jules Verne fan and we talked about stuff like time travel—silly married people things we never talked about with anyone else. It was the sort of stuff that made us married—the sort of thing that marked her as mine and me as hers. I only wish I had figured that out a few years earlier.

Glenda chewed on her lip. "I'm sorry. I can tough it out if you need me to."

I wanted to laugh. Glenda *was* tough. I was the one going

soft. "No," I said, starting the car and pulling out of the diner's parking lot. "We won't go tonight. We'll come back here later and see if Ray might call."

"Do you think he will?"

"No."

She touched my hand. I didn't know how I felt about the touch of her hand on mine. Or maybe I did and that's what was bothering me. I liked Glenda. More than I wanted to admit. She made me feel like a man . . . like someone strong, someone who could be counted on. I only hoped I could avoid screwing it up.

We drove in silence for awhile. We couldn't sit inside the diner all night long, and I couldn't take her back to the hotel, so we meandered through the streets reminiscing about Kansas City and talking about what we both wanted out of life.

The bullet holes in the windshield made us a little conspicuous and I started thinking about how I didn't want to get pulled over. "Maybe we should get off this road."

Glenda took my empty coffee cup and set it on the floor beside hers. "I want to show you something. Turn here."

She directed me out of town, away from traffic and street lights and up into the hills onto Mulholland Drive. We climbed for several miles, until the road emptied into a wide overlook high above the city. L.A. sprawled below us in a million lights. There were several other cars around. Some of them rocked wildly and all of them had steamed over windows. Glenda smiled.

"A friend told me about this place," she said. "I always thought it would be fun to come up here and look at the city. Isn't it beautiful?"

It was beautiful and I said so. But there was a lot of uncomfortable stuff going on around us and I didn't know what was expected of me—or what I expected of me. Something squeezed in my chest. I think it was panic. "Glenda, I—"

She touched my chin and gently pulled my head around until we faced one another.

I thought of Laura—the last woman I'd been with. Years now. Two years. Glenda sat before me, fragile, almost broken. I wanted to protect her . . . but maybe it was less than that. Or more. Maybe I just wanted . . . *her*.

She leaned toward me and my breath hitched. I tried to whisper her name but no sound came out. She leaned forward until our lips touched.

I had expected softness, tenderness. But there was no softness to the kiss—not on my part. I searched for her mouth the way a drowning man searches for air. My hands tangled in her hair and her nails raked at my neck. Suddenly she was on my lap, loosening my tie. I moaned and pulled her closer, feeling parts of me—dead for so long—come back to life.

She moaned my name and suddenly my shirt was unbuttoned and her hand was touching my chest through the thin fabric of my T-shirt. I was frantic and even now I can't excuse my behavior. I reached up and touched her breast, growing even more excited as she moaned my name again. She was soft and lovely and I was flattered that she wanted someone like me as much as I wanted her. I was a broken-down P.I. with a dead wife and a dead partner in a car with a girl half my age.

And then the folly of it all hit me—a middle-aged man with a girl in his car. What was I doing? I wasn't any better than the johns she picked up who took advantage of her for what she was willing to do. The only difference was that I wasn't paying for it.

The excitement I'd felt changed to shame.

I pulled back from the kiss and took her hands from around my neck. I held her fingers gently to my lips and pressed my forehead to hers.

"What's wrong?" Confusion darkened her eyes.

I looked past her and focused on the lights of L.A. swimming below us. "You deserve so much more, Glenda."

She slid from my lap. "Oh. I get it. This is the brush off. The thanks but no thanks speech." She busied herself with straightening her skirt and hair. "No sweat."

This time it was me who touched her cheek, turned her head. "This is not a brush off, Glenda."

"You don't want me. I call that a brush off."

I smiled. And it only got bigger when anger flashed in her eyes. "I do want you. I want you more than I've wanted anyone in a long time." I sighed, not knowing how to make her understand. "But I won't do this with you here . . . in a car. When we're together it will be someplace beautiful. And there won't be bullet holes in the windshield."

Her eyes narrowed. "You really mean that or are you just feeding me a line? Because you are still a bull in my book you know."

I kissed her hand. "I mean it. You don't know how much I mean it."

"So you like me a little?"

"More than a little." I buttoned my shirt and fixed my tie. Glenda used the rearview to redo her lipstick. I studied her in the dark interior of the car and hoped she would forgive me. When she looked at me and smiled I felt a little better.

I started the engine and pulled away from the rocking cars and fogged windows. There was nothing to do but go back to the hotel or to the diner. Glenda didn't want to sleep. So we went to the diner. Again.

I was on my fourth cup of coffee when the pay phone rang. Glenda and I stared at each other as it rang a second time. We climbed from the booth and waited. She reached for my hand and our eyes met. When it rang a third time Glenda gave a little nod. I picked up the receiver.

"Hello."

"Fokoli? It's Ray."

31

RAY

I hung up the phone in a daze. I'd just talked with a ghost.

Was it possible Fokoli was alive? It was like he just stepped out for cigarettes and I'd fallen asleep and dreamed a terrible, very realistic dream. Maybe it was this damn city. The whole place is a factory for fantasy and lies. You get here and you can't trust your own thoughts. Everything turns Technicolor, the women are too beautiful, the strings are always swelling. It messes with your head enough to think Dean could have survived like the hero in a Saturday matinee serial.

The blood on my shoes told me it wasn't a dream.

I left out the details when I explained to Dean about finding Audrey. And what happened after.

I stood looking up at her hanging body for awhile. I tried to reconcile the blank stare with the light emanating smile I saw in her photographs. How could shadows on a sheet of paper have more life in them than the real girl?

She was ingenious, fashioning a rope out of braided bits of curtain ties and torn bed sheets. It was not an act of impulse but of desperation, it took time. She must have known she was next for a film shoot with Enzo. Must have known the last girl didn't come back.

A black pit of emptiness inside me began to fill with hate and anger. I refused to start thinking that I'd killed my sister because I got there too late. I hadn't killed her, but I let her down. She asked me for help and I didn't come through.

What did she expect? I'm not a professional. I'm just a boxing manager. What did she want from me?

Tears strained against my eyelids. The flood of hate continued. Did she think, during the long night it took to braid her noose, of her lousy brother and how he disappointed her? How I ignored her cry for help?

Outside in the hallway the man returned. Seeing the open door he started speaking to her before he turned the corner.

"Finally wised up, huh? Well get your ass downstairs, we got custom—"

He saw me first then his eyes went quickly to the figure hanging above us both. He went slack-jawed.

I punched hard and fast. His gut took the shot and I felt all the way back to his spine. He doubled over and I grabbed an arm and spun it around his back.

I pulled him up straight and hissed in his ear, "How many others?"

He nearly fell down the stairs as I prodded him on, straining the limits of the tendons in his shoulder as I wrenched the arm like a chicken wing behind him.

We entered a lobby area where Lloyd was waiting on a couch with two girls in lingerie on each side. He stood and stammered. The girls made futile attempts to cover themselves.

"Who else is here?" I said to Lloyd.

"I . . . I don't know. I saw him," he pointed to the chicken in my arms, "and I heard voices from down there." Lloyd pointed off to the left.

Again I spoke into the chicken's ear. "Who else is here?"

"Danny. Maybe Enzo, I don't know."

Enzo. I should have killed him in Palm Springs. Time for take two.

"Why are they here? Some kind of meeting?"

"They're waiting. T-t-to meet with Baron. They rolled in, said it all went to shit in Palm Springs. Enzo's running the show now. That's all I know, I swear."

I aimed the chicken down the hall and pushed hard, calling over my shoulder to Lloyd. "Round up all the girls and get them out."

I slid on the brass knuckles as we approached the door. "Knock," I commanded. He did.

"Yeah," came a voice from inside.

"Go on," I said.

He turned the knob and I shoved. He fell out ahead of me, tumbling to the floor inside the room.

There were three other men inside sitting around a table, playing cards. I recognized two of them, Enzo and his pal from Palm Springs. I also recognized the room.

The wood paneling, the cot in the corner, the tripod with a black 8mm camera. This was the room from the films in the red and yellow cans.

The chicken's body fell forward and hit one table leg clipping it off and sending the green felt card table down to the floor in a shower of chips and hands of five card stud. It was distraction enough that I could get a clean swing with the brass knuckles to the back of the head on the guy nearest to me. He went down in a heap. Enzo's pal from the desert went for a gun and I swung out a backhand with the brass knuckles and opened a gash on his cheek that he instinctively reached for, dropping his gun as he did.

I reached down and picked up the black pistol. Four against one wasn't fair and I wasn't in the mood to prove anything about my fighting skills just then. Brass knuckles or hot lead, I needed all the help I could get.

I held the pistol on Enzo. He raised his hands slowly, the hint of a smirk on his face.

"Audrey's dead." I don't know why I felt they had to know.

"Which one's that?" Enzo said. It was all I could do not

pull the trigger right then.

"You, you, over there." The guy I hit stood up rubbing the back of his head. I made them all line up in front of the cot. "Who knows how to run the camera?" They exchanged sheepish looks. The chicken raised his hand. "Did you run the camera when the girl was raped? How about the one who was killed?"

He didn't answer. I knew I must have sounded like a madman, and in that moment I was one.

"Get over here. Turn it on."

He obeyed the gun more than me and he lifted the tripod out of the corner and set it in a spot I could tell would have been the same as for the other films.

"You," I gestured to Enzo with the barrel of the gun. "Over here."

"Sure thing, boss."

He came over slowly. My fist was still wrapped in brass knuckles and I threw a jab to his nose. The skin split and blood began to run. He kept his cool but put both hands up to stop the bleeding. "Did you like it?" I asked. "You looked like you did."

"The girls, you mean?"

"Yeah."

"Did you like watching?" The smirk was back.

"Show me," I said. Enzo raised an eyebrow. "On him. I want a live performance."

His pal looked shocked. He didn't know who to fear more.

"Sorry, Ray. I don't swing that way."

"Just give me the finale. Cut to the chase, as they say."

"Or what?"

"Or I shoot you. Do it and then you can answer some questions."

His pal tried to protest. "Enzo I—"

Enzo put up a hand smeared with blood. "Shut up."

I raised the gun to Enzo's eye level. We stared at each other across the room for a long moment, then he turned and put his hands around his pal's neck.

The other two did nothing to stop it. Well-trained dogs.

"Are you rolling?" I asked and then heard the whir of the camera start up.

It took longer than with the girls. He fought back more but Enzo had a vice grip on his throat. The body went limp in his hands and Enzo held on a few more seconds to be sure before letting him drop to the floor.

"Cut," I said. The whir stopped. "Now him." I pointed the barrel at the new friend, the poker buddy, who wasn't happy about it.

"What the fuck, man!"

"You or him," I said to Enzo. "Maybe you want to take your clothes off? Be more in your element?"

Enzo let out a long breath like he was trying to calm himself. The air caught in the blood clogging his nose and whistled. He stared daggers my way. When he grabbed his poker buddy by the neck I knew he was picturing what he was going to do to me.

I didn't have to ask, the camera started turning.

The poker buddy spit and kicked. He clawed at Enzo's fingers locked around his throat. Enzo was turning red, holding his breath with the effort. The strain made the new cut on his nose bleed harder.

I wondered if the men who paid for the girls, Mr. Butler or Mr. Heathcliff, would get the same thrill from the movie we were making now.

Enzo grunted as he squeezed and I heard something crack in the other man's neck. His bones breaking? His windpipe crushing? He had bitten his tongue and blood came running down from the corner of his mouth. I saw one of his eyes bloom red as a vessel burst. I'd seen that in the ring a few times. Takes a long time to heal. This guy wouldn't need to worry about it.

Enzo tossed his body onto the bed. It lay there, a clothed male imitation of a movie I'd seen before.

"Nice job. You must have had practice," I said. Enzo was out of breath, sweating. He extended and clenched his fingers then wiped away some of the blood running from his nose. The chicken behind the camera tried swallowing but his throat caught and he coughed instead. He must have been doing the math in his head of how many people remained in the room and how little convincing it took for Enzo to kill two of his associates to protect his own skin.

"What do you want, Ray?" Enzo asked.

"I told you the first time. I wanted to find my sister."

"That's Audrey?"

"Uh-huh."

"And now she's dead."

"Uh-huh."

"I didn't do it." He wasn't apologetic or pleading. "You got the wrong guy."

"I know. But the thing is, you would have."

"How the fuck do you figure that?"

I turned to the chicken. "You had another shoot scheduled, didn't you?"

"Um, yeah."

"With Audrey?"

"Well . . . he requested her."

A black ball of hate was growing in my gut. I wanted the night to end but the list of men involved kept getting longer. "Who did?"

"The client. I don't know, Mr. Butler I think. She'd been out dancing at the house. So he picked her."

"What did you have planned for her? A red can or a yellow can?"

"Just a yellow. I swear," he said, as if that made it all better.

"And then what? If he liked what he saw, then you make another one? Is it like an audition reel or something?"

"Ray," Enzo said, "You have no idea what a pile of shit you're stepping into."

"Oh, I don't?"

"No, you don't. These are powerful men. You think you're hot shit because you got to Silvio? He was small time. You saw him, couldn't find his own dick with a flashlight and a magnifying glass. But listen up, we don't make girls come here. All of them, your sister included, came here on their own. We promise them roles in the pictures and that's what they get."

The black ball in my gut was growing. I fired. The shot hit a few inches to the left of Enzo's shoe. He and the chicken jumped.

"You may have suckered them in here but why do all the doors lock from the outside? Huh? And on the movies I saw, I don't think those girls wanted to do those scenes."

"Maybe they're just good actresses."

I raised the pistol, aimed it at the chicken. "Turn it on!"

He flinched at first, but then he started the camera rolling. "Over there," I pointed next to Enzo. Hands up, the chicken walked into frame. I tossed Enzo the brass knuckles.

"Time for the finale."

"Then what, Ray?" Enzo asked.

"Then you answer some goddamn questions I have."

"Jesus Christ!" the chicken said.

"Action!" I said.

The first blow from Enzo was enough to send any man down. Right in the temple and the chicken crumpled into a heap. A one shot K.O. But Enzo didn't stop. He knew a knockout wasn't the end of the fight.

He raised the brass knuckles up to his ear and punched down ten more times. With each hammering blow the blood coated Enzo's fist more until it looked like he'd dipped it into a bucket of paint.

Enzo stood, stretched out his back and flexed his fingers still wrapped in brass. The camera buzzed next to me. Enzo struggled to catch his breath. He was spent. Dots of blood spattered the front of his shirt.

"Well?" he said.

There was no satisfaction. The black ball didn't shrink. No matter how many bodies piled up on the floor it wouldn't bring Audrey back.

"It's not *Gone With The Wind* but it'll do for the cops."

"Fucking hell."

"Or you could tell me where to find Butler."

"I don't know."

"Bullshit."

Enzo sat back on the bed, his legs brushing the legs of the dead man. He let the brass knuckles slip from his fingers and clatter to the floor. "I don't. He's got a beach house and a place in Beverly Hills. That's all I know. Why don't you go door to door? I bet it's only about a hundred thousand homes."

"But he's your client."

"I told you Ray, these guys are insulated. They're very high up. They buy and sell guys like us and they always keep their hands clean."

If a loaded gun aimed at his head didn't do the trick I was out of ideas how to get Enzo to spill. Then I saw it. The cardboard box from Silvio's office was in the corner of the room. Two other boxes were around it and a pile of papers.

Keeping the gun on Enzo I went to the corner. His face tightened as I sifted through the papers until I found the torn address book pages. I licked my finger and turned to B. Butler was there. An address in Malibu.

I turned back to Enzo. "How long does one of these film reels last?" I pointed the gun at the camera.

"A few minutes I guess. Maybe five."

"Guess I'd better hurry then."

I fired. A red hole opened up in Enzo's putty face. A spray of dappled red hit the wall behind him. The camera clicked to a halt before he hit the ground.

I felt sure I was doing the right thing, but there was no feeling of accomplishment. I was glad killing gave me no peace. I'd hate to get any more used to it than I was.

I bent down to pick up the brass knuckles, then turned and walked out.

I left Lloyd in charge of the girls. He sat numb as I told him the news about Audrey. I think he expected it more than I did.

I came back to the hotel because I didn't know where else to go. Didn't want to have to explain it all to the police. It would be hard to justify all the killing. I had a hard enough time explaining it to myself.

I got back around 6:30 and found Fokoli's business card with a phone number written on the back. It could have been left days ago, I didn't know. I thought the handwriting was a hallucination. Then I actually spoke to him and now we had plans to meet.

Guess I'm not done yet.

32

FOKOLI

"Jesus Christ, Ray."

He stared at his shoes like a kid who knows he's in trouble.

I didn't give a shit. "You're alone for two days and you kill how many guys? Are you trying to get us killed? I didn't come along with you so you'd get us both sent up the river and that's exactly what's going to happen." I pounded on the trunk of the Ford.

Glenda was leaning against the hood smoking a cigarette. She crushed it out and said, "Everybody just calm down. You're going to draw attention to us."

"Shut up," I said.

Ray looked up then and I saw that he'd been through the ringer once or twice over the past few days. Some of the spark had gone out of his eyes. "Don't talk to her like that," he said.

I shoved my hands in my pockets and paced around the car, muttering under my breath. He was sorry, he said after he told me everything. Sorry for killing people. Sorry for making a big fucking trail of blood that any cop worth his salt could follow. He lost his temper. It wasn't his fault. Audrey was dead.

And now here we were—two Midwestern hacks and a woman—all of us wanted by thugs and cops alike. I stalked back to where he stood, leaning against the car, his arms crossed at his chest and his feet crossed at the ankles. I pointed a finger in his face. "Did you stop to think about what you were doing? Did you stop to think that sometimes it's best to be subtle? To try to find things out before you kill the people with the answers?"

"I got answers," he said in that dangerously quiet way of his.

"You got us in a shit load of trouble."

His eyes narrowed and he took a step forward. "You weren't there, Fokoli. You don't know—"

"I saw a girl get her head stomped like a grape," I said.

Glenda pushed herself between us, glaring at me, her eyes wet with unshed tears. "And you did nothing to help." She hissed it at me.

"I got you out of there," I said. "I got you someplace safe."

"You let my friend die."

"You can barely remember her name, Glenda." I yelled it in her face. We were fighting. Our first fight. Did she think of it that way too? The tears that had been swimming around finally spilled over her lower lids and down her cheeks. Ray pulled his arm back like he wanted to punch me.

I laughed. Harsh and angry sounding. "Aren't you forgetting your brass knuckles?" I asked.

"Fuck you, Fokoli," he said, but he lowered his arm.

Glenda coughed. Her upper lip was starting to sweat. She needed another shot. Well fuck that.

I strode to the end of the lot and stood under a billboard that encouraged people to EAT AT BOB'S. BEST CHILI WEST OF TEXAS.

Hamburger wrappers and paper cups fluttered in the wind, held in place by long, brittle grass. I kicked a paper cup, sending it up into the air. It traveled about four feet and then got stuck in another patch of weeds.

I wondered if Ray thought he was some sort of superhero—some sort of Lone Ranger sent to rescue everyone. Sounds of muffled conversation from him and Glenda drifted in my direction. I couldn't make out what they were saying but it was obvious she was crying. I wondered if she felt rejected—if what happened between us, and my stop to it, was why she was so angry. I stared out into the nothingness beyond the billboard. After awhile, the crying sound stopped. A car door opened and closed and the heavy tread of Ray's shoes sounded behind me.

"Glenda's not feeling well." When I didn't respond he said, "Fokoli, I don't know what to say. I told you everything that happened because I wanted you to know we've got a leg up on these guys."

I shook my head. "Here's what you don't get, Ray. These guys you killed are just like ants crawling around on the outside of an anthill. They're out there scrounging for food to take back to the queen. Follow the ants, find the queen. Step on the ants and not only do you not find the queen, you've got a million more seriously pissed off ants under the ground. There is no 'leg up' on anything." I rubbed the back of my neck. "There's just us versus them now and there's a lot more of them."

I fished around in my pocket and pulled out a syringe and a bottle of morphine. It was nearly empty. This would be the last dose.

Ray took a step back. "What are you doing?"

"For Glenda," I said, shoving past him to the car.

Glenda wasn't happy to see me, but she rolled up her sleeve and took the shot without protest. I showed her the empty vial and she gave a sharp nod.

I held her arm longer than I had to, but I needed to touch her. I needed her to know I cared. "Look, Glenda. I'm sorry. I'm really sorry." She stared at me for a minute and then softened. She leaned into my chest and cried. After a minute she wiped her eyes. I kissed her then. And this time it was tender and soft, the way a first kiss should be. It was the kind of kiss a guy gives to a woman he cares about.

I helped her lay down in the backseat and then, because it

felt so good the first time, I kissed her again. She sighed softly and shut her eyes. When her breathing slowed to the even rhythm of sleep, I backed out and closed the door.

Then I returned to face Ray. "There's something I need to tell you."

He arched an eyebrow at me. "What?"

"I had to take out a couple of guys in order to save Glenda." He didn't say anything, so I continued. "I drugged them. Left them in the hotel."

"Do they know your name?"

I nodded. "I had to give the fat guy my business card. Pretended I was looking for a girl on behalf of a client."

"And you used Dean Fokoli as your name?"

I nodded.

He chewed on his lip and looked like he wanted to punch something. "So you drugged some guys. In a hotel. And they know your name." I opened my mouth to say something, but he held up his hand. "You left a trail. A big fucking trail," he said. "Stepped on an ant."

Sarcastic fucker. I blew out a breath and raked a hand through my hair. I remembered then about Audrey and I felt like a heel. I guess maybe he had an excuse to be mad—but Jesus Christ he was tough to work with. I cleared my throat. "I'm sorry again about Audrey. I'm sure she'd be proud of you."

Ray looked around and I figured he wished there was a punching bag nearby so he could work out some of his frustrations—like maybe whacking seven or eight guys hadn't been therapeutic enough for him.

"So what now?" he asked.

"We get Glenda someplace where she can rest."

I headed back toward the car. It was late—after midnight—I was exhausted. It was true Glenda needed rest but so did me and Ray. I wondered if cops were after him. And if they were, how close on his heels were they?

We climbed in and I started the engine. Ray didn't talk and

I was too tired to try to make conversation. Glenda slept. I kept my eyes on the rearview for a tail. We were on a deserted stretch of road in a broken down part of L.A.—the sort of neighborhood that doesn't notice a car full of holes.

I paid close attention to the cars on the road. They were few and far between. Two or three passed us and I tried halfheartedly to note the make and model and all the stuff a good P.I. is supposed to do. But it was late and I was tired from days of living on the run.

I was careless.

Glenda didn't rouse when I pulled into the lot of a motor lodge and stopped at the office to ask for two rooms—one for Ray and one for me and Glenda. I didn't care what Ray thought. I wasn't letting her out of my sight.

The manager looked pretty alert for a guy who'd been sitting behind a desk all night. In fact, he looked so alert the hairs on the back of my neck stood up. Call it my cop sense, call it anything you want, but everything about that place suddenly seemed wrong. I tried to pin it down—to hone in on what it was that was off. A bead of sweat trickled down the side of the manager's forehead, along his cheek and to the edge of his jaw where it stubbornly held on. He made no move to swipe it away.

He slid the registration card across the counter to me. I filled out a fake name for Ray, letting my senses focus on the back room, the broom closet, the parking lot outside. "Quiet night?" I asked.

The man gave a tremulous smile and swallowed nervously.

I backed toward the door. One step. Two. The lot was silent. Nothing but night breezes and crickets.

No one jumped out at me. No one shot at me.

The car was still running and I could see Ray's silhouette. I moved around to the driver's side, trying to peg the feeling in my gut.

Ray leaned over to say something, his mouth opened, the

words frozen there. I had my right leg halfway into the car. I was almost sitting when headlights blinded me. Ray didn't finish what he was going to say. It would have been impossible to hear over the sound of spinning tires and flying gravel from the approaching Buick. I jumped in and put the car in reverse.

The oncoming car had the advantage of speed and struck the Ford just as I started to move. Ray was thrown back and then forward against the dash, hitting his head. In the back, Glenda was thrown to the floor. I pushed the accelerator to the floor and looked over my shoulder as I careened backwards through the lot.

The car had paused for a moment after striking us, but was coming full speed now. I had the pedal to the floor and we still didn't move fast enough.

I didn't see the second car waiting. I have no way of knowing if Ray saw it or not. It hit us from the side, sending the Ford into a spin and popping two of its tires. I felt the bandage on my shoulder rip, felt the skin tear and the wound open. Then I felt glass against my head and the wet smear of blood.

Blackness crept into the edges of my vision. The world went sideways. The back door was wrenched open and Glenda moaned. Glenda. I needed to help Glenda.

Through the starred windshield, I saw her dragged away. Ray's head was against my shoulder. Dizzily, I shoved him off of me and fumbled in my waistband for the snub nose. I climbed out and managed to get two blind shots off before the car disappeared into the night.

Ray climbed out and stood next to me. "What happened?"

"They got Glenda."

He swore and clenched his fists at his sides like he was trying to control his temper. Sirens sounded in the distance.

"Come on," I said. "We need to get out of here."

Three blocks away we stood in an alley and assessed ourselves. Ray had some bumps and bruises but was okay for the most part. My shoulder wasn't as bad as I thought so I left the bandage in place.

"We got to go after her," Ray said.

"We will."

"Now."

"No," I said. "Not now. Let's think about what we'll do first and then we'll do it." I turned and looked up the alley. "Maybe we can avoid leaving a trail of dead bodies behind us."

"If we go now maybe we can avoid letting any harm come to Glenda." Ray was a man of few words. When he said something he meant it. Maybe he was right. Maybe I was right. Maybe we both were.

All I know is that right there, right then, I hated the situation I was in and I wanted to hit somebody. And Ray just happened to be the closest guy.

I pulled back with my right before thinking things out. He blocked it easily and clocked me one on the chin. I don't know how long it was before I opened my eyes again but when I did, he was there, standing above me looking angry and impatient.

"Can we go now?" he asked.

33

RAY

Lloyd didn't owe me a thing but he loaned me his car anyway. I think seeing Fokoli with me and the fact that I didn't ask Lloyd to come along made him highly agreeable. Before we left he told me the girls all scattered to the wind like pieces of trash, which I told him was a regrettable turn of phrase. I saw fear in his eyes like he was afraid I was going to start punching. I deserved it. I deserved to be put behind bars like an animal.

He also told me there was one girl unaccounted for, even if you factored in Audrey. The girls, before they ran, did a head count and one girl, Darlene, wasn't there. Like a good junior detective I filed away that tidbit for later in case I needed it.

Fokoli drove. I had Lloyd write out directions to Butler's Malibu address and I acted as navigator.

I marveled at Fokoli, just the fact that he was alive. He looked a lot like a boxer coming back to the corner after a good ten rounds. Taking a bullet will do that to you. And I didn't like the way he was so Johnny-on-the-spot with that morphine needle. Still, this guy was tougher than I thought. I was even more thankful than ever he hadn't caught up with me sooner during all the trouble in K.C.

I noticed Fokoli gripping the wheel like he was trying to choke it to death.

"They better not hurt a fucking hair on her head," he said out loud but I suspected it was more for himself and not for me.

"We'll get her back."

"We fucking better." His palms rubbed on the black disk of the wheel. There was something there. Something that made Glenda more than just a whore with a morphine addiction. Fokoli was taking it personal. Now maybe he knew how I felt about Audrey, but I didn't dare mention her. That wasn't the best advertisement for my track record at saving damsels.

And my God, Glenda. The sweet kid who just wanted to dance on the silver screen, the girl my brother had loved and who had saved me back in K.C. It was so easy to forget she was a prostitute. Part of the deal, as she explained it to me, was when she made it out to Hollywood she would quit that business. I couldn't help but think that by me dragging her into my fight back in K.C. I must have accelerated her journey west and somehow forced her to take a job working for this Baron character.

So now on my conscience I had my sister—a girl I couldn't save—and Glenda, a girl I drove to danger. Christ, I have a way with women.

"So we get there, you drop me off and then you go after Glenda alone," I said. "Is that it? Or are you staying to talk to Butler?"

"He's yours. I can't believe I've wasted this much time already."

"Where will you go?"

"Baron. It's got to be him. I stole his property. I have a feeling he won't do anything to her until I show up, but then again I've seen what he's capable of when he wants to prove a point."

"I wish I could go with you."

"No. This is my fight and Butler is yours. Faster we get this wrapped up the better."

We turned north along the ocean. Fokoli lit a cigarette. I was in no position to tell him to put it out.

"We could still call the cops," I said.

"Too late for that. You kinda fucked us. Not that I'm entirely clean in this deal. Besides, men like that, they don't deserve a trial and free room and board."

He was starting to sound like me.

"Aw, hell. Maybe they do and maybe they don't," he said. "I know I don't want to go to jail so it's your call if and when you want to bring the cops into it. Just leave my name out. And do me a favor, whatever happens," he turned to me, "try to talk to him before you start swinging. Remember what I said about the ants. Find out if he's the Queen first."

"I still don't get how a man could do that to a girl," I said.

"It takes all kinds."

I knew it was true but I was depressed having to admit the world was capable of such cruelty. Then again, who was I to talk?

Outside, the ocean exhaled a thick fog onto the land. The air chilled and as crowded as the rest of Los Angeles was, out near the beach turned desolate. I kept expecting Bela Lugosi to jump out of the shadows.

Fokoli pulled over and killed the engine. "That's it up ahead. You walk from here."

I could hear the ocean surf but couldn't see the water. The fog blocked out any moon so everything over the water was black, like those old maps where the world is flat and just spills over into nothing and someone's written something ominous like HERE THERE BE MONSTERS.

I thought momentarily about going with Fokoli, saying screw it to Butler. Audrey was already dead. Silvio and Enzo were gone. Would they really start all over again?

Yes. Even if it was a maybe I had to see this thing through. My rescue mission now was for all the girls yet to come. For all the other Audrey's out there. I hoped I could do better by them.

"Good luck, Dean," I said.

"Yeah. Good luck, Ray." We shook hands like two proper

gentlemen. They were hands, sure as anything, to have blood on them soon enough.

The tires spun as Fokoli gunned it back to the city in search of Glenda. Better for her to have a professional on her side anyway. My rescue skills had a lousy track record. As I approached the beach house I thought maybe I could improve on that record.

I didn't have much of a plan—go up and knock on the door. A man answered, young and movie star handsome. He was tall and sturdy and I could tell he knew his way around the ring.

"I'm looking for Butler," I said.

"And who are you?"

"Just tell him I bring a message from Silvio and Enzo."

His eyebrow crooked up in a high arch. "This way." The handsome man ushered me inside. He told me to wait in the entryway. This must be when they release the lions. Dispose of me for good.

No lions. He returned quickly and told me to follow him.

The house was big and when I reached the living room I saw that the entire back wall of the house was windows, outside just a black curtain.

In a tall chair beside a dying fire was an older man in a velvet smoking jacket, a cigar pinched between his fingers and a glass of brandy on the side table. It looked like a stage set.

"Butler?"

"And you must be the man who is causing such trouble lately. I thought there were two of you." He spoke with a fake aristocratic air. A trace of English accent he probably got from a dialogue coach. I hated him instantly. Hell, I hated him before I even got there.

"You just get me. My partner is visiting Mr. Baron."

"Ah, yes. Vile man. If he didn't provide the . . . services . . . I desire I wouldn't associate with him."

"But, you do."

"As I said, if not for necessity."

Two other men appeared from nowhere, each as good looking as the other and just as strong. They hung at the fringes of the room silently but let me know they were there. I felt the weight of the brass knuckles in my pocket.

"So you know all about me?" I asked.

"One hears things. After the trouble in Palm Springs," he paused, gestured at me with his cigar. "That was your handiwork?"

I nodded.

"Yes, well, after that mess I started getting phone calls. It threw off our production schedule considerably. Naturally I wanted to know who was responsible."

"And if you were in danger."

The three men inched forward. Butler waved them off. "No, boys. You can go now. There will be no more violence tonight."

The trio seemed unsure but followed orders and faded out of the room. I had no doubt there were still close though. Butler eyed me up and down.

"No one seems to know anything about you."

"I know about the films," I said.

"Do you now?" said Butler. "You know the whereabouts of the missing film, perhaps?"

"You mean the one in the red can?"

Butler swallowed hard. "Yes." I knew more than he thought, or maybe I was confirming his worst fears.

"I did know. It was gone from the last place I saw it. Went missing when someone murdered my friend."

"Baron's men," he said, on the defense. "I don't deal in murder."

"Not from what I saw." He tried to take a drink but his brandy got caught in his throat and he coughed. I continued, taking small steps forward. "My sister was living in the apartment. The one with all the girls. Audrey. Do you know her?"

"I can't recall. She worked for Baron you said?"

"She was about to work for you is what I heard. She was going to star in one of your pictures. But not anymore." His body stiffened. "She's dead."

Butler reacted as if he hadn't heard. He just lifted his brandy snifter, spun it twice, then sipped. "That's a shame. She was a pretty girl. A very pretty girl." He spun the drink in his glass, a look of remembering in his eyes. I hated that her image was playing in his head.

"So you don't deny it? You were going to make one of those films with my sister." I took a step closer to Butler and he sat up in his chair.

"Mr. Heathcliff is the one you want. He called for that particular story line."

"The red films?"

"Yes."

"It's anyone's fault but yours, isn't it? Baron, Heathcliff. Your hands are clean, is that it?"

He set down the brandy glass. "Look, what do you want from me? If you're here to make threats, or call the police, I assure you I have many friends on the inside. But I will assume since you haven't done that thus far it isn't on your agenda."

"I prefer to handle things on my own."

"Yes. Very clever. I'm not Baron, you know. I'm not some two-bit flesh peddler living in the gutter. I make over forty pictures a year. Last year I had three films in the top ten. You can't just make me vanish like Silvio. You found your sister. Now is the point when the picture fades to black. The end."

"I want to know why."

"Why?" he repeated.

"Why you do it. Why did you make those films?"

Butler sighed. "Do you go to the movies, son?" I nodded. "How often? Once, twice a month?"

"Maybe."

"I see movies every day. All day. I see them half finished, too long, I see them over and over again. I'm here to tell you, there's nothing new out there. We're all just regurgitating the same old stories in the same old ways. We've made all the movies anyone is ever going to want to see. We've gone to talking pictures and we've gone color. What else is there?" He leaned forward like he was telling me a great tale before bedtime. "Son, I've seen it all."

He puffed his cigar. I stared, listening, waiting for an answer that would satisfy me but really I knew one would never come.

"But then, ah but then. Sex. The great taboo. We realized you can film people having sex. It was a great revelation for my friends and me. I started a small film society. Other like-minded fellows who think there's nothing new under the sun. We meet on occasion and show each other films that get the blood flowing again."

"So you hired Silvio to make them."

"A cog in the wheel. We couldn't do them in our own studios, it would be publicity suicide. A nobody like him needed the cash to finance his B pictures. And the girls were more than happy to oblige. Oh, the girls. They're delivered by the busload to Hollywood every day. Do you have any idea how many beautiful girls promenade through my office every day of the week? The cream of the crop. I'm here to tell you there are no more pretty girls in Peoria or Ann Arbor or Pittsburgh because they've all moved to Hollywood."

"Where you're waiting to make them stars." I chewed off the words like plug tobacco.

"Exactly. No one did anything they didn't volunteer to do. But . . ." He drifted in thought for a moment. I took another step closer to him. That brought him around. "But after awhile, even that gets boring. So where do you go? More taboos. I started making requests. A girl would get hurt, a girl would get slapped. We happened upon Mr. Enzo who seemed to quite enjoy it. It was perfect casting."

"He won't be enjoying anything anymore."

Butler went a little pale. "Is that so?"

I nodded.

"Well, it was he who started hurting the girls more. Then one day we got a film in a yellow can to show at our get-together. Silvio said it should be kept separate from the others. It wasn't for any new members of the group. When we watched it . . . Oh, it was wonderful."

I pulled my fist tight and inched closer, about six feet from his chair. Behind him the fire flickered, nearly dead.

"To see such a raw performance, such genuine emotion, well it's not something I see every day. You see, those girls from Peoria might be beautiful but most of them can't act. They can't do or say anything that a sane person would believe was real. But you get them in a room with Enzo, then you see some true human emotion."

"So what you're telling me is that you made these films because you were bored."

"That's an over simplification—"

I stepped two broad steps across the carpet and grabbed the lapels of his smoking jacket. The velvet was soft in my fists as I hauled him halfway out of his seat. His cigar spilled ash on his leg and the chair like any other cheap stogie. His face was stricken. I could tell he had been anticipating this moment since I walked in. I didn't know how much time I had before his handsome friends came to his rescue.

"What are you going to do?" he wanted to know. I wasn't sure. There had been too much killing already.

Behind me the three men appeared like shadows. They advanced steadily the way Hitler was moving across Europe.

I reached down and slid the loose belt out of Butler's smoking jacket, then let him go. He fell to a soft landing in his chair. I wrapped the belt around my right fist quickly, leaving a long tail of burgundy velvet because I only had time for two loops before I spun to my left with my fist ready for business. It hit the jaw of Handsome Man #1 and he went to his knees. I smashed him again at the base of his skull and he fell to the floor. I reached down and quickly drew the gun sticking from his belt and tossed it. I hadn't been aiming for anything but it landed in the fire, making the coals spark and the fire jump back to life.

I spun to my left and swung at the face of Handsome Man #2 but he blocked me with his forearm. I quickly kicked up and hit a bull's-eye to his crotch. My, God, I'd become a real back room brawler. But at three-to-one I wasn't taking any chances. I snatched the gun from his belt and brought it up.

I was face to face with the last Handsome Man, the one who'd answered the door. He raised his arms to a fighting position and began bouncing on his toes, a grin creeping across his face. I was right about him doing time in the ring and I could read by his expression that he felt confident he had the drop on me. A good old fashioned boxing match suited me just fine. Enough of this junkyard scrapping I'd been reduced to. Time to fight with a man who knew his stuff. I tossed the gun far back into the hall. It rattled along the tile floor into the darkness. I felt the brass knuckles in my pocket but ignored them. If Fokoli had stayed here he would have known for sure I was an idiot.

I lifted my hands into my familiar position. Microphone, telephone was the new slang for it. Like your left hand was holding a microphone up to your mouth and your right was holding a telephone at your ear. Good defense was what I called it.

We countered each other's movement without a word. The Doorman didn't need to call out boastful threats and I admired him for it. I would have felt better about my chances if he'd started telling me all the ways he was going to tear me apart. Instead he was quiet and patient, like boxing into a mirror.

I could have drawn out the brass knuckles but this was a real bout and I had too much respect for the art. Besides, he could easily draw out his gun and this round would be over quick.

Thinking he had me beat already, he advanced into striking range. Behind us Handsome Man #1 was still moaning as he crawled on all fours dripping blood from his mouth and feeling on the carpet for his canines.

The first punch came and I dodged left. I didn't try to hit the Doorman; I'd wait until I knew more about his technique. He threw two quick jabs that both missed the mark. He nodded approval.

"You fight," the Doorman said as a statement.

"I have," I answered, trying not to reveal too much.

He came at me again and I deflected a right to the head and a left to the body. That pissed him off.

Butler watched from his front row seat as the Doorman attacked again. He threw a flurry of punches to my midsection so I balled up and took them through my defenses, waited him out until he tired or decided to swing for my head. He swung for my head.

I ducked under his arm and came up fast. Two quick jabs to his face and both landed. The velvet wrapping kept them from full impact but it was enough to knock him off his balance. He leaned back on his heels and I charged forward. He held his hands up in defensive position lifting his elbows out in an attempt to maintain balance so I threw a big right to his middle.

His stomach muscles were solid but he staggered back. I threw another. Lungs nearly empty, the second blow did more damage and he wheezed audibly. Most men would have gone down already but he held it together and swung out at me, clipping the side of my head. My head rattled and my ear stung with tiny needles. A few more of those and I'd have that most hallowed of boxer's calling cards—the cauliflower ear. I stepped back and it gave both of us time to regain our equilibrium.

Off to my left I saw Butler start to rise. I slid back one step and put an open hand on his chest, shoving him back to his chair.

"You stay," I said.

The Doorman was coming at me now. I could almost sense

the beer and spit bucket smells of the ring.

I dodged another right and hooked a left to his gut that caught him on the side. He swung out a tight fist into my kidney and I grunted in pain. He slapped a wide cross to my cheek and I reeled backwards. He followed. When he caught me he slammed a fist into my chest. I took it and lashed out at his exposed head. I rammed my burgundy-wrapped fist into his chin—dead center. His jaw knocked back straining at the hinges that held it in place. He staggered.

I stepped forward, putting my entire body weight behind the next punch. I pivoted my shoulders over my hips and followed through, a textbook demonstration on how to throw a punch.

My fist landed dead center on the Doorman's mouth and under the velvet I felt teeth crack. His jaw was sent rocketing back a second time and some ligament, some muscled attachment broke free.

He screamed but it was muffled by his off-kilter jaw line and the hands he held to his mouth. As he went down, his eyes wondered what just happened.

He fell backwards and tripped over Handsome Man #2 just as he was starting to recover from my crotch shot. The Doorman fell toward the fireplace and flopped down hard on the slate hearth. A tremendous crack filled the room. The Doorman's head pitched forward and a spray of red spat out from behind his ear.

Another crack and the man straining to recover from his crotch injury took a bullet to the stomach. The gun in the fireplace had become superheated, the gunpowder in each casing exploding and firing random shots across the room.

I rolled away from the fireplace, stood and grabbed up Butler again by his lapels.

Butler pleaded. "It's Heathcliff you want. He was the one who suggested that girl should die." His fake accent was slipping back into pure Brooklynese.

Another crack. I heard wood splinter somewhere in the

corner.

"He's making another one," Butler shouted. "On his own."

"Another what? Another red film?"

"Yes, yes. He's got a girl and he's going to star in it himself. He got tired of seeing Enzo. He wanted the full effect. He's an actor you see—"

I cuffed him across the face. "Where?"

"At his bungalow. I'll tell you where just please don't kill me."

I remembered the missing girl Lloyd told me about. Darlene. I was too late to save one. Maybe I could make it in time to save another.

"Let's go," I said, dragging him toward the door. "You drive."

A final gunshot echoed through the big house.

34

FOKOLI

I made my way through the fog, heading back to the car and thinking about Ray. I didn't know if leaving him at the beach house was the right thing to do. I did know Ray could take care of himself—it was the possibility of more bodies that made my skin crawl. Did I really care if the bad guys ended up dead? No. Not really. But I hated the thought of so many men dying at Ray's hands. What was he becoming? What had I helped him to become?

I blew out a breath. I was turning into an old man.

The air was chilled with the dampness—almost as if the fog had grown claws that dug in and held on. And Glenda was out there in it—with Baron. I turned the car on and pushed the pedal to the floor as I moved toward the city.

Glenda was probably still okay. Baron would want revenge—and he'd get it by hurting Glenda, but he wouldn't do anything until I was there to see it. Baron was a guy who loved an audience.

I talked to myself while I drove, spitting all the pieces out, trying to make sense of them all. I used to sit in the tub, throw a rubber ball against the wall and talk to myself when I was working on a case—that was in the days when I gave a damn. I hadn't spit it all out like this in a long time and it was good to feel my brain flexing like it used to.

Baron went after Glenda for revenge. He may or may not have had anything to do with the movies in the red and yellow cans. Probably he did—because he was a pervert—but he was too sloppy, too much of a pig to be much of a big brain. Ray had killed just about every decent mark worth interrogating, and for now that was okay because the girls on tap to be in any future films were free—scattered to who knew where.

L.A. was as busy as ever and as I passed all those nameless, beautiful people, I couldn't help thinking we were insignificant. Did any of us matter? Did anything we did matter? The memory of Glenda's eyes danced in front of me. She mattered. And saving her mattered. I didn't know about anything else, but right then, with everything that made me human, I knew that. I parked the car and checked my gun. There was no point in taking it in with me. I'd be searched and they'd take it. I put the snub nose, and Charles's gun in the glove compartment. Then I took a deep breath and stepped out of the car.

Baron's theater was lit up like a Christmas tree and men made their way in and out with no apparent worries about police. Live and let live. If L.A. was anything like Kansas City, over half the cops here were on the take and those who weren't were too scared to do anything about it.

I shoved through the crowd, approached the doorman in front of the theater and started to explain myself—who I was, why I wanted to see Baron. A heavy man in a blue wool suit pushed into me. He smelled like rotten meat soaked in gin. "Hey there, Benny," he slurred at the door man as he put a fat hand on my shoulder. "Is Loretta available for an appointment tonight? I could use a massage." He pushed me to the side with the hand on my shoulder. The other hand he extended toward Benny. I caught a glimpse of the corner of a one hundred dollar bill in his palm as he shook Benny's hand. Benny pocketed the cash with the slickness of a pro and opened the door. The drunk stumbled past, knocking me into Benny.

"I need to see Baron," I said.

Benny ignored me, taking tickets from patrons who were there for the show and accepting bribes from others who wanted more personalized service. I pulled a bill from my wallet and handed it to him. "What?" he said.

"I need to see Baron."

He continued to methodically take tickets, nodding at the faceless men who pushed into the darkened theater. "Nobody sees Baron." His mouth curved up a little as he said it, like it was one of the more amusing things he'd heard all day.

"He'll see me," I said.

Benny's mouth tightened. "Beat it."

I ground my shoe onto Benny's foot, enjoying the grim-ace of pain that crossed his face. "How about you go tell him I'm here."

"How about I rearrange your face?" He leaned over and rapped some sort of secret knock on the front glass. I pulled my foot back, adjusted my tie, and waited.

After a minute the doors opened and two men in tuxedoes pushed their way into the crowd. Charles and his friend from the hotel. They looked a little pasty, no doubt still recovering from the morphine I gave them. They also looked pissed and it was obvious at first glance that they recognized me. I gave a half smile as my old pal Charles took my arm. "Thanks Benny," he said. "We'll take it from here."

After the inevitable frisking, I expected Charles to take me into the theater, to one of the back rooms where Baron would sit in his oriental chair and twist the rings on his fat fingers while he stared at me and offered a choice on which way I'd prefer for Glenda to be killed.

But Charles pushed me back out onto the sidewalk. "Let's walk," he said. "It's not far and it's a nice night."

So we walked; Charles and me in front with his hand on my arm, the second thug behind us with his hand in his jacket pocket and the unmistakable shape of a .45 aimed in the general direction of my kidneys.

After two blocks Charles stopped in front of a Chinese

restaurant. "Ah," I muttered. "Of course." A nudge in my back from the .45 propelled me through the front door.

"Mr. Baron is in the back," Charles said.

The restaurant was dimly lit but not overly crowded. Couples watched our trio with hooded lids, barely looking up from their plates of fried rice and Peking duck as we passed. A waiter in a red brocade jacket bowed and, as Charles nodded in his direction, the waiter led us through the building. The restaurant divided at the back of the dining room. On the left, large swinging double doors opened into the kitchen. The sounds of dishes clanking and the smell of frying food drifted out as waiters opened and closed the doors. To the right was a long, dark hallway. Naturally, that's the direction I was propelled by Charles and his friend.

Three doors lined the hall. Charles knocked on the first one. The door opened a crack and a dull eye stared out at us. Charles was silent. The door opened wider and we were allowed inside. The waiter who had granted us entrance bowed and left.

Baron sat at a large, round, black table surrounded by ornate chairs in the middle of the room. The table was heaped with plates of food. "You do realize you're not Chinese, right?" I said. Charles used his foot to sweep my legs out from under me. I fell to the floor.

"Get him up," Baron said.

Charles pulled me up, but stuck a fist in my gut for good measure. I started to keep score in my head.

When I caught my breath, the guy with the gun shoved me in a chair.

"Would you like something to eat?" Baron asked, gesturing with his chopsticks to the feast in front of him. "Young Glenda wasn't very hungry. She's gone to have a little rest."

My chest tightened. Glenda wasn't hungry. Was she here someplace? I looked around the room. One door. No windows. I'd have to get past Charles and his friend if I wanted to get out. I was banking she was behind one of the other two doors along the hall. "Where is she?" I asked.

Baron shoved an eggroll into his mouth and chewed a little before speaking. "You'll see her."

I had no patience for this. Baron was crazy. I stood up. Charles rested a heavy hand on my shoulder and made to push me back into my seat. I covered his hand with my own and spun around behind him, twisting his arm up until his hand rested between his shoulder blades. He arched back and I used the leverage to swing him around and into the gunman. The two went down in a heap and the gun flew across the floor.

Baron ate another eggroll and looked bored.

I picked up the gun and waved the barrel at all of them. "Where is Glenda?"

Baron only stared at me.

Charles and his friend climbed to their feet, looking angry, but at least they had their hands up. "I said, where is she?"

Baron still said nothing. I waved the revolver in Charles's direction and cocked an eyebrow. "Tell me or I'll shoot him."

Baron shrugged. Charles looked as if he wanted to tell me anything I wanted to know, but he kept his mouth shut. I supposed it was fear of Baron that was responsible for his silence.

I pulled the trigger and Charles collapsed, holding his knee and moaning.

"Where is she?" I asked again through clenched teeth.

Baron only stared at me, lifting his fork in a monotonous cadence to shovel food into his mouth. The second man's jaw started to work as I swept the gun in his direction. A second shot rang out and his head exploded. I looked at the gun in my hand. I hadn't pulled the trigger. My eyes drifted back to Baron, who placed a smoking revolver on the table next to his plate before picking up his fork again.

Jesus Christ. My mouth dried out. The rage in me was sudden and ferocious and matched the disgust I felt when I looked at Baron. But I also felt fear. Glenda's name threatened to spill out of my mouth in a cry, but I squelched the urge and remained still.

Baron looked at Charles. The warning in the fat man's eyes was unmistakable. "Terrance was always loose-lipped. Charles knows how to keep a secret."

Charles was too busy moaning to acknowledge the compliment.

It was pointless now to ask about Glenda. Baron could have shot me any time he wanted. I backed up a step. Then another.

"I'm a good shot you know," Baron said around a mouthful of fried rice.

The room smelled of blood and fried duck and I was starting to feel overly warm. I had a chance. Maybe only one. I stopped moving back and moved forward again. "So I'm just supposed to stand here and watch you eat all night?"

Baron's eyes narrowed, but he didn't stop eating. And he kept his right hand on the table now, right beside the gun. I would have to move quick. "We'll talk when I'm full," he said.

I didn't wait for him to take another bite. I grabbed the edge of the table and pushed, dumping platters of duck and rice and gai pan all over Baron. His gun clattered to the floor.

I turned and ran into the hall, closing the door behind me.

35

RAY

I made him drive. Butler must have been used to having a driver because he kept veering over the white lines and running the tires off on the shoulder. He cowered and flinched every time we went over a bump, just like if I had a gun on him. All I was holding were my fists. That seemed to be enough.

Butler seemed older. His hair was gray and he wasn't about to score a touchdown for Notre Dame or anything, but from our first meeting in his oversized living room his confidence had drained, and with it whatever youth he was clinging on to.

I hated the thought of Fokoli all alone trying to rescue Glenda but I had to see this through. Besides, if I could trust anyone in the world to get the job done it was him: a man who already came back from the dead.

I had no idea what I was going to do when we got to Heathcliff. If I could make it there before he started shooting the film with Darlene the rest would work itself out.

Huh. Shooting. Jesus Christ this town gave me a headache.

I had every intention of calling the cops. Honest I did. Butler scared me a little with his talk of who he knew in the department, although something like this isn't just a pot bust, or an underage girl at a party. This can't be swept under the rug.

We didn't drive far before Butler pulled the Packard onto a

small driveway. What Butler had called a bungalow the rest of us would call a mansion. It was higher up in the hills of Malibu, overlooking the ocean from the cliffs, not on the sand.

"This is it." He swallowed, his throat was tight and dry. "Now, you'll let me go?" He pleaded.

"Come with me." He was easy to maneuver. He stayed a few paces ahead of me and walked slow and tense, reminding me of the girls so easily forced to go where they didn't want to go, knowing nothing good could be behind the next door.

The house was isolated. No neighbors peering in over the hedges. Up on the cliff the fog was thinner. I looked down on the beach houses, all shrouded in a thick soup, and imagined how easy it was to think of this as a world that you owned. A world with no consequences. A world where girls felt no pain.

I nodded to Butler and told him to knock. He did, weakly. No one came to the door. I peeked in through a window and saw light coming from the back of the house. I tried the doorknob. Locked.

"Louder," I said.

He banged like he was trying to wake the dead. I hoped we weren't that late.

I heard rustling inside, then footsteps coming down a hallway. I slid my fingers into the brass knuckles.

"Who's there?" came from behind the door. I nudged Butler in the ribs.

"It's Mister Butler."

The door opened and a young man with a familiar face stood there dressed in a short robe like you'd wear in a sauna. "Jesus Butler, can't you wait until—"

The man was young, handsome, familiar. He looked at me, then Butler, confused.

"Heathcliff, I—" said Butler.

I shot out a hand wrapped in brass and smashed the knuckles across the bridge of his nose. Heathcliff staggered back into the house and I followed, pulling Butler along with me.

BORROWED TROUBLE

I slammed the door shut behind us and threw Butler aside. I knew he wasn't a threat.

"Where is she?" I said to the hunched figure clutching his bloody nose.

"Who the fuck are you?"

I grabbed the robe and straightened him up. "Answer my question first." I pounded another fist at his face. It rammed off his hands covering the broken nose. He cried out as he hit the floor again. He was in too much pain to answer so I followed the light into the back of the house.

Never turn your back on an opponent. It's a rule they teach you before they'll even let you in the ring to spar. I didn't care, I had to find that girl and hope like hell she was in better shape than Audrey.

Down a short hallway I found the room. Two hot lights made the room brighter than high noon in summer and bleached out the color on the tiny bed and the girl tied to a scrolled iron headboard. The room was nicer than in the other films. The girl was just as scared.

She was alive. Her mouth gagged, hands and feet bound and she squirmed on her stomach in just her undergarments. The look in her eyes at the sight of a stranger was pure terror.

A camera was pointed at her. I checked but it was not rolling. I slid the brass knuckles back into my pocket and went to her.

"Darlene? I'm Audrey's brother. I'm here to take you away from this. It's over."

I undid the gag in her mouth and her first sounds were deep sobs. I worked at the ropes while she cried but it took me some time since they were tied in sloppy knots. Once she was undone I told her to stay put. As I left the room I saw a small table stacked with a rope, a necktie and a pistol. All ways he could finish her off for the big finale of the film. I guess he was waiting until the moment came to decide which way to go.

I went back to the living room where Butler and Heathcliff were recovering. Heathcliff had managed to get himself into a chair and Butler stood flat against the wall next to a bay window. The kind of men I was used to would have figured out by then how to gang rush me and beat me senseless. These two were a pair of country club swells who spent more time manicuring their hands than using them for brawling. The only gloves they'd ever slipped on were white.

Even through the blood spattering his face I knew Heathcliff immediately. Leonard Sutherland. He'd been a song and dance man, then did that biography of Thomas Jefferson and since then he was considered a serious actor. He'd appeared with most of the top actresses in the pictures and still it wasn't enough. He could have his pick of any woman in America, but this was how he chose to get off.

"Get up," I said. He didn't move. "I said get up." He slowly rose. "This piece of shit already told me why he did it. I want to know why you had to star in your own show."

"What? Who the fuck are you?" The blood in his mouth made his speech slurry.

"Just watching Enzo wasn't good enough? You felt like you could do a better job?"

I felt the black ball in my gut again. His death would be covered up. A fake story, something romantic to go with his image—a jealous lover, an angry husband—this would never come out. I needed him alive.

"I'm sorry," he said.

"What about Audrey? You have any plans for her?"

Butler spoke up from the corner. "Look, you've made your point. Take the girl. Take her and the car and go."

He spoke like the girl and the car were of equal value.

"I want to know what he would have done with Audrey. Would you kill her or just rape her? Would you watch it over and over and tug at your own dick? Would you even remember her name?"

For the first time, I cried over my sister. I wept as the two men watched me, afraid I was coming apart at the hinges. I was a little scared myself.

BORROWED TROUBLE

I was snapped out of it by a gunshot. I spun quickly to see Darlene in the doorway holding the pistol. A trail of smoke drifted from the barrel forming a lazy S. I followed her aim back to Leonard. He'd fallen back into the chair. I looked for blood but it was hard to tell what was new, and what was my fault.

"What the fuck are you doing?" he shouted. He seemed unhurt. A prop gun. Probably what he used to get her out here, to make her do what he wanted. Fake. Like everything in this town.

I held out a calming hand to Darlene. Her eyes were wet and angry. "Just put it down," I said.

She fired again, not understanding why the gun wasn't killing him. The sound was small, like a week-old puppy when you were expecting a German Shepherd.

"They're blanks," I said. "It's just a prop from a movie. Put it down."

Her eyes let go of the tears they were holding and she dropped the gun to the floor.

"Good. Now go call the police. Tell them where we are. Describe the way up here the best you can, okay? These guys are gonna get what's coming to them, don't you worry."

"Yes, call them," said Butler. "Call them so we can get this over with. I'll take my chances with them, over a madman like you."

I turned to him with my best madman eyes. "You still think you've got enough friends to make all this go away?"

"Better than friends," Leonard said. "I've got money."

I looked at him. He might have been right. Getting them arrested might be futile, but then so would killing them. I had to trust that the cops would do the right thing.

But . . . I did have one thing I could take from him. And it would satisfy an itch.

"Darlene, wait in another room please," I said.

She sobbed heaving breaths. "Why?"

"Because you've seen enough."

"Are you gonna kill him?"

"No," I said. "Worse."

She took a few hesitant steps backward and then turned away. Leonard started to rise again from the chair. "What are you doing?" he asked.

I walked forward, slipping my hand into my pocket for the brass knuckles.

"What are you doing?" he asked again.

Butler shouted an angry plea from his place, shrinking against the wall. "For Christ sake, you've got your revenge. Don't be an animal. We're done. It's over! We won't do it again."

I stood over Leonard Sutherland. Millions of women wanted to be this close to him. If they only knew.

"Do you even remember her name?"

"Who?"

"My sister. What's her name?"

"What? I . . . I don't know."

"Did you film anything with the girl?"

"What?"

"In the room back there, did you film anything?"

"No. I was getting ready. I . . . I couldn't load the film the right way, I—"

"You missed your chance. You'll never be on film again."

I took one punch for each girl in that apartment building, and one more for Audrey. When I finished, that famous face—the matinee idol—looked more like a pound of fresh hamburger meat. Even more like the scraps you bring home for the dog.

He coughed and spat thick blood. I knew it ran down the back of his throat the way it does from a broken nose. His nose wasn't the only thing broken on that million dollar face.

His career was over. He'd live, he might even get off from the charges. The red film can would disappear and magically never have existed, thanks to several greased palms at the L.A.P.D. But no doctor in the world could put him back together again. And no one would ever pay to see his face again unless he joined the circus.

Butler slid down the wall and cowered on the floor, covering his eyes. The blood was too much for him, the violence too real, and after all he'd seen and been so bored by. I guess the thrill only worked if it was on film.

I found Darlene in the kitchen and I led her out to the Packard.

"We'll get you cleaned up and then I'll drop you at the police station." She nodded. "Do me a favor, huh?" I leveled my eyes at hers. "You don't know me. You don't know who I was."

"I never seen you before."

"And you never will again."

I needed her help with directions but I managed to get us pointed back to my hotel room. We were silent on the ride and the city around us kept a respectful hush.

I thought about Audrey. I thought about Glenda. I thought about train schedules and tickets back home.

36

FOKOLI

The heavy smell of Chinese food mixed with the smell of cordite and blood in the air of the small dining room. Baron had tipped over in his chair before I ran, Kung Pao beef spilling all over his brocaded robe. Any other time I probably would have found the sight of a fat man covered in his dinner funny. But now all I could think about was Glenda and getting the hell out of L.A.

The plinking sound of oriental string music drifted down the corridor from the dining room, along with the muffled voices of a dozen conversations. Kitchen sounds permeated the drone. It was all business as usual and I noticed that in the split second it took to close the door and check the next room. Empty.

That left one room. I checked the knob. Locked. I kicked it open. Baron had one guard on Glenda. A tall guy with an enormous Adam's apple. I took him out with one good punch to the throat. Guys like that are always expecting to get hit in the stones because that's the place most of us normal folks can reach. But a punch to the throat, while not as painful, is far more terrifying. A guy is less likely to punch you when he's trying to catch his breath.

He crumpled at my feet, spitting blood and clutching at his neck.

BORROWED TROUBLE

Glenda saw me and started to cry.

Baron had dressed her in a green satin dress and tied her to a bed covered in red velvet pillows. Her hair was done up and held in place with what looked like black chopsticks. What was it with these guys and tying dames up?

I got one arm untied and she clutched me, sobbing wildly, making it almost impossible to get the other arm untied. "We've got to go," I said. "Baron's coming."

That brought her around. The dress she had on was tight, but she slid from the bed and stood on legs that seemed sturdy enough. She pulled the chopsticks from her hair and held them in front of her like daggers.

I almost smiled.

The hallway was deserted and the door to Baron's room was still closed. We had two choices for exit—out the front, or through the kitchen. I motioned for Glenda to get behind me and we moved toward the dining room. The sounds I noticed before—music, conversation, dishes, were conspic-uous now in their absence.

The dining room was empty. The front door stood open and patrons scurried around on the sidewalk, frantically hailing cabs. Glenda started to whisper something to me, but I motioned her to be quiet. I needed to think.

It would be an ambush most likely. Baron was probably waiting in the kitchen or out front. And if he wasn't waiting, then one of his goons was. I calculated my odds. No matter how I did the math, me and Glenda came up dead.

I turned to her and said, "I think you should lay down under one of the tables. Wait until you get a chance and then go for the cops."

Her eyes narrowed. I hadn't known Glenda long, but I'd been around enough women to know that when a dame gives that look she's either been insulted by an idiot, or she's just stepped in a wad of chewing gum left on the sidewalk.

No chewing gum here. No sidewalks. Just and idiot and a gun.

I blew out a breath. "Fine. But if I go down, don't hang around to see if I'm okay. Just run."

She nodded and looked less offended.

The front door was the most obvious choice, and the most tempting. So I figured it was where Baron would have positioned the nearest thug with the best aim. That left Baron either in the private room where we left him—not likely since he wouldn't have had time to get everyone to leave the restaurant—or the kitchen.

My money was on the kitchen.

I pulled Glenda in that direction. "What are you doing?" she hissed. "Let's get out of here."

I turned around and gave her a look of my own. She shrank from me a little. I turned around before her eyes got narrow again.

The kitchen was empty but the stoves were still on. The pungent smell of vegetables had changed to the stench of burning meat. Pots of cooking rice boiled over, spewing drops of starchy water all over the floor. We tiptoed over the mess and moved toward the back door.

Steel pots and pans stood on a long table that lined the middle of the room, separating the kitchen into two corridors—one for chefs and one for wait staff. Glenda and I took the chefs' side.

Plates, some filled with food and some only half-prepared, were lined up along the counter, interspersed between the pots and pans as if everyone just stopped what they were doing and left. We made it halfway along the length of the table before someone cut the lights.

Glenda hissed but, to her credit, she didn't scream. Flames from the stoves gave enough light for us to see where we were standing, but the rest of the kitchen fell into in total darkness.

"What now?" she whispered.

I didn't answer. I reached behind me for her hand, felt the long chopstick she held and grabbed her wrist instead.

I thought about taking her back out through the dining

room to the front door, but it was too late. The kitchen door swung open and for a moment the dark shadow of a tall man taking ragged breaths was silhouetted there. It was Adam's Apple. I hadn't double checked him. I pushed Glenda down and lifted my gun. I fired once toward the door, but the bullet sparked off a kettle and ricocheted around the room for a few seconds before falling harmlessly to the floor. Somewhere in the dark, Baron chuckled softly.

"Not a good place for shooting, Mr. Fokoli unless you have impeccable aim." He squeezed off a shot that whizzed past my ear. "Like me."

My chest tightened painfully and from her spot on the floor, Glenda whimpered. "The cops are on their way, Baron," I yelled.

The burning food began to smoke, filling the room with a thick haze that stung my eyes. Baron gave another soft chuckle. A footstep sounded behind me, in the direction of Adam's Apple. I pocketed my gun. In this place I would be firing blind and I couldn't risk it. I picked up a pot and threw it, satisfied when I heard the thump of metal against flesh. That sound was followed by the sound of more metal pans clanging together and a body hitting the floor. But the movement didn't stop. Adam's Apple got back up and moved closer. He was on the wait staff side of the counter, almost even with us. I backed up, into a hot stove, propelled forward by the heat just as Adam's Apple squeezed off a shot that grazed my cheek. If third time was a charm, I'd be dead on the next one.

Glenda grabbed me by the belt and pulled me down. She pointed to the pots of boiling rice on top of the last stove. "It'll work. I know it." Months of morphine use had left her malnourished and wraith thin. She was weak. I didn't know how much help she would be, but I didn't see any other way.

I pulled her along after me on the floor, moving closer to Baron. We slid through slimy water spilling over from the pots of rice, some of it still scalding hot. Adam's Apple followed along on the other side of the counter, tossing plates of food over on us and occasionally dropping an empty pot on my head. With his damaged windpipe his breathing was too loud to be discreet so he made no effort to hide. And that was fine. We were getting closer to where Baron was hiding and we had a plan.

We stopped moving when we got to the last stove. We were still ten feet from the back door. I couldn't see beyond the tight halo of blue light cast by the gas flame. The room was filled with acrid smoke much thicker than I'd realized at first. I imagined there was a walk-in refrigerator back here, as well as a pantry where Baron could hide, but I didn't figure he would give up the chance to have me in plain sight.

Adam's Apple's rasps grew more strained, colored with the effort of coughing from the thick smoke. Somewhere in the distance a siren sounded. Fire department? Baron must have had the same thought. The sound of his fat flesh scrabbling over the linoleum tiles toward the back door was audible even above the sound of pots Adam's Apple kept throwing in our direction.

"Now," Glenda whispered, struggling to rise.

I knew she'd lift one end of the pot and spill it down her front. I motioned her to be still and in one fluid movement, I rose and grasped the kettle of boiling rice. My skin sizzled as I held the handles and lifted, raising the pot and throwing it at Adam's Apple. His scream was a hoarse cry of agony. His gun dropped and went off, sending another bullet ricocheting around the room.

I lifted a second pot, no longer able to feel my hands, and ran forward. Glenda stood before me. In the darkness I could see she was poised above Baron. I yelled at her to move. When she didn't, I kicked her to the side and dumped the pot on top of Baron. He didn't flinch, didn't cry out. I stared at his still form as the siren sounds grew louder. Red lights pulsed through the dining room window, casting an eerie light in the smoke-filled room. "It's okay now," I said to Glenda. "The cops are here."

She looked at me with haunted eyes. "I killed him."

My tongue grew thick. "What?"

She pointed to Baron's body, showing me what I could already see. Two black chopsticks protruded from his thick neck. His skin bubbled, already distorted from swelling and overcooked rice. Glenda gave a laugh that sounded half crazy.

There was movement in the dining room. Had to be cops. Fire department would have come in through the kitchen.

Had Glenda killed Baron in self-defense? I hadn't killed him. I only dumped boiling water on him after he was already dead. But I'd killed Adam's Apple. I tried to look at this entire situation from the perspective of a good cop. And then I tried to look at it from the perspective of a cop on the take.

It was a no-brainer. I pulled the chopsticks from Baron's neck and grabbed Glenda's hand. Then, for the second time that day, I ran.

We didn't notice that my hands were bleeding until we got ourselves checked into a motel. Suddenly the bullet wound in my shoulder didn't hurt as much. My hands were blistered and swollen. Glenda had to rip my sleeves so I could get my shirt off. She bandaged the burns and packed the suitcase. My mouth got dry when I saw her put her clothes in on top of mine.

She called a cab and helped me change. And then she kissed me.

It was soft and sweet and made my heart ache a little. "Thank you, Dean," she said.

I cleared my throat and nodded. As the cab pulled away from the motel I thought about our clothes resting together inside my small suitcase and wondered what, exactly, her kiss meant.

37

RAY

I completely ignored the soaring cathedral ceiling of Union Station. I couldn't take my eyes off Glenda's arm resting in Fokoli's bent elbow as they walked ahead of me. If not for the bandages I'm sure they would have been holding hands.

Could be that she was just clinging to her knight in shining armor but the way Fokoli looked there was no shine to him at all. Hollywood had run him through the ringer and hung him out to dry, then run him through again for good measure. I was leaving in better physical shape but with a new, fresher hollow place inside. At least it would keep the other ones company.

All this way, Kansas to California, all those men beaten and killed that trailed behind me like the miles of track across the desert floor. And the girls. There was no way of knowing where they all ended up, except for Audrey. I'd paid for a nice plot in a cemetery overlooking a big movie studio in Burbank. A thick headstone was carved with: Audrey—loving daughter and sister. The light in her eyes still shines.

I hadn't seen it, the carving would take a week, but I knew it would be there.

"You gonna be okay, Ray?" Glenda asked.

I looked them over once more. They must have felt my stare because Glenda unhooked her arm from Fokoli's. "Yeah, I'll be fine. Going to get me some barbeque as soon as I get off the platform. I'll leave Hollywood to the make-believers." I turned to Fokoli. "Thanks, Dean. I owe you a fee. Don't think I've forgotten."

"We'll work it out. When I get back, I'll look you up."

"I have a feeling that might be awhile."

Fokoli looked at Glenda. She smiled back at him. "As long as it takes."

"I'll wire you the money. Once I get back I'll get a few kids to manage and I can start making some dough in no time."

"No rush. This town has as many P.I.'s as a dog has fleas but everyone is booked solid. Soon as I hang out my shingle I'll be crawling in cheating husbands and broken promises. Don't know why everyone comes out here to be in the pictures, the real money is in the dirt trade."

I held out my hand to shake and quickly felt foolish. Fokoli smiled. I noticed the red markings along my fingers from the brass knuckles before I folded my hand away again.

"Glenda," I said. "You take care. And look after our boy while he recovers, okay?"

"Least I can do. This mug saved my bacon. Besides, I think we've both got some healing up to do. Maybe we'll head out to Palm Springs for a bit."

I shook my head. "I don't recommend it."

I turned and started out for track twelve. A big silver engine with Easterliner written in script across the nose had just pulled in and was letting out car after car of people taking their first breath of California air.

I noticed one face in the crowd. She was small, still a teenager. She wore a new hat in the latest style and a new outfit, but from the size and condition of the suitcase she was holding I figured it was her one and only set of nice clothes. She looked around at everything like she'd just taken off blinders. The wide open room of the station seemed to take her breath away for a moment.

She was taking the first steps in her new life, the life of a movie star. I hated myself but my mind flashed forward to a future she wasn't planning on, one she couldn't even conceive of.

Dean saw me watching the girl. I wove my way through the crowd and stopped in front of her.

"Need any help, miss?"

"Why sure, thanks. Can you tell me which way is it to Warner Brothers? I have to get there early to get on the audition list."

She trusted me, and why shouldn't she? After seventeen years on the farm, she'd never met anyone she couldn't trust. Her flat Midwestern accent gave her away.

"Kansas?" I asked.

Her wide smile got even wider. "Why, yes. How'd you know?"

"I'm a Kansas City man myself."

"I'm from right outside Wichita. Pleased to meet you. Cindy Mae Morningstar." She dropped to a whisper. "That's my stage name. Do you like it?"

"I like it a lot. Cindy, let me introduce you to my friends, Dean and Glenda, a pair of old Kansans just like us. Why don't you let them show you around town, get you settled in?"

She turned to Dean and Glenda, confident this was the type of person she would meet in Los Angeles. Eager to help out a young lady with a dream. "Oh, would you? That would be so kind of you. Wow, you sure are pretty, ma'am. Are you in the movies?"

Glenda smiled. "Well, sugar, with pretty little lambs like you gettin' off every train, how do I stand a chance?"

I let them take her and hoped I'd be seeing Cindy's name on a marquee someday soon.

I followed the three of them with my eyes as they fell into the river of bodies making their way out into the Los Angeles sunshine. Against a far wall, twirling an unlit match stick in the corner of his mouth, was a tall guy in a pinstripe suit. He watched her as well, drooling like a wolf who'd just lost the sheep he was planning on having for dinner.

Nothing was different. My coming to town was only a momentary interruption. The girls would keep coming, the wolves would keep howling.

But, no, there was something different. My sister was gone. A sister I'd never met. Not a real person, just a photograph tucked into my suitcase and a name carved in stone I'd never see.

Had the violence all been pointless? No. Men paid for their crimes. What I'd done wouldn't bring Audrey back, but it might save someone else's sister.

I boarded the train and found an empty compartment that would be my home for the next two and half days. I was looking forward to the steady rolling of the train car, the rise and fall of the Rocky Mountains, and the slow settling into the flatness of the Kansas plains.

Hollywood was too bright for me. And the brightest light casts the darkest shadows.

About the Authors

JB Kohl and Eric Beetner have written four novels together and have still never met in person. Weird, they know it.

JB Kohl is the author of *The Deputy's Widow* (2008) which Eric read an admired. When she read a short story of Eric's she decided to pester him until he agreed to collaborate on something. Resistance was futile.

And so, *One Too Many Blows To The Head* and its sequel, *Borrowed Trouble* were created.

JB continues to work on her own novels in addition to working as a physician assistant in the very flattest part of the midwest. Rumors of her belly dancing have not been confirmed.

Eric Beetner is author of several novels and novellas as well as over 60 published short stories. His books include *The Devil Doesn't Want Me, The Year I Died Seven Times, Criminal Economics, Dig Two Graves, White Hot Pistol, Blood On Their Hands, Stripper Pole At The End Of The World*.

He has also written two novellas in the popular Fightcard series of boxing pulps under the name Jack Tunney – *Split Decision* and *A Mouth Full Of Blood*.

And some of his finest work remains unpublished, waiting to be released on the world.

For more visit ericbeetner.blogspot.com

JB and Eric's latest collaboration, *Over Their Heads*, will be released soon. It is a contemporary crime novel filled with over the top action and violence. Exactly the kind of book Ray Ward and Dean Fokoli would read in a ten cent paperback.

Made in the USA
Middletown, DE
16 September 2017